The Battle

The Battle

Connor Chronicles Book III

Dormaine G

Published 2017 by Creativia

Book design by Creativia (www.creativia.org)

Cover art by Cover Mint

This book is a work of fiction. Names, characters, places, and incidents are the product of the author's imagination or are used fictitiously. Any resemblance to actual events, locales, or persons, living or dead, is purely coincidental.

Books by Dormaine G

The Connor Chronicles
The Keepers (Book 1)
The Revealed (Book 2)

Madame Lilly
Madame Lilly, Voodoo Priestess (Vol. 1)
Madame Lilly, Voodoo Priestess: Soulless (Vol. 2)
Madame Lilly, The Time of Sanura (Vol. 3)

Micco
Micco, Anguta's Reign (Book 1)

Coming Soon:
A Time Not Forgotten
Madame Lilly (Vol. 4)
Forbidden Hunger (A Vampire's Tale)

Read more about Dormaine G:

I have been writing stories for many years, both in my head and on paper because I've always had a love for books ever since spending Saturdays at the library as a young child. Within a book, the mind can travel to worlds of the imagination and the beyond.

I finally took the plunge and published my first novel in 2013. Since then I have released several books and plan on staying locked up in my office in Colorado spinning more tales

Website: http://www.dormaineg.com/

Blog: http://dormainegblog.blogspot.com/

Goodreads:
https://www.goodreads.com/author/show/7329928.Dormaine_G_

Amazon Author Page:
http://www.amazon.com/Dormaine-G/e/B00HNE9GOC

Facebook:
https://www.facebook.com/profile.php?id=100004470074838

Twitter:
https://twitter.com/dormaineg

Please email me at:
DormaineG@gmail.com

Acknowledgments

I want to say thank you to my husband, Kenny, for all his patience and understanding. Without him I would not be grounded.

I need to thank my bother-in-law, Mathew, for his continued support and his eye for detail. Without him Madame Lilly would not be what it is today.

My good friend and author Janice G. Ross as she has helped me through the rough patches and has kept me moving forward. Without her guidance, I would not have strived as hard.

A special thanks to Creativia Publishing but especially Miika because he has spent long hours scrutinizing over my books. I appreciate his patience and understanding. Because of him I am proud of my work.

Chapter 1

Connor

Ronin gripped me firmly through the gushing wind that pushed me backward. I had to shut my tear-stained eyes against the sudden light that blinded us. It felt as if Earth was spiraling out of control behind us and I was losing my footing on reality. I had no control over my body when a sucking force took hold, cascading me onward. Blackness took over, compressing my body so profoundly, I thought my insides were going to concave—but, just as quickly as the pressure began, it stopped, and suddenly, a new world appeared.

Ether—a foreign world that might have been, in fact, my final resting place.

We touched down in a dreary wet alleyway and my mind reeled from such a rush. I fell against a building and Ronin caught me.

"Are you all right?" His eyes narrowed, examining my lack of coordination. I responded with a nod but my head felt like it was going to split in two. "The first portal jump is always the hardest, but it gets easier," he explained, but his words did nothing for my dizziness. He helped me lean against a building, then worked his way closer to the street.

I rested my head against the cool brick and took a long breath, then choked on a disgusting odor that caught in my throat. It smelled like a garbage truck. I covered my nose, not believing how horrible Ether reeked.

"Over here." Ronin motioned for me to come closer. After straightening my shaking body, I wiped my mouth and walked closer to Ronin, a guy who not too long ago had been my enemy. He was the prince of Ether; he lived here but didn't seem too sure of our present situation. His hand grabbed mine again and I took it for no other reason than to gain stability.

We hid behind a large blue metal box that also smelled and waited for something but I had no idea what. It was night time here, as in Earth, or early morning—I had no idea about the interplanetary time difference. But no matter, the dark, purplish sky that released its mist and rain did nothing to protect us against the muggy weather.

From what I could see, people hurried to wherever they were going, probably to get out of this heat and yet, strangely, they were covered in mostly leather. I leaned forward to get a better view of the Ether but Ronin eased me back and shook his head.

Again, I rested my back against the cool, comforting wall, anxious to merge in with the crowd, but Ronin kept checking a device on his wrist. I glanced down at my own wrist and remembered the bracelet he had given me a few weeks earlier. It had saved my life; only I hadn't known that when I'd put it on—or, should I say, when he'd slapped it on my wrist without my consent. My chest, being a traitor to my mind, felt the loss. Then I thought of my mother and wondered if she'd survived. My heart sank from thinking of our last moments together. It was like it used to be before the fights and the lies. Knowing she was upset with me right before she was attacked forced me to hold back a gush of emotions. The only consolation of possibly never seeing them again was knowing I was doing this for my family and the people back on Earth. If we could stop Monlow from attacking Earth, then all of this wouldn't be in vain.

"It's time." Ronin shook me out of my nostalgia. "Keep your head low and stay calm or the beings here will sense what you are." His tone was stern and his stare was stony.

"All right," I said, put off by his cold mood. Not that he was the warm and friendly type, but he seemed eerily dark.

"Let's go," Ronin ordered and tugged on my arm. His glower informed me that what we were about to do was dangerous but I had no clue why.

I pulled him back. "What's with the serious looks?" I asked him.

"You can't sense the abnormals—what you call nunans?"

"Yes, but we've faced those before on Earth."

"Not like the ones here." He glanced out into the street.

He was right. My body temperature rose in anticipation of an encounter from a nunan. After taking in a long breath, I attempted to subdue my anxiety. As he pulled up his hood, I placed mine upon my head. Although I did not have leather on, I figured my dark denim and hoodie should blend in well enough. Honestly, I had no other choice.

We eased our way out of our temporary safe haven and kept our heads low. Ronin made sure to grip my hand firmly. Every time we bumped into anyone, he gripped it even tighter. He made sure I was close to his side, every step of the way, as we weaved through a crowd that showed no mercy against anyone's shoulders. My nerves kept firing and this reminded me that we were among more than just humans—not that I could forget. My tension lit up. The wetness against my face helped cool me a bit, but not much.

I felt like I was his child. I hated it. But as much as I didn't like the feeling, his tight grip helped keep me grounded. I wanted a fight against whatever scurried next to us. It was my nature.

Actually, I didn't know what this planet consisted of but it was made clear to me that the people, who looked just like me on the outside, were different somehow, like abnormals, and they were in abundance. I tried not to look up but my nerves tingled and the more I looked around, the more others became aware of me. A few even stopped and gestured towards me.

"Keep your head low," Ronin mumbled under his breath, hastening his steps. I took a long breath, then lowered my head back down. I could not see much of the scenery except the sidewalk and others' boots that had pounded a lot of pavement. But so far, from what I'd seen, the place appeared to be overcrowded and dirty.

By the time we crossed the sixth street, the crowd had thinned, but I was still on edge. Now knowing Ronin was San, his senses must have been amplified, too. It was clear that we needed to get to where we were going and fast. Actually, I didn't know where we were going. I put a lot of trust in Ronin and I hadn't second guessed him once. What choice did I have?

"Just a little more to go." He looked back at me with a tense gaze.

We stopped in front of an old boarded up green building, which looked like an old complex of apartments, stacked incredibly high. He unlatched the gate and turned left. We cut across wet yellow grass and a lot of trash build up, hurrying down a corridor lit with flickering yellow lights. Half the fixtures were hanging on for dear life. Straight ahead was a dark parking lot and I hoped a car would be waiting for us. Every nerve in me was now on fire.

We made it halfway and I yanked Ronin back.

"What?" he asked, then looked to the right.

3

The door burst open and a strange male stepped out and pointed a purple weapon at us. He was a nunan. I'd never seen his kind before.

"Ronin," said the tall skinny being with a lizard face. His pinkish-reddish skin stretched tight against rounded cheeks and his hands were large and scaly.

"Shanuk," Ronin addressed the male, easing his way in front of us.

"Where ya been?" The being spoke with a harsh accent that was almost hard to understand. His long, thin tongue didn't help his speech, either.

"Where have I been?" Ronin repeated. "Who are you to question me?" Ronin stepped in close and they almost touched noses. Shanuk stepped back. Ronin may have been my age or close to it, but he spoke like he was much older. I've always noticed that about him.

"Who's she?" he asked, trying to peer around Ronin who was blocking a full view of me.

Shanuk stepped back again. "You know, Ronin?" He chuckled but there was nothing funny about this situation or the tension. "Monlow is very worried about you." The male fidgeted with his weapon but did not lower it.

"No, he's worried about everyone, including you." Ronin poked him in the chest that was draped with a long burgundy cloth-like jacket. "I just came down here to get some Elonium fresh air; what's it to you? I didn't know I had to run my schedule by my father's drudges."

Shanuk's yellow slits rolled over whatever part of me they could see as he sucked his front jagged tooth. "So many pretty girls at the palace and you come slumming. Tsk tsk. She must be worth the stench of this place. Let me see her," Shanuk ordered, but before Ronin could protest, two blue goons with elongated features appeared. One stood behind Shanuk and the other behind me. No wonder my nerves were lit up. We'd probably been followed for some time.

"No, what you're going to do is let us pass and mind your place." Ronin slowly eased forward but stopped quickly. He glanced back at me and the message was received loud and clear, especially when I heard a weapon charge.

"Don't make me use it," Shanuk threatened him, although his hands shook.

"It will be your last regret," Ronin said.

"Watch out!" I warned Ronin, then kicked the weapon out of Shanuk's hands. The burst of light shot off in the hallway, taking out an already failing light.

As Ronin walked the wall to take on both creatures, I rolled over onto the damp concrete and tripped the big blue creature behind us. The huge lug was too busy staring at Ronin to even notice what I was doing. Big does not equal smart. He hit the ground with a thud and bumped his head. I snatched his weapon when his arms flew up but realized I didn't have a clue how to use it. There was no finger trigger or button.

In the split second it took me to notice this difficulty, I looked back at Ronin to ask but he had Shanuk wrapped around his neck, while the other blue creature was trying to get out of Ronin's leg lock.

Peering back at the contraption, I realized that my blue creature was up on four legs. Its back was severely arched, exposing protruding vertebrae. In moments, it grew immensely in size and its fangs dripped some sort of foul green liquid.

"Holy crap!"

The creature yanked the device out from my hand and smacked me in the gut with its tail. I flew back and hit a window. My arm broke through the glass but, surprisingly, I wasn't cut.

I looked over at the four-legged creature's open mouth and saw its neck jerk back awkwardly. A noise released from its throat right when it hacked its slimy mucus at me. I dove away and noticed the cement warp where the slime landed. When the four-legged creature scampered sideways towards me, I quickly lifted my hand and sent it flying back to the gate. Surprisingly, the thing landed a lot farther way than I would've expected.

Is it possible that I'm stronger here or is the gravity lighter?

After it rolled back up, it rushed towards me a lot faster so I yanked a long, slick vine from the ground and whipped its back with it. The creature let out a loud animalistic sound at me and jumped over in my direction. I leaped out of the way but it quickly reverted back to two legs and tossed me against the building with one of its elongated hands. I landed on my neck.

Rolling over in the muck, I grabbed the slick vine again and lassoed it around the creature's neck. But instead of the beast reaching out for me, it tugged on the vine.

I wrapped the slip around my hand and held it taut. Placing a foot on the creature's chest, I choked it. It clawed, gagged, and kicked violently but I kept my foot in place until it passed out. But even then, I held on, making sure it wasn't faking.

When I was certain, I let go of the vine in relief, but that was short lived when alarm took over. The slippery weed unraveled itself from around the creature's neck and elevated upward. It had a mouth—one that opened wide, revealing more than twenty sharpened teeth. It slithered so quickly that I fell back and only managed to crawl away. I reached for a stone but a shot fired and blasted the serpent away. Ronin held up the weapon I could not manipulate. I looked back at my so-called vine and kicked it away from me.

Ronin walked over to the blue creature and bent down next to its still body. "Next time, just use the Taser."

"I would have if I knew how to use it," I said and stood to wipe myself off.

He stepped back and pumped the handle underneath, shooting the other creature once in the head and another time in the abdomen. I looked up at him in shock. "We leave no witnesses, Connor. No one can know that you're here," he said, then tossed the gun in the bushes. "Let's go." I was not innocent to harming another life but he seemed so cold, so detached from what he'd just done.

Back down the hallway, we hurried and stepped over lizard eyes and his goon. Both of them lay unmoving, their necks twisted unnaturally. Their lifeless body positioning was disturbing. I faced away, thinking, did we have a choice?

We reached the end of the corridor and took a quick right. By a metal fence, we squatted low as Ronin pressed buttons on what appeared to be a very advanced watch. But not two seconds later, a bright light shone above. I covered my face from the whirlwind it caused but was more in awe of the fact that a car hovered over us.

Upon descent, it cut off its lights and just hovered. We ran over and Ronin lifted me up by my waist, pitched me inside, then jumped in behind me.

I peered back at him, annoyed at having been tossed in like that. "My bad, but we don't have time for it to touch down or wait for the hover lift."

After cutting him a curt glance, I got on my knees and gazed out the tinted window. I forgot all about him during our ascension and was utterly amazed that I actually found myself in a flying car.

"Take a seat. The ride can get bumpy," Ronin said as I sat across from him. I kept looking between him and the window. Something about him was off, but when blood seeped through his shirt, I knelt in front of him.

"You're hurt."

He covered his shirt up with his jacket and glanced over at me. I forced his hand and jacket away and lifted his shirt. He was sliced on his right side, through his rib cage. Lowering his shirt back down, he grunted. "No wonder."

"No wonder?" I repeated. "What does that mean?"

He ignored my question and pointed under the seat. "Grab a red aid kit and take out the foam. It will help with cutting down on the blood loss."

"What?" I said, feeling under the seat and grabbing the box. I opened it up but saw nothing that could possibly make a foamy substance. He obviously saw my puzzled face when he pointed to a flat silver round canister. When he bent the thing, it made a popping sound and grew in size.

"Twist it open and apply the material on the wound." He sounded so unruffled compared to my ever-growing panic. He did not appear well at all. His skin had already gone pale and felt clammy to the touch, all just from a knife wound. I applied the pink and white foam as instructed onto his cut. It adhered to his skin, sealing the wound.

Once fully covered, he grabbed for a cloth but I slapped his hand away. He looked at me in surprise. "I've got it. Just sit still," I ordered. I applied the cloth and kept my hand there for pressure.

"More pressure." He pushed my hand down and shifted in his seat. He was in pain. "Normally, the foam would be enough, but for this this kind of wound I'll need you to keep steady pressure until we get to where we're going." It sounded as if he was becoming short of breath so he laid his head back on the seat.

"Yeah, where exactly is that?" I wanted to know, tired of being left in the dark.

"My place."

I turned back to his wound, feeling some sort of relief knowing where we were going, even though he could be lying and this might be a trap. We could be on our way to turning me over to his father. I shook off the negative thoughts and refused to let worry creep into my thoughts. It was too late, anyway. I would just fight as I always did if it came to that.

"It looks more like a knife wound than a Taser wound. Not that I'm an expert but I've seen enough knife wounds lately to know what one looks like." Ronin did not respond but just rested his head back on the seat and it seemed as if he was going to pass out. "You don't look so good. How deep did they cut you?" I asked.

"It's not the depth of the wound that I'm concerned with but the poison encased tip left inside me. It's done on purpose… it slowly releases a toxin." He gripped the seat as I applied more pressure to stop the trickle of blood.

"What kind of poison, Ronin?"

"The kind you don't ever want in your system. If it stays in too long, then I will die. You're going to need to remove the tip of the blade from inside me."

"Me? I'm no doctor."

"You are today." He grunted.

"Don't you have a doctor on staff for emergencies?"

"Yes, but Monlow may have gotten to him. We don't know who to trust; that is why we trust no one." He gripped my arm and sat up. "You understand? No one but us and the ones we know for sure who want to get rid of Monlow. Okay?"

"Yes…yes, okay. Now sit. Lean back." I removed his hand as he fell back further onto the seat.

"I'm going to close my eyes for a minute. The car will take us home. Wake me when we get there. That was the last thing he said before passing out.

All I could think of was, how did we get this far? And, Ronin might not even survive. If something were to happen to him, as hard as that pill was to swallow, how would I get home? Screw that; if this all went up in flames, I would find a way home and we'd just do things the San way.

I observed his chest rise and fall more frequently as if he was not getting a full breath. Beads of sweat encased his head and his color turned sickly. Every so often, he would adjust in his seat but I held the pressure.

As soon as the car touched down, Ronin instinctively woke, jolting up and wincing as he did. He lifted his shirt and the wound area was both black and bloody. He lowered the material down and held onto the foamy mess.

He pressed a button on the car and the door lifted up to a forest. It was pitch black outside; not even the car lights shined. It was more of a purple-reddish color that greeted us as we eased out of the vehicle. Ronin tried to walk by himself but I grabbed onto him and, at first, he seemed uncertain of my help, then gave in when I didn't let go. Letting others help—a concept I'm sure he wasn't too familiar with.

We passed numerous enormous trees, the largest I'd ever seen. They seemed to reach the stars. Even in the dark of night, their pink and red colors shone brightly. Little winged creatures fluttered above and they seemed to escort us, guiding the way to his home. But I'm sure they were just following, curious about us.

Eventually, the ground angled downward, which proved a little difficult for Ronin to manage, and although he did it without a grunt, his face betrayed him. Once we made it to level ground again, he gripped the closest tree and stopped to rest.

He did not say anything when I asked, "Are you all right?" Stupid question because I knew he was not. I just didn't know what else to say. He faced the ground and nodded.

Eventually, he looked up and searched around. I did the same and took note of the size of his home. Being too focused on getting to safety, I hadn't paid attention to it, but the sight of it now left me speechless. His place was massive and in all rights, it was truly a palace. There were people outside, uniformed guards with weapons actually, and I wondered if they had been placed there to protect Ronin or keep him in.

Ronin mumbled, "This way," bringing me out of my state of wonder, and nodded to the left. This time, he reached out for me to assist without hesitation. He was obviously feeling worse.

About fifty feet to our left, he knelt down and held onto his wounded side, then gripped shrubbery and removed it from the ground, revealing what I could only assume was an entryway that led to a secret chamber. I was right. There sat a metal door with two round handles.

"I had it made a long time ago when I first moved here in case of imminent threat, but now it's proven a necessary evil. Very few people know of its existence." His brows scrunched as if to warn me not to tell anyone about it.

Ronin grabbed hold of one handle but I bent down quickly to retract his hand. He threw me an odd look as I pulled open the heavy doors without lifting a finger. He nodded a thank you and we crept inward down the dusty, cemented stairs, which led into dimness. A faint yellow light glowed ahead, imbedded within the stone walls, but it provided very little help. We both stopped at the bottom of the stairs and I listened out but heard no one nearby. I shook my head, telling him so, and onward we walked. I shut the door, encasing us in a sort of tomb-like environment.

From his pocket, Ronin pulled out something round and tossed it in the air. It lit up and stayed no more than five feet in front of us. "It's a boun...umm, a levitating light," he explained before I asked.

He guided our direction as I helped with our steps. It was a coexisting relationship at this point. Neither would make it far without the other. The place was a damp, dimly lit maze but at least the boun helped when it came to needing to see where we were going. We came to three forks and even Ronin second guessed himself at this juncture. The toxin was messing with his mind. He kept wiping the sweat from his forehead and trying to control his breathing but he was suffering. We trekked down a few more halls until Ronin fell against the stone wall and gasped in order to catch his breath. The poison was winning.

I waited for him to catch his breath and, when he shut his lids, I shook him. "Ronin!" His lids jolted open, startled. Without a word, he pushed off the wall and once again, we helped each other. We'd been down here so long, I wondered if we'd ever get out.

"Are we lost?" I asked while helping him against the cool stone again. "Ronin, you have to focus. I need you to stay with me." I shook the crap out of him. "I would levitate you but you'd probably pass out and I need your mind to keep working."

He bent over to take a few long breaths, then straightened up and braced himself against the wall. "This way." He pointed to the left.

We headed forward and up a ramp to a metal door that eased open to a small, quaint, red velvet sitting room, with cushions on a long lounge chair. The door proved to be the back side of a bookshelf—how fitting. I quietly shut it and we headed out of a tall wooden door leading to a spacious hallway. In the middle, stood a huge opening where you could peer over to see downstairs.

It was so peaceful and I wondered if we were the only ones there. I listened carefully and faintly heard people talking and moving throughout the place, but not close by. After walking about twenty feet, we took a left through double doors which led to a foyer with two doors. We chose the one straight ahead and entered one of the largest rooms I had ever seen.

His bedroom — a magnificent sea of turquoise, black and ivory. Standing by the door, I took in the extravagance that overwhelmed me.

"Connor," Ronin's raspy voice called me as he struggled to his bed without my support. "There is a multicolored wooden chest hidden under the sink behind the fifth tile in the lavatory. Can you retrieve it, as well as some towels?"

After he pointed in the direction of the room, I hurried up. Of course, there were three sinks in the bathroom. I just picked one, then another—on my second attempt, I found the bag, grabbed plenty of towels behind a curtain, and headed back out.

I stopped short. A chill washed over me. Ronin lay on his dark oceanic blue covers awaiting my return. His blade lay at his side. It reminded me of a time when dead men were sent out to sea upon a bed of wood with their swords in arms.

"Connor," Ronin called to me again and I gathered my thoughts. "I'm going to need you to clean the area, cut the wound open an inch with that blade." He pointed to a small cutting device on his night stand next to his leather belt. "Dig in with your finger until you find the tip, then pull it out with pliers. Immediately throw it in the liquid jar with the plyers." I noted a small jar with clear liquid on the chest and placed it on the nightstand. "Do not touch it after you pull it out. Remember to put it in the jar. Afterwards, stitch me up and inject my left arm with a dose of meds." He explained my expected duties while he sluggishly rummaged through the chest I just handed him. He removed the scissors, then started to cut his own shirt upward.

"Ronin, I'm not afraid of blood or anything but you know I've never done…"

"No one has ever done anything until they do it for the first time." He coughed and his scrunched-up face made it clear that staying conscious was unbearable. "You can do this, Connor." His eyes pleaded with me. "Hurry before I pass out again."

"Okay." It was all I could say. The poison worked fast. He'd made a drastic change from the car to right now. Ronin was dying.

When I got everything ready and put on my gloves, Ronin took a tube-like canister and slammed it into his right thigh. An exhaust sound released. "Antibiotic," he answered at my amazed expression. "Remember, use it again afterwards." He placed his leather belt in his mouth and bit down like in the olden days. I didn't ask about pain reliever because I already knew Ronin would not take it. I could not help but watch him maneuver in agony. Sometimes, Ronin reminded me of an old soul.

I swallowed hard, took a nice long breath then did as he instructed. I took the blade to his already red and tender skin but, when he winced, I hesitated, like he'd done to me when a branch was sticking out of my leg. He nodded for me to continue. "I need you to hurry. Don't stop for anything."

"Okay." I stood from my seat next to him on the bed and sliced up, giving my right index finger room to fit in as he bit down on the belt and gripped the covers. I dove deeper inside him in search of the poisonous tip. Blood seeped out the cut the farther I went. I ventured slowly so as to not slice myself with the same poison.

At last, I felt an odd shaped object that did not feel like bone—round with a sharp edge. He winced when I moved it.

Why doesn't he pass out already? How much torture can a person take?

I just looked at the perspiration traveling down his face and his breathing was worsening, but I ignored him, needing to get this done. Picking up the small surgical pliers, I dug them downward, where I had left my index finger. I reached for the object and tugged on it, but it would not give. It was firmly planted in there. I twisted and turned the pliers and Ronin's eyes rolled up in his head. He finally passed out.

I had to use all my strength to pull it out and when I did, I immediately held it away from my face. Ronin said it was just a tip but it looked more like a bio-organic weapon. It had thin metallic legs and its slit for a mouth squealed in my grip. Its four thin extremities reached for me as its round belly swished around with black poisonous liquid. I was grateful Earth was not this far advanced yet. Remembering the jar, I placed the contraption in it and it screamed while it sizzled. I held up the jar to watch it fight to climb out but its extremities were melting.

Turning back to Ronin, I applied pressure but every so often turned back to the poisonous object that still had fight in it. The liquid was turning murky as the poison released into it. Refocusing on Ronin, I observed that there wasn't an overabundance of blood, so that meant the weapon hadn't nicked a major artery or vein.

Thank you, Mom, for being a practitioner. It helped.

After a few minutes, I stitched him up as neatly as possible, cleaned around the wound, and applied a bandage. The last step was to inject him with more medication in his right shoulder. He didn't even flinch.

I sat back down, bloody gloves and all, and watched him breathe. The little monster in the jar no longer moved. I took a long exhale, appreciating the fact that the weapon was dead.

After a minute of calming my shakes, I took his bloody shirt and towels from around him and hid them behind the curtain in case someone came in and saw them. After cleaning the bloody utensils in the bathroom, I laid them out to dry. That took about fifteen minutes; then, I headed out to the room to check on him. He was still asleep. His chest rose and fell more restfully now—a good sign.

I walked over to his huge, semi-frosted covered window and was able to see out. Lights lit up the nearby area and, from what I could see, the groundskeeper stayed busy. There was a heck of a lot more greenery than where we portal jumped.

In the middle of the estate, I spotted an enormous, glossy, metallic water fountain with the Ether military crest, the Vuszen, in the middle. The creature stood on its wolf hind legs as its eagle wings spread wide, its head held high. Water spewed from its open beak into the fountain below, surrounded by that same glossy material wall. Around the jet, a spread of grass covered the whole area. Each bush was cut in the shape of different animals. Different colored flowers decorated the garden with benches and steps leading down into where I could no longer see.

Guards stood at several key points holding unique weapons or at least ones I was not familiar with. Some looked over-sized, strapped over their backs, and others were small, gripped tightly in their hands.

The beautiful purple-red sky now had a hint of yellow in it. There seemed to be another gigantic planet hovering so close, you could touch it.

Will it one day fall on Ether?

"Connor." The sound of my name brought me back down from the stars. Ronin blinked his eyes open. In only a matter of an hour or so, his coloring appeared healthier.

"Yes." He reached his right arm out to me, and I walked over to him. "Are you in pain?"

He didn't answer me but instead grabbed my waist, lifted me over him, and positioned me next to him. It happened so fast. I didn't expect it or for him to be so strong. He rolled over and hugged me from behind, whispering, "Thank you." Then, he drifted back to sleep.

I stiffened up, unsure of what to do—guilty. Never in a million years would I have imagined being here on Ether, let alone through Ronin's help. I thought about getting up once he was asleep but it felt so good being next to him. Before I knew it, my mind drifted off into slumber, knowing that, for this brief moment in time, we were safe.

* * *

"Finally. I thought you'd never wake up," Ronin said when I stretched out on what had to be the comfiest bed I'd ever slept on. He stood by the window holding a mug of steaming liquid.

He sat down next to me, leaned over, and kissed me on the lips. Butterflies took flight. When he pulled back, I asked, "Why did you do that?" I blushed, feeling anxious, thinking of how dangerous he was, but that trait somehow made him more appealing. His heterochromia stare—one eye green and the other brown—mesmerized me.

"I don't... I don't know." His voice cracked. It was the first time I'd ever seen him unsure of anything. "I just wanted to." He got up and grabbed his shirt from a chair. "Anyway, thank you again for helping me last night. There is breakfast in the sitting area." He pointed to the adjacent room, avoiding my gaze.

"Sitting area?" I sat up, pulling my knees in, and saw where he was referring to. Across from the bed and down three steps stood indeed a sitting area with three white couches, two orange lounge chairs, and a long metal table in the middle with a huge mirrored wall. All surrounded by windows and a sliding glass door.

As he donned his shirt, I could not help but stare. He was in great shape. He had a tattoo of a Vuszen, the Ethos military crest featuring the head of an eagle and the body of a wolf that covered his back. Crisscross daggers shielded his heart. His left upper arm was covered in a foreign language with tribal markings surrounding it. They stood out against his sun-kissed skin. His dark, shoulder length hair had carefree waves and it reminded me of the ocean.

He glanced over at me. I inhaled deeply and quickly faced away. I felt hot, the embarrassed kind.

He seemed so much more mature than the boys back home. Being royalty I'm sure played a part in that. He was probably used to mature females too, not girls who wore superhero shirts and baggy jeans like me. Then it dawned on me.

"Ronin, how old are you?" I asked, shifting over feeling a bit awkward just sitting there while he was up getting ready for the day.

"Why do you ask?" He walked into his closet.

"Just curious." I began to blush. "I mean, you look young but I just wondered..."

"Eighteen. Why, I ask again?" He came out of the closet holding two black and gold daggers and looked between me and them.

"I don't' know." I pushed a piece of hair behind my ear, now sitting on the edge of the bed. I watched him examine each weapon like I would a shirt. "It just seems like..."

"That I'm older?" He stared at me. "My speech and my demeanor are a product of my upbringing and title. In addition, going off world one needs to appear older than what they are. It's about survival. You're not the first to tell me that." He went back in the closet and I heard him shut a cabinet, then walk back out with the bigger dagger. He sat on the window seat and applied black boots. "Let's eat. I need ten thousand calories a day. I can assume you do as well."

"Is that how much we eat a day? I never counted. I just ate."

"I can only imagine what you eat. Yes, our metabolism calls for that. We burn a lot of calories in a day."

"I'm going to ignore that remark about what I eat and use the facilities." I stood and pointed towards the bathroom.

"There are accommodations for you," he said before I could even ask that question. "Mindalous made sure what you need is at your disposal."

I nodded politely, then walked over to get cleaned up. I hurried up cleaning my face and attempting to tame my wild mane. I was starving, but then again, when was I not? Then, it hit me. I felt no aches or pains like I did on Earth. First, my strengths seemed heightened when I fought the blue creature and now this. Ether may come with some serious perks.

I cut off the light and headed to the sitting area where Ronin was waiting. A bright light cascaded through the window behind him as he read over a binder in one hand and held a piece of fruit in his other. Sitting on the couch, I began to put different meats, cheeses, and breads to my plate. He barely noticed me.

"How are you feeling? You seem miraculously better," I asked. When I looked up, he stood right in front of me and offered me a colorful plate filled with an assortment of fruits. I took the whole plate.

"You saved my life, Connor—thank you for that. It means a lot to me." I was not used to this gentle side of him—only his darker side. But I didn't really know him. "I owe you a lot. I could have easily called for the doctor once we landed but you being here didn't expose us to any questions the doctor might have had."

"Ronin, bringing me to Ether to hide from your father is what got you into trouble in the first place. Me helping you last night was payback for protecting me, and don't forget the bracelet that saved my life back on Earth. I'm supposed to be dead right now but because of you, I'm alive."

He clasped his fingers together behind his back. "Last night you were just another excuse Shanuk used to attack. He's hated me ever since we were young lads. He's wanted to be second in command for as long as I can remember. Don't fret; being the prince keeps me in harm's way."

"Is it that bad here? I'm not trying to be naive but…"

"I should have never said that to you before: you being 'naïve'. And yes, it's that wicked here, but how could you possibly know my way of life? To do cruelty is natural to Ether. A title does not hold much value unless you enforce it." He spoke so matter-of-factly. His face held no expression, which I'm sure was a product of his upbringing as well. "And in the past, I most definitely enforced it upon the San. Ironically, it always affected me somehow."

"Because you are San—that I know—and instinctively, we're not supposed to harm one another," I explained.

"Is that so? I've harmed San, supposedly my kind, as you and Bynder say. Maybe I am San but a tainted one, Connor. Nurture holds a powerful sway."

"But your father lied to you. He probably had you, I don't know, use your confusion and anger towards us. He forced you to do things against us because he is twisted and you had to, right?"

"Yes, hatred for my upbringing and my father was my dictator at times, which all made hurting the San possible. But looking back now, I would go into seclusion afterwards." He faced away for a split second, then quickly back to me.

I was about to ask him more about his world but there came a knock at the door. He held a finger up to his lips, advising me to stay quiet. "One minute," he said from across the room. "Stay here. Whoever it is cannot see you from the door."

I lost sight of him and heard a male voice. I didn't want to eavesdrop so I got up and peered out the window onto the garden of greenery. When he returned, I noted his demeanor had darkened. "Monlow is summoning me to the Dom."

"Where?" I asked, glancing at the piece of paper in his hand.

"His palace. I'm to arrive at his throne room at once." He stood at the top of the stairs and crumbled the telegram in his hands. His tranquility appeared to have been crushed with it.

"Wait a minute. You two have different castles?" That was a stupid question; of course they did. Why would he take me to his place if he lived with his father? "Sorry, ignore that question." I felt a little embarrassed. Then I thought of the bad conditions in Elonium. Two luxurious homes versus those poor conditions. How unfair was that?

"If you knew Monlow, you would, too. He's watching me more closely ever since I've failed in bringing you to him. I've never failed him before. So, either he is truly confused as to how you somehow continue to elude me, or he thinks I'm betraying him. But ever since visiting Earth, my thinking has changed towards him and when Tanikka started telling me bits and pieces of my past, I've started to see him for what he is."

"Ronin, you can't go." I grabbed his arm when he turned away.

"I have to." He observed me as if bewildered by my reaction and I abruptly let go of his arm. "He will just send guards to retrieve me anyway."

"If he suspects you of treason, then why hasn't he killed you?" I followed him up the stairs into the other section of the room.

"Monlow is a sadist. He loves to make others agonize, not knowing where they stand so he could come for them at any time. It's more torturous that way," he said so coldly, without inflection. He then walked into the closet to grab another weapon from his cabinet.

Ronin stood facing the cabinet. He didn't move and I could not blame him. Monlow sounded awful and being in a room with him must have been ten times worse. "No matter, Ronin. Just hold true to the fact that you are San. I don't doubt it and neither should you."

"Somehow, those words provide me with little comfort." He held up the blade and stared as if contemplating a decision. After a moment of silence, he looked at me. "How can you be so sure of what I am, Connor, when I'm not? You all say that I am San, but that parasite sitting up there on the mountain gnawed away at my soul for so long, he has infected me with disease. So, I ask you, Connor, how much San is even left in me? What's left of me after he's eaten away at my sanity?" His tone brimmed with resentment.

What being could cause one's mood to change so quickly? Monlow must have been a cruel and insane monster. I needed to say something, anything to Ronin so he would not do anything drastic. "Ronin, this world he built for you, his world, is all lies. It was his anger towards the San, the misery he held against them—that's what he fed you. You did what you did to survive and that meant hurting our kind at times but it ate away at you as well."

"He's killed his own kind, him being a San himself, so easily by the hands of others. Killed to get the throne, not trusting the innocent, taking from the ill begotten ... the list goes on." Ronin twisted the device in his hand. "Yes, I was pulled in two different directions, so what is left of me?" he asked, standing so close to me. He gripped the dagger tightly as his eyes bore into me.

"Strength." I refused to back down. "You are no Monlow, Ronin. I don't know what you're contemplating with that knife, but you've managed to survive in an existence that has ripped you apart and yet, here you stand. You're fighting that plague called Monlow and you've found your kin in order to do the right thing. That alone should tell you something. Trust in that. Right now, you must play whatever part you need to in order to survive, then heal later."

"All I can trust is my anger and need to survive." He rushed around me and grabbed his long black leather coat, applied his belt, and sheathed his daggers within their holders. Then, he stopped by the door. He glanced back slightly. "Don't leave this room for anything and don't open this door for anyone. Do you understand?"

"Yes," I said.

"If anything happens, someone will come for you," he ordered, opening the door.

"Be safe," I said as he walked out. My stomach turned thinking what it must feel like every day not knowing if it would be your last by your own father's hand.

Chapter 2

Ronin

Out the door I went after another summoning by the man I had once called father, the one I used to look up to and habitually followed orders from—but no more. Now I have to bide my time until the ceasing of his existence. If Monlow knew I was no longer a true believer of his, then he would rid himself of me just like he'd done so many others.

As of late, he's questioned my loyalties and that in his mind is just cause for these incessant summons. Rather than Monlow confronting a person outright, he loved to toy with their psyche in the hopes that they would break. It was tiresome—he was tiresome—but to blatantly refuse his request could prove fatal.

I could only assume the reason for this summoning was because Shanuk and his assailants had gone missing. Lately, paranoia was his only ally and this vicious partnership was running rampant.

Although I now knew that Ether was not my place of birth, it was, in fact, my home. Monlow might have kidnapped me as a young lad but he'd made sure I'd done enough damage to make a name for myself here, and I could no longer stand by and let this planet rot away like my insides had by his influence.

"Tessie," I addressed my driver. "I will take the aero-glider out myself." The short, swollen man politely bowed his bald head. I normally had a chauffeur but today I needed to make a stop before reaching the mountain, and having witnesses to this unplanned trip was not an option.

I hopped in the aero-glider and pressed the ignition button. Easing the vehicle out of the carport, I flipped on the internal propellers and lifted off in a hurry. I ascended into the air, rushing to get to Tanikka's home. My keeper, the one who watched over me so dearly, the one I cared for against my father's order and never knew why.

As I veered through the air, I could not help but think of our relationship. She'd always held a special place in my heart when my father taught me nothing but malice. I'd always protected her, made sure she was cared for, and never forced her to live in my palace. I'd assumed it was because she was my den mother of sorts, not just my caretaker, but now, I knew differently. She was San.

What it must have taken to watch me grow into anything else but what I was destined for. What anguish she must have borne to not say anything, to desperately want to protect me and not be able to. Monlow, gifted in the art of taking another's abilities, must have taken her powers years ago. How hard it must have been to live here alone and exposed.

I slowed down on the outskirts of Flinus and cruised near her pod, where she felt safer. Touching down on her cobblestoned street, I hurried to her place hidden by saplings. I did not knock or call out to her, but instead, stormed into her humble home and observed her in her normal attire of earth toned top and long skirt. She was stirring a brew or possibly mixing herbs but no matter what, it always smelled welcoming even though I'd never told her this.

Standing at the door, I gripped my belt and watched her expression of surprise slowly turn to bewilderment. "Ronin..." escaped her lips but her words failed her when I rushed over and hugged her tight. Her lungs gasped at my sudden, out of character behavior.

At first, she didn't know what to do or say, clearly scared to embrace me back, but when I would not let her go, she wrapped her frail arms around me and I shut my lids. Something as little as a hug from her felt so good.

"Ronin..." Her voice cracked when I got down on one knee, kissed her aged hands, then looked up at her. With her free hand, she gripped her chest and I watched the tears swell on the base of her lids. "How does the prince of Ether come to bow before me?" she cried.

I stood back up and cupped her face in my hands. "Because I am not the prince of Ether." I shook my head. "I should have never been."

"How do you know this?" she asked.

"I've always known something was unique about you, us, but I could never quite figure it out. Then, there were your subtle but persistent teachings of love, honor, and life warping what Monlow showed me." I walked away to clear my throat. "Then Connor..."

"Connor?"

"She's here, hiding in my palace. I have sentinels watching over her." I turned back to her.

"Oh, by the great council, you're protecting her!" she cried out and, this time, it was she who placed my face in her hands. "She is far more special than you can imagine."

"The Keepers could not tell me everything, actually very little, but…" I cringed at asking the question but I needed to know. "Did he kill my biological parents, mine and Cheyenne's?" My jaw had already tightened before she answered the question that I already knew in my heart the answer to.

"Yes, Ronin, I'm so very sorry." She placed the tips of her fingers over her mouth, something she'd always done when she was saddened.

I acknowledged her with a long exhale. What was I to expect—hope that they had survived? No, I was more realistic than that. "I cannot stay longer but I need three things." I watched her wipe her tears away. "Last night, I was stabbed by Shanuk's poisoned blade. Connor was able to pull it out but I need you to look at it."

"Yes, of course." She went to her other room to retrieve her basket of medicinal herbs, oils, and ointments. I removed my shirt, sat on a stool, and awaited her healing touch.

"Two, I need you to go to her today and make sure that she is all right." She agreed while she unwrapped the dressing and started applying medicinal herbs to the wound.

"It's already starting to heal. You know that is a San trait." I just looked at her, thinking of mine and Connor's conversation.

"And three." I gently touched her petite wrists, stopping her movements, but she could not face me. Direct eye contact was only allowed in limited doses. "Don't ever bow to me again." She gazed up at me and her expression was one of shock. "Nor call me 'My Lord'. To you, I am…"

"Vincent," she whispered. "Your true birth name. And to you, I am…"

"Herina, my Keeper." I finished her sentence as she had done mine. After a long moment of her smiling up at me, I asked, "Are you almost done? Monlow does not like to be kept waiting."

"Yes … that should hold you and I will bring more by later." She finished wrapping me up with a new dressing. She wiped her face dry with the back of her hand and wiped the leftover ointment on her long skirt.

After reapplying my shirt and coat, I headed for the door. Stopping short, I looked back at her. "Lock the door," I advised.

"I will, Vincent." She smiled, walked over and shut the door behind me.

What she said added to my resolve. Tanikka had confirmed who I was. Not that my gut did not tell me what the other Keepers were saying was not true, but it was not in my nature to believe so easily. But I've always known that there was more to me and it had something to do with the San. Hurting others had never been a second thought until I dealt with them; then, I betrayed my father for the San. Betrayal—something I was vehemently against. But I still felt like I lived in limbo. Who was I—the cruel son of Monlow or the tainted long forgotten San? Truthfully, I had to wonder how much influence being a San held.

* * *

I soared over the palace, which stood imbedded into the moss-covered mountain. Actually, only half the mountain covered the palace and the other side was exposed to the sky. A truly remarkable sight. Monlow had always had such extravagant and overbearing taste.

I flew over the long red carpet leading up to the monstrous double doors of the main entrance and I decided to drive into the back. As soon as I set down on the stone, my mood hardened. Each visit with Monlow worked my every nerve.

"No driver today, my Lord?" asked the attendant, a tall, skinny human who probably only ate when allowed.

"No," I answered. I voice-activated my aero-glider, allowing him usage. I had already deleted my hard drive in case he was ordered to check my last destination.

"Thank you, sir." He bowed but I said nothing back.

I strode off through the lot doors, thinking how ironic it was that Monlow had mostly humans working in his palace. Was it to remind him of home? Did he miss that place called Earth, his true home of centuries ago? And did he mistreat them because of his own self-hatred of being human? The San might have abilities but so had the species of human birthed on Earth until people came to be without abilities. That, I discovered on my own.

I headed up the stairs, passing many partitions made of glass—a visible barrier. Monlow was adamant about being able to see what others were doing. He'd always been eccentric but, having been informed of his polluted past, I figured more of his behavior added up. He was paranoid, not just bizarrely controlling, and it had gotten worse since he was slowly dying.

I turned left instead of my destined path and met the head chef, Genab, in the kitchen. Everyone stopped and bowed to me. "You may rise," I raised my hand in an upward motion.

"Are you hungry, sir?" Genab asked. "I can make you whatever you want." He tossed a live five-legged sea urchin in boiling water. It squealed as it attempted to suction away from imminent death. I focused on it, thinking of how our lives could very much be paralleled, when Genab locked the latches on the top, I snapped out of it.

"What do you have in the ice box?" I nodded for him to follow and he did.

In the cold storage that could fit a small home, we walked to the back to look at a variety of food that needed to be ready at a moment's notice, nourishments that fed Monlow's ravenous appetite. "Listen, if I don't leave here by nightfall, then I need you to get word to my house maiden, Mindalous... stop salivating," I said to the poor sap who had been in love with her for years. "She will know what to do."

"At your service, as always." He slightly bowed.

"Shut the hell up." Genab and I had known each other since childhood. He respected my title but was one of the very few I saw as a pal; being who I was, those were scarce. I grabbed a few things and headed out the kitchen.

I tossed it all, but the fruit, in the hallway bin and trekked to the grand chamber, the one where my father resided.

The hominids at the door were going to announce me but I shook my head. "Never mind; he knows that I'm coming." Taking in a long breath, I opened the double doors. I entered the main room decorated in red and white walls with a gold trim. It was gaudy.

There, Monlow sat, high in his gold and white chair, dressed in a long robe above everyone else who had to bow up to him. I no longer had a taste for my fruit. I spat what I had in my mouth out and tossed it in the waste.

"What took you so long, son?" He asked, right before ordering four men on their knees to the torture chamber. His deep, aggressive voice thundered across the chamber as he asked me the same question every time I arrived in his presence.

"You haven't been waiting long. Ether has barely rotated. I do have other duties, Father."

"None more than me, I'm sure."

"Of course not," I said as I ascended the three stairs, making my way closer to him and passing both the standing and kneeling onlookers awaiting their sentencing or to beg for a deal, I surmised from the blue bostuge guards to the staff. It was a daily ritual he performed but each session got shorter with each passing day the weaker he became.

Next to him, I could see his translucent skin that no longer grew hair as the black tarry veins pulsated underneath the stretched flesh. His eyes no longer turned back to their brown state. Truthfully, I didn't remember their natural color, so instead, black remained their hue.

"Everybody out!" he snarled, rising up in his chair to almost my height, then slowly lowering back down. Everybody rushed out, helped by the tall, elongated guards. Soon, it was just him and me in the huge dome that felt devoid of air when the doors shut.

"What's the big secret?" I leisurely headed back down the stairs to the opposite side's glass partition overlooking the hellhole below. It was a large room the size of his chamber, known as the soul taker. This was where beings went after being sentenced to death by either stake, hanging, some contraception of death, or other means. Watching others suffer was his form of entertainment. I just preferred the capturing and left the rest to him. Watching was not my thing.

Monlow extended his long, bony fingers with cloudy fingernails towards where I stood. "I made this." He was referring to Ether. "I am the ruler and yet there are those that dare to defy me. They see me as weak, old, brittle even." His jowls took a second to close. He stood up tall on his legs that I could not see under his long black cover. His bottom half moved in a fluid motion, like a devilfish would if it could walk out of the sea.

"Why do you think so?" I asked.

"Because Shanuk has not returned since yesterday. He has not checked in as instructed."

"Maybe he is busy as…"

Monlow snapped his head quickly towards me and bones rattled. "Why did you drive yourself? You have escorts for that." He changed the subject just that quickly. Something I found myself doing from time to time.

He wanted to know what I was hiding or if I was keeping secrets. "For no other reason than wanting to. There are plenty of days when I drive myself."

"But you literally drove and did not use autopilot."

"So, everyone is your spy now?" I folded my arms and leaned against the glass. "Is nothing I do sacred? Shall I check in every time the planet turns so many kilometers to give you updates of my whereabouts? Should I implant a tracker in my wrists?" I held out my arms. "Like the rest of the minions you order about so you will learn my daily routine?" I asked, furious that I had once again been summoned for this nonsense.

Within a blink, Monlow had me suspended in the air to his height, by the tip of a finger. He didn't have to touch me but it was more personal this way. His mind proceeded to squeeze the life out of me. "You try me, son. Do not think I did not hear that detestable tone you took when you said 'father' as you entered the room. You're hiding something. I could snap you as I do a pauper." He had his face so close to mine, I could smell his foul breath. The species he now craved were horrid and his odor reflected that.

"Then do it," I encouraged as his hand pressed on my recently acquired wound, but I refused to beg for mercy. He squeezed my body tighter. "No, huh?" I grunted. He was close to cracking a rib. I could have taken out my knife but that would have sealed my fate at that moment so I did not challenge his strength—still far superior to mine, no matter how sick he'd become. "This is why I moved away years ago. Your paranoia has gotten worse," I retorted when he dug his finger inside my gash.

Monlow quickly let go of me and rushed away. "That is because the ones closest to me are deceiving me!" he bellowed, waving his arms around, afterwards hugging himself tightly.

I took long, deep breaths after his death grip. "Then end their existence. Why do you ritually summon and punish me for others' wrongdoings?"

"Because Shanuk would never have disobeyed me."

"Then where is he? Huh? I stand before you, once again, to prove my loyalty, and yet he is nowhere to be found."

"He's only ever wanted to serve me."

"He's only ever wanted to be me," I shouted and carefully walked closer to Monlow, but cooled my tone. "Maybe he's realized that will never happen, that he will never have the throne when you've passed and decided to either flee from your constant berating, relentless questioning of deceit, or take it for himself." I taxed him. If I backed down from him, then he would know not to trust me. I had to maintain my rebellious attitude. Yes, I followed my father but never once did I refrain from testing him. "So, if you feel that I am hiding something, then check my palace, question my staff, shackle me." I held out my wrists once again for him to take. "Do what you must so I can live my life and help you find these traitors. But if I were you, I would start with Shanuk." I had to divert the blame elsewhere and that grunt would be the best scapegoat for now. I placed a hand on my wound as it started to bleed again.

Monlow let a low guttural growl and, even from where I stood, the lewd, acidic stench insulted my nostrils. He said nothing while his cold, murky globes examined me; quickly, his attention diverted elsewhere when someone entered the room unannounced.

"Dear, high Lord…"

Foolish man. I shook my head at the man who stood petrified for interrupting us.

Before the man could finish, his head was ripped off his body. I didn't even flinch. This display was nothing new. The court announcer knew never to interrupt our conversations but the fatal horror Monlow inflicted upon the man did help settle his temperament. He slithered his way back to his chair.

"I need not check up on you." Monlow exhaled, sitting down. One would think him old and tired but I knew better.

"It seems that you already do so."

"Yes, I guess, but within reason. I have not lived this long, Ronin, by taking threats lightly. I need the blood from that human girl. It has healing abilities." And there it was. The truth without saying it. We answered to him but he never gave all his untrustworthy truth. He needed Connor's blood to survive, she was his cure, because in truth, she was his descendant, which meant he was San, but he would have us all believe otherwise. We were just supposed to accept that her blood was somehow special with no other explanation. I said nothing as his brittle hands waved me closer. "You find her and bring her to me. I haven't much time."

"As you wish." I kneeled in front of him. "I only said your namesake snidely because I grow tired of being questioned for treachery. Forgive me, Father." I played my part as a dutiful son.

He gripped me by the shoulder and, as I stared into his cold, deadpan eyes, he leered over me and ordered, "Then locate her." He hissed and sat back. "See that someone takes care of that mess." He was referring to the decapitated man. "Check on the soul taker chamber. Make sure all deaths are repulsive as I so ordered." I nodded, stood to my feet, and left the room.

Halfway down the hall, my knees all but gave out. I used the railing for support and gathered myself. Each visit was becoming more intense. One day, he would lose all patience with me and I would be just another decapitated man on the floor.

Chapter 3

Connor

After Ronin left, I forced myself to eat something. My stomach was in knots but I could not remember the last time I'd eaten. I grabbed some food and walked over to the huge window. I nearly dropped what was in my hands when I saw a beach—an actual beach.

How is this possible? I swear there was a sea of green as in trees and a water fountain before?

His bedroom door suddenly opened and a pretty female came into his room and handed me clothes. At first, I was caught off guard.

"I am Mindalous." She curtsied. Petite, she had tan skin and the prettiest big brown eyes I'd ever seen. She had to have been in her twenties and her smile made me smile in turn. She appeared human. "Ronin wanted me to bring these to you so you would have something to wear when you venture out."

"Oh." I awkwardly held out my hands. "You don't have to curtsy to me."

"Of course I do." She kept smiling.

"No, I mean Ronin is royalty I'm..."

"I know exactly who you are. You are here to save us." She headed towards the lavatory. "I will run your bath water and add soothing salts."

I was surprised. Save us. What exactly did Ronin tell her? Who knew? We don't even have a plan and I'm supposed to save other people. I'm not even sure if I can help myself. I rushed after her in the lavatory. "I can do that myself. You don't have to wait on me," I explained, clinging tightly to the clothes in my hands. I wasn't even sure what she handed me but it served its secondary purpose in being my stress reliever. I just wasn't used to this pampered treatment.

"Of course you can, but if there is anything I can do to make your transition here easier, I will do it." She spoke so sweetly as she poured pink and blue salts into the water. It was almost too much to take in. She got up from sitting on the dark stone floor; after simply touching a knob, water escaped a wide spout, raining down like a waterfall into a gold Egyptian sized bathtub. "Let me help you with your clothes." She reached for my shoulders.

"Oh, no." I eased away, blushing. "I can do that."

"Oh, nonsense. Let me help. Ronin believes in a stress-free environment at home."

Surprised, I stepped back again when she reached for me. "No, I'm okay." I stood off to the side and she went back to the tub.

"I saw your shocked expression when I described Ronin's home environment. We—all of us who live here—are aware of his outside curricular activities. Do not judge him on that basis alone. This world is different from yours, Connor. Outside these walls is ugliness, but inside, he insists on there being serenity."

"You're aware of everything?" Blown away, my eyebrow raised as far as it could go. Who was Ronin?

"Enough." She glanced back at me. "I myself have washed the blood from his clothes. There are things he won't talk about and it is not our place to ask."

There goes that 'don't ask questions' comment again.

"So, who exactly lives here?"

"All the staff that work here. In our free time, we can do as we wish. But mostly, we visit the beach and the market downtown."

"Yeah, about that. Last night there was grass outside and now the ocean." I squinted at her waiting for an answer.

"Ronin likes the sea and we are able to rise high to reach the beach on the other side of the planet."

"This place doesn't seem real."

"Remove your clothes. If you would like I could bath you…"

"No, I'm good," I squealed, and she giggled at my response.

"All right then. The body sponge is in the basket over there. I will be in the room cleaning up if you need me. Where are his bloody clothes from last night?" I crawled under the sinks and handed them to her.

"Okay, I will take care of these right away." She bowed again. I felt so awkward at her doing that.

When she left, I immediately removed my clothes and stepped into the mini in-ground pool. The water temperature was perfect and the bath salts smelled heavenly. I sat on the built-in seat and leaned back on the head rest, letting the environment take over. My eyes popped open.

Did she say 'transition' here? Why not say 'visit'?

I chose to ignore it for the time being and allowed myself to enjoy this tub. It might have well been the last calm moment I'd have in a while.

* * *

After time had passed, I forced myself out of the most deluxe bath ever. Now I see why my mom loves her turbo jet bath and never lets us use it. Freshening up was just what my nerves needed to relax. After drying off and applying the scented lotions in the basket, I squeezed into black leather pants and black fitted top. Leather had never been my thing, let alone a tight, stretchy top. My preferred attire was very childlike, but it was me.

When I stepped out, I noticed the place was immaculately clean. Mindalous had taken care of the bed, the food, and replaced it with fruits—some I'd never seen before—a variety of nuts, and cheeses. Several carafes had been filled with different colored drinks.

"Connor," called a woman to the left of me as she was talking to Mindalous, and immediately I knew she was—Herina aka Tanikka. Overwhelming emotions filled my chest as I ran up to her and hugged her with all I had and she did the same.

"Let me look at you, child." She pulled me back by my arms and examined me from head to toe. "You are much prettier than I imagined. I remember when you couldn't even walk. Now look at you, all grown up into a woman.

As she spoke I could not help examining her too. She looked a lot like my other Keeper, Tanzia, from Earth, or maybe it was just that they both had hazel eyes.

As Mindalous excused herself, Tanikka led me to the adjacent room and we sat on the couch facing each other. This reminded me of home, and the numerous times I had lounged on the couch with my mom as we watched an old classic movie or just hung out. But, as of late, she barely wanted to speak to me and with good reason. I'd changed so much in such a short time.

"After all the years I've waited for you … we've waited for you."

"What do you mean, 'waited' for me? I heard Mindalous say that I was here to 'save us'. What am I missing?"

"It is prophesied that the descendant of Monlow is the savior of us noncon-formists. You are the one being that can save Ether. He's searched for you ever since you were born but he was never able to find you. Your mother saw to that."

I lowered my head thinking of the woman who gave birth to me that I would never meet. "She killed herself so Monlow could no longer read her thoughts."

Tanikka lifted my head by my chin. "Don't lower your head in sorrow. Be proud of what she did. It was the honorable thing to do. Just know that she did it because she knew that you were—no, are—special."

"But Tanikka, I don't feel so special. My powers haven't even fully developed yet. How am I special?"

"Are you not stronger here on Ether? You do feel it deep down inside." She touched my heart. "Don't be afraid to tap into that. You will do what needs to be done when that time presents itself." She seemed so sure. "But you are not alone. You have followers you've never even met so don't ever doubt your power. You are blessed with gifts far more than you can fathom."

"I... I have followers?" I blinked back this new humbling reality. "Stronger? Yes, and only yesterday on Earth my body ached just to move but as soon as we portal jumped, I felt almost invincible." I shrugged.

"Ether is definitely special to us and that is why Monlow fights to keep con-trol over it. The San do well here, which makes our gifts most valuable, but then there are those like you and Monlow who excel on Ether. Plus, I have a strong feeling it has a lot to do with your prophesy. You are also stronger be-cause instinctively, your body is aware of impending doom. I've even noticed a change in Ronin especially after he met with our kind, the San."

"What do you mean?"

"Ronin was most loyal, always stuck with Monlow because he had to in order to survive, but something within him is different. He's more insubordinate. I noted his mental struggles years ago, but waited for him to come to me in case I was wrong. There were times he would come to my place and just sit there. I could see his mind churning as anguish clouded his thoughts. I was his safe haven in this terrible world forced upon him. He wouldn't utter a word, then he'd rush out without a backward glance. Until one day, he divulged things to me and started asking me personal questions, but I was very careful in my answers."

"Like what?" She'd piqued my interest.

"Well, about his mother, other family members, foggy memories of his childhood, and his distant familiarity with Earth. Monlow, I'm sure, had a hand in ridding the world of your kin but he really was adamant about retrieving your mother."

"Why?"

"Monlow's mind is warped; why does he do any of the things he does? I'm sure it had something to do with her being royalty."

I had a feeling she was holding something important back but I let it go for now. "What things did you tell Ronin?"

"I told him bits and pieces, never all the truth. I could not speak against his father for fear of punishment. Also, I was not sure how much he was going to accept. He never pushed any harder than what I gave. But when I spoke, I could see the deep sigh of relief that he, in fact, was not imagining things. Deep down, he knew the truth, but even that needed to make sense before he could accept it."

I shook my head, feeling awkward intruding into Ronin's personal space, so I changed the subject. "What does Monlow look like?" Tanikka immediately dropped my hands and hugged herself.

"A monster. A true one." Her body trembled, thinking back. "Even years ago, when we were forced to Ether, he looked revolting. His skin appeared sickly, his pupils would enlarge and unexpectedly change from brown to black, his veins would pulsate under his skin so profoundly, it seemed as if they would burst. And I swear there were times things would move unnaturally under his skin. He walked on two legs but now…" She shook her head and I could see the disgust on her face and hear it in her tone. "Make no mistake, he is no man." She pursed her lips. "I have to visit the castle once a week to drop off natural herbs and he takes pleasure in my repulsion." She took a sip of water and it took her a second to swallow.

"Now his skin is thin, so thin…white…even translucent…" she stuttered, then took a longer sip of water before wiping her dress clean, as if she'd seen a speck of dirt. I gave her a second to calm her trembling hands. "His black veins are permanently visible on the sides of his face and head; his speech is a deep animalistic one and his fingers are bony and brittle. He always wears a long robe to cover his deformed body, which moves in an unnatural fluid motion, like he has snakes for legs. Some even say he has a tail. I've never seen it though." She rushed over to the window and quickly opened it.

I was left speechless as I watched her try to control her fear. She no longer had her abilities and to be afraid like that must have been overwhelming. I walked over to her and sat next to her.

"He's always been a monster but because of his greed, he could not stop. I think he likes that he is altered so he can intimidate others."

"I say it's working." I shook my head in revulsion. "So why didn't he try and take my mother's blood?"

"It's only over the last decade that he's been sick. Your mother passed away sixteen years ago. Between mine and the doctor's remedies, we kept his sickness at bay, but now he is truly dying. He is still powerful, although weaker." She paused, then stared at me for a minute. "And that is why he needs your strength within your blood, while it's still pumping.

"If we lose, am I expected to end my own life?" Before she could answer, I silenced her by holding up a finger to my lips for I heard footsteps getting closer to the door. Tanikka pulled me up and hid me behind a hidden doorway that was covered by a curtain. I found myself in a storage closet of shelves lined with old books and files. I was hoping what I heard was the sound of Ronin's steps, but I didn't know his stride yet. It just hit me that I knew everyone's pace back home. A waft of sadness washed over me but vanished when the door was snatched open.

"Ronin." I was glad to see him.

"Come out, it's safe." He stepped back, giving me room to exit.

"Thanks," I said, not sure what else to say at his apparent darkened mood. I wondered if that was normal for him after a visit with Monlow.

I exited the storage room and allowed him to shut the door behind me. He walked over to Tanikka. "What news have you?" he asked her without as much as a glance my way when he passed me.

Tanikka took out a small scrap of tan parchment paper from a hidden pocket in her long green skirt and handed it to him, a look of worry crossing her face. "Thank you," he said a bit awkwardly, but a smile stretched across her face as if he'd gifted her the world.

It touched my heart that something as simple as a "thank you" made her smile. I felt terrible about this world she had tolerated. A San, a powerful being, had resorted to living as a servant. I rushed over and gave her a hug—I don't know why … maybe just to say I was sorry for everything she'd endured on the planet that hated our kind, and for her being so alone. She squeezed me back, wiping yet another tear away.

When we released each other, Ronin was watching us with narrowed eyes, as if our behavior was foreign. Sentiment—must have been a rarity to him. He blinked back an expression, one I could not catch, and quickly replaced it with tension as his gaze glossed over me. He refocused only on the parchment and unfolded it. His lips tightening as he read the note.

After reading what it said, he faced us to explain. "The professor wants to see me—us." He nodded toward me. "As soon as we can arrive." His jaw tightened.

"The professor?" I asked, wondering about his guarded disposition.

"An old friend." His tongue lingered on the last word as he marched away to remove his gear from his person.

"Okay, I'm confused. Why do you seem bothered if he's a friend and why does he want to see us? Wait—how does he know I'm even here?" I headed over to him but he had yet to turn around.

"Connor, can't you just leave it at that? I answered you." He placed his gear down on the table and only faced me through a hung mirror.

I gave him space. "That's not my thing. I know you are not used to answering to people but I came all this way…"

"For me not to trust you," he said, finishing my sentence.

After stepping away irritated, I took in a long breath. I had to remember that it truly took a lot for him to trust anyone.

Then I stopped cold. A cold chill ran up my spine. It wasn't so much trust this time as it was the fear of something. I eyed him through the mirror. The idea that he felt anxious about anything almost startled me. Somewhere along the way, I'd come to revere Ronin as fearless. "Jesus, Ronin, what?" My words caught in my breath.

"Let it go, Connor," he advised, still not moving.

I could not. I tried to think of what it could be with him as his lips refused to move. I stared at them, waiting for him to speak—but nothing. We both stood there, frozen. "You're worried that if I know too much and get caught then they could get information out of me? Is that it?" I decreased our distance. "Because they won't…"

He spun around to face me. "This thing…"—He clenched his hands tight as well his jaw, "…we have is most confusing. I pride myself on my discretion." He stormed away as if to get some space from me and I backed off, giving it to him.

"How do you think I feel, Ronin?" I snapped, not meaning to sound so annoyed but it bothered me, too. Only I needed answers.

He marched up to me. "Unfortunately, I know exactly how you feel." He sounded pissed.

"Yes…" I trailed off feeling a bit exposed. What have I let him sense about me? We stopped speaking for a moment. I didn't know what else to do other than continue discussing the letter. "I would never betray the San."

"You won't have a choice, Connor." He wiped his mouth with a cupped hand before continuing. "Monlow's mind reader will be in your head and you won't even know its happening. You cannot withstand the magnitude of the pressure, especially after he tortures you, simply because he likes it. My father will have you beaten for the pleasure of it and you are not trained in the art of torture like I am."

"You're trained in torture?" My jaw dropped at this revelation.

"Monlow is my father after all." His stare was chilling. "As I've told you before, you know not of my world."

"But why torture you?"

"Why do you think? If I were ever caught then they could…"

"Never retrieve intel on him." This time I finished his sentence.

"Exactly."

I shut my lids for a long period of time, rehashing the words "he likes it", then opened them to find him staring at me. I took in a long breath, trying to release my tension. "But he will know that you helped me."

"Yes, but if he does get me, at least he won't know everyone who is involved," he said coldly.

"And we have to keep it that way," I said. We observed each other for a long time.

"It can be no other way," he agreed. Even though we were both apprehensive we at least agreed on that subject matter.

"So what else is there? There is more, Ronin," I pried but he appeared to be bothered. He folded his arms and watched me cautiously like I did him. When he said nothing, Tanikka came up to me. "What?" I asked her as I stared at an angry Ronin, but I was not even sure why.

"It's the journey getting there," Ronin finally answered before Tanikka could speak. "We cannot hop in a car and drive there and we cannot be taken. We have to travel like vagabonds. It will be a bit of a hike and if either one of us is caught then..."

"I got it—mind readers, torture," I said with a heavy weight on my chest. I truly may have come this far only to die.

"I am amazed." Tanikka clasped her fingers together and brought them to her lips. "I've only heard of such a joining but I've never seen it firsthand." Ronin and I glared at her. "I understand the lack of privacy but we can use this to our advantage." She grabbed both our hands and squeezed.

"And what exactly is this "joining", Tanikka?" Ronin asked, removing his hands from her grip and backing up. "Would someone like to clue me in?" He looked between Tanikka and me.

"Oh, Ronin. There are so many things I've wanted to tell you but you weren't always open to the truth."

"Then tell me now." He pointed at the rug.

She nodded. "Of course, come sit." She gestured towards the couch.

"I will stand, thank you, but, please do sit."

They were so formal to one another; unlike Selena, my Keeper and me, but then again, she had always been a caretaker to him.

"As you wish." She took a seat, then took her time explaining herself, making sure he heard her well as she related the tale that had been told to me several times already. I almost felt as if I was imposing on their time together so I went to the balcony, but she called me back in. I stood at the doorway as she continued. "...There is Destiny, two beings so drawn to each other with such a unique link that they will forgo all logic and reason to be close to one another, for their true role is to govern as one over all others." She explained all about governing the land and not about having to abide by such a link, when the pair concerned did not believe it existed.

When she finished, Ronin stared at Tanikka as if what she'd just told him were either lies or a made-up story in her head. It took a minute for him to respond. "And you believe in such fairytales?" he asked through pursed lips and folded arms.

"I believe in what I see and even you cannot deny your bond with Connor, Ronin." He stood there tight jawed.

All of this was hard for me to register, as well. So much had been thrown at us in such a short while, it was a wonder neither of us broke. Both our worlds were a lie and we had no control over any of it.

"I see." He nodded to himself as if to answer a question that lingered in his head. "Let Lannet take you home. I insist," he said, and she agreed with a nod. And just like that, Ronin was done. He had no more questions, nor did emotions have a role to play in this revelation. He was so very diplomatic.

When he left the room, I asked, "That's it? He has no more questions? Because I had a lot when I was first told."

"That's Ronin. His mind will ponder things and absorb when ready. He's not an emotional person like you are. He prioritizes and that will help balance you two during this mission. Please be safe and protect and trust in each other on your extensive journey." She clasped me tight. "Until we meet again." She rushed out the door and as she left, I wondered if I'd ever see her again.

On the balcony of his sitting room, I sat on a cushioned cove and stared out into the sky. Eventually, Ronin came over and handed me a drink. "Thank you." It was a sweet, fruity beverage. One of the best I'd ever had.

He sat by my propped-up feet on the seat, looking out into the night's sky with me. The stars were bright but dull compared to the planet so close to us. The breeze from the ocean smelled like back home. For a second, I closed my lids and pretended I truly was there. Listening to my brother Kane whine about something silly, my sister Ebony complaining about an issue she had, and both my parents fuss at me for the umpteenth time for disappointing them with my lies. I would have never imagined in a million years that I would miss them, but I did.

Water fell on my hand and I wasn't even aware that I was silently crying. As I wiped the tears away, Ronin gave me an inquisitive look. I stared back at him in wonder that he had once been my enemy but had somehow become my protector—and I his supposed savior. I opened my mouth to explain the tears but he stopped me.

"It's okay," he graciously said. I rested my head back on the pillar and focused on the water.

He leaned forward, putting elbows to thighs, twirling his drink between his hands. "This thing between us..." He glanced at me briefly, then slowly turned away and my stomach wildly reacted. "What do you think of it?"

I sipped a drink, trying to slow my thoughts. I hadn't expected that question or at least so soon. "I don't know." Moments drifted between us as neither of us spoke.

"What made others aware of it in the first place?" His stare was intense.

I got up and placed a hand on the railing, admiring the water. "The night we first met."

"When I didn't force you through the portal back to Ether." He twirled his glass between his hands again. "There was this moment... I had you pinned... everything in me wanted to, but..." He gripped his glass tight. "I just couldn't."

I remembered it well. It had been the first time I'd ever felt so helpless—the beginning of the end of the world we knew. "And the fact we never reported each other all those times you came to my house."

"You never told anyone?" He arched his brows.

"Only when I was forced to," I whispered—words that left my mouth without my permission.

I wasn't even aware that Ronin stood next to me until his finger rested next to mine. Electricity shot through me and it was hard to breathe. Something as simple as a touch from him made me lose control. It felt both terrifying and exciting. "When we were caught?" He was referring to the night Tony had caught us kissing in the park.

"Yes," I whispered, staring straight ahead.

We stood there, letting the night breeze take us over. Neither of us spoke any more about our so-called destined path, only took this moment for ourselves.

Chapter 4

Ronin

We had just left the palace grounds via the tunnel. I had left word with my staff that I was taking a short business leave to Vonvere, a small villa a great distance away. If my father was so inclined to call on me there, I had servants and allies who would cover for me. Furthermore, I had a lookalike who would make small appearances so others could say they saw me. My tracks were covered on that end.

Now, Connor and I needed to travel smart in order to arrive at The Wall where Kenrick Henrique, the professor, resided. The wall had been built centuries ago to keep out the creatures that dwelled in the forest surrounding the place. It was a well-established area with a scholarly society and rich, fat nobles. Not as wealthy as us, since my father ruled all over Ether, but he allowed them to live as they saw fit as long as they brought in wealth. This was the main port of interplanetary trade on Ether.

Being that Henrique sent for me, things had to be coming together. Visits from me there had become forbidden in the last year. Too many people lived behind that wall who loathed that man on the throne.

I'd gone to school there from age eight to sixteen. I lived there during the week, then returned to the palace during the weekends. Horror did not begin to describe my childhood. I needed to be well educated, properly versed, and, as required by him, I graduated two years early when my abilities came to be or—as he would have me believe—granted upon me. My father was ready to set me on a course of pure destruction. For as long as I could remember he'd never been a loving man, always cold and harsh.

But for some reason I've never feared him, not once—to this day. I know he senses it and it vexes him. Truthfully, I fear nothing, not even death. There were times I even welcomed it. The terror he put me through made me that way.

On any given day or weekend, never knowing what torment he had planned, I endured. Getting locked in a cell with monsters, left to starve, watching thousands of others being put to death and my own hand forced to take lives against my will—what could I fear? I lived with a fiend so how could I fear any man or foe for that matter?

He wanted me tough, he wanted me cruel, so he got it; only, he never planned on me not fearing him. That, he never anticipated. But, I did as I was told because it was all I knew or he would take from me all that I had. If I ever cared for anything, he took it. If I ever enjoyed something, he perverted it. If I ever loved something, he killed it. I learned at a young age never to care, want, or love anything other than to get up from under his endless watch.

At times, I was rewarded when I did right by him. He showered me with money and gifts. Grown women threw themselves at me from when I'd reached the age of sixteen but all I desired was my freedom. That desire, I kept hidden. So, I played my part, and played it well. Sometimes too well. The more I hurt others, the more lenient he became; he rewarded me with freedom so I came to long for hurting others as I silently suffered. A weak emotion—suffrage.

I was an unconscionable person, like he wanted, until I got my own palace at eighteen. A final reward—freedom. I was no longer constantly under his warped thumb. It had barely been a year and now he wanted to take it back. If I had to survive under his thumb again, I could, but my heart had already started to thaw.

For some reason, I'd always felt envious of the kinship between the Keepers and the yougows. I had resented the yearning of warmth I'd desired from the professor and the fact I cared for Tanikka so much.

And now, Connor. Far too often, she reminded me that I was human and that could prove fatal. I needed to remain hard, calculating, very much like my father, but how else was I supposed to live in this world? As much as I'd always longed for a family as a child, I grew up and let that fantasy die long before my eighteenth year of advancement.

No matter what I'd done in the past or what I'd come to be, this planet was my home and Monlow was destroying it. If chaos erupted, thousands would go missing daily until one day no one would be left. Knowing my father, if he had to die, so would millions along with him. No one was safe, not even me.

As I pondered my past and unknown future, Connor and I cut a path through the unruly debris. Taking a car was out of the question and walking alongside the road was not an option, either. We needed to get through the unmanned and droid-free side of the twelve mile long, wooded stretch behind my palace.

I chopped away using a machete while Connor didn't even have to lay a finger on her axe as it hacked away. Her mind did all the work as we made something of a path to the other side. Despite the temperature being in the seventies, I was feeling the heat. We each were fully covered in leather but the cool breeze that found its way to us helped a lot.

Strapped to her back was a heavy pack of supplies but not once did she complain about being tired or the fact our task was too hard. She was different, oddly different. I thought most girls whined, but not her. I'd worked alongside some of the best female fighters who were without question harder than most fellows I knew, but I always figured they were an exception to the rule. I was used to seeing pampered and spoiled girls in the palace.

"Are you tired?" I asked when she stopped to take out her water.

"No," she said before taking a swig. She wiped her mouth with the back of her sleeve, then placed back the bottle in the bag. "Are you? Do you need to rest?"

Should I be offended? "No, I was just wondering about you," I replied, getting back to work as her mind did the same.

"Worried! About me? Why, Ronin, I'm flattered that you are concerned about my wellbeing." She batted her lashes.

"What?" I was baffled by both her words and demeanor.

"Relax, Ronin, I'm kidding. I keep forgetting that we are from different worlds, even though I'm standing on another planet with a notorious villain." She rolled her eyes and kept moving forward.

"Notorious, huh?" I never really thought of myself that way.

"Don't look so shocked, or am I not allowed to talk about the Prince of Ether? Shall I be banished?"

She was mocking me. "I have to remind myself that you are not from here or yes, you would be punished. It's the law that I have to enforce or I will appear weak. Ethosians rarely speak out of line to me but every so often, one challenges me. Sometimes they are simply disciplined or I fight them, against my father's orders. It depends on the situation but the females… they know their place."

"Excuse me?" She stopped cutting and tossed me a vicious scowl.

"It's the way here, Connor. You don't have to like it but you must respect it."

"I cannot believe that in so many ways Ether is far more advanced than Earth but some of your customs are so primitive to us. You know, females have equal rights there; well, at least they are supposed to."

"In certain ways, they do have rights. They have careers and own businesses but you forget we have a ruler. This planet is not ruled by a democracy. He's a dictator. Each planet has their faults, Connor," I explained. "I feel ours is more advanced because people will work harder and prove their worth. Fear is a powerful influence. Your people can be quite lazy."

"And what was that shady part of town we arrived at? That didn't seem more advanced. Okay, the buildings were, but it sure was seedy," she said very animatedly with her hands.

"Yes, Elonium is known for its poor habitat but even they fight hard to work and when they do, they receive more money that day."

"Wait, they have to fight to work every day? That's barbaric. Please don't tell me you're defending that crap." She folded her arms.

"Yes, I am. And why are you taking it so personally?" I asked, puzzled by her sudden mood change. I stopped chopping to clarify further when she didn't budge. "Connor, this is my planet and I will defend it. It may be different from yours, but that doesn't make it wrong." I was becoming pissed that I needed to defend my planet's ways against one that was inferior to mine. "With every government, ruler or laws, nothing is perfect." I started slicing again but when I didn't hear her next to me, I stopped. This was getting tiresome fast. She stood there with her arms down at her side but she no longer appeared mad. "What?"

"I'm sorry, Ronin," she said now with a softer tone I didn't understand. She was throwing me off. "I'm not saying that psycho stuff you've done in the past was right and I may only be here because it serves our plans, but I'm sorry you were taken from Earth. It could have been any one of us but it was only you."

I turned my back to her. "You're confusing at times, Connor." I checked our surroundings. "You know you're the only person who has ever said that to me? But I don't need your pity."

"It's not pity." She hurried in front of me. "It's called being human, empathizing." She rushed up ahead but stopped short. "You know, Ronin, forget it. You're an ass."

"What?" Her mood swung again. I truly think she's cracked.

"Yeah, I said it to the Prince of Ether. I was trying to…"

"I know what you were trying to do, Connor, but I don't have time to waste energy on being sentimental."

After a moment of silence, we both went back to chopping. Then, for some odd reason, the words "Thank you" slipped off my tongue. I refused to even glance her way. As I'd admitted before, she got under my skin.

"You're welcome," she remarked, not looking at me either. After a moment, she added, "So, was that our first fight?"

"Are you insinuating that we're…?"

"It was a joke, Ronin. Joke. You know what that is. I'm trying to lighten the mood. Jesus!" Connor stopped moving. "Get down. I hear something." She grabbed my arm and yanked me down.

"I don't hear anything," I whispered but my back was against a tree.

"They're about a hundred feet away. It sounds like three men but I don't understand what they're saying," Connor described what she heard while we remained covered by greenery.

"You have enhanced hearing?" I was amazed that she had another ability. Most San only had two.

"What?" she asked as I stared at her.

"You have four abilities," I told her as if she didn't know it herself.

"No, three." She checking the area, half listening to me.

"No, Connor." I pulled her closer. "Four—invisibility, telekinesis, enhanced hearing, and telepathy. You told me to 'watch out' in my head before Shanuk shot at us. You just never put two and two together since these powers are not fully developed."

"Oh snap, you're right." Her eyes widened. "Wait, Ronin, you have three abilities: enhanced combat, invisibility, and teleportation, and not the typical two."

I was stunned. She was right. It had never dawned on me either. *Maybe there was a reason we have come together after all,* I was going to tell her, but I finally heard the men. "They're close." In a bent position I squatted over to a larger tree.

Who are they?

Through the bush, I peered over at Connor when her voice sounded in my head. "Poachers. They are looking for wildlife," I mumbled under my breath aware now that she could hear me.

I motioned for her to stay down the closer they got to us, and took out my knife to stop them when they approached.

No! I grabbed my head. Her words reverberated so loudly. *We don't need to hurt them. Let's let them pass and we can go around.*

I cut her a look of irritation due to the high volume. She needed to learn to control her emotions. "Earthlings," I mumbled and she cut me sharp look "They are on my property." When her face showed resolve, I held up one finger. "I will you give you this one. Just one."

"Thank you," she mouthed.

We let the pilferers pass as we headed toward the other side of the forest, I could feel the tension in the way Connor killed the bushes with the blade.

"What?" I hesitantly asked in anticipation of another interrogation.

"Were you really going to hurt them?" Connor asked me as her blade savagely killed the wildlife.

"Yes," I responded without reluctance.

"Why harm someone when you don't have to?"

"You don't understand, Connor. What you don't rid yourself of now comes for you later."

"That's sounds like an excuse to hurt someone."

"Not an excuse, but a reality." I told her making way through the uncultivated foliage, angry that she asked so many questions and angrier at myself for answering. Yet, the best way to appease her was to just answer, and get to the point quickly. That seemed to work for both her and me. She wasn't the 'beat around the bush' kind of girl.

"Whatever, Monlow. You sound very similar to how they describe your father."

I grabbed her shoulder and spun her around. "Don't you *ever* compare me to Monlow. You got it? Ever!" Those words fueled me with such anger, my mind was sweltering. "I assure you, by the end of this trip you will have seen things you could never imagine and done horrible things just to survive; then, I'd like to see how quickly you judge me." I was furious at Connor but she was right. My attempts to not be like my father proved a constant internal battle.

"Fine." She clutched my hand, warning me to let go. I did. "You may not be like him yet but you're sure well on your way."

"That may be, but at least *he and I* don't share the same blood," I reminded her.

"Wow, you went there, huh? Yeah, he and I are related but like you said, nurture plays a big part." We both stood there and neither one of us backed down. I clenched my hand tightly out of anger but then released it. "You want to go? We can do this right here," she threatened. Her blade spun past me and dug into a tree behind me.

"Your powers haven't even fully developed." I towered over her. "I would wipe the floor with you, Connor." Gritting my teeth, I backed off, even though her offer was one I wanted to oblige. "You know what, Earthling, let's get this excursion over with before one of us kills the other."

"Fine with me," she cocked her head. "I don't want to have to kick your ass." She bumped me as she passed, then pulled her blade out of the tree.

I swore it was my face she envisioned as she now personally slashed away violently at the taut vines.

* * *

Somehow, we were on schedule when we made it through the woodlands, which was actually the safest part of our journey. Not talking towards the back end helped. We hid behind two saplings, making sure no one was on the road we needed to pass.

"So far we are on time but we should try and hurry. The road ahead is long and there is much to encounter from here to our destination."

Connor let out a giggle and I could not stop my sigh "Sorry," she covered her mouth. "Sometimes you speak like in the movies. You know, like back in the day when men where manly and saved the day."

"No. I've never seen a movie."

"You've what… never seen a movie?"

"No. I know what they are but I've never seen one." I checked the road again from our squatted positions. "Now can we get back to the journey?"

"Sure thing, Robin Hood." I shook my head at her remark, assuming it was a character from a movie. "Never mind. I don't hear anyone coming," she said. "Why can't we just Credo? I mean, go invisible?"

"I know the word but unlike Earth we have the technology to see things that go hidden and tracking faunae, they're like hunting dogs, but more vicious, anyway, they can sniff you out." I smirked. It was a childish dig comparing Earth to Ether but it felt good nonetheless.

"Good one, Ronin," She cut me a side glance.

I headed out onto the tar road and down the hill on the other side with Connor close behind me. The area across the road was not as dense so we needed to be more careful. Besides the occasional poachers, not many dared to step on the land surrounding my palace. Furthermore, I liked to keep certain areas on my land untamed to deter too many unwanted visitors.

When we reached a large steel dairy tank, we stopped. "There is a laborer's home not too far from here." I eased her in front of me so she could take a peek. "See, it's just down the meadow below the row of shrubs."

"Yes, I see it," she answered. We crouched when the owner of the house came outside.

"Every day around this time he leaves to go down to Elonium. It may be seedy there but it's plentiful in just about whatever you need for one reason or another. We're hitching a ride on the back of his truck. He uses the road instead of taking flight, where patrol is more rampant. That means less of a chance him being stopped and searched. Someone who has something to hide knows which roads to take and that in turn helps us."

"I hate to complain..."

"But you will." I sighed, watching the man load up his truck.

"Whatever, but that truck looks old and full. Explain to me again why we can't drive to the Professor's house, which you said is half a day away by car?"

"As I said before, my father trusts no one and as of late, that includes me. He has spies everywhere— not to mention the tracking devices he's installed in my vehicles that we have to find and remove every day. We have to hitch the whole way, leaving no trace of us. And remember, I'm supposed to be in Vonvere," I explained, looking down at her unappeased face. I'm sure she had another question but I gave her no time to ask. "Let's go. Place your hood," I reminded her, and took off. She ran beside me to the side of the house.

"He's alone in the garage," she whispered, and instinctively we went credo when there was no more cover.

We snuck to the back of his lorry. I lifted her in and shoved her forward, trying to ignore her squeal. Smacking my hand away, she looked back at me. "We need to hurry." I suppressed a grin, then slid in next to her. My back was to the bed wall and she faced me—a bit awkward. Not too long ago we hardly spoke and now, we were going to ride a good distance huddled up under each other.

"Just out of curiosity, would you have taken this route if I wasn't here?" she asked.

"Wait," I shushed her when I heard him coming around.

The man lifted the flap but only I could see him from my angle. He didn't appear to be able to see us but instinctively, my hand went to my knife. He tossed a long metal rod in the back of the truck and I bumped it out of the way before it hit Connor in the head. He stared in our vicinity, unable to see us, no doubt wondering how the object had bounced in another direction, but after a few seconds, he lowered the flap. He got in the automobile, started the engine, and we took off before either one of us spoke again.

"To answer your question—yes, but I'd prefer a companion to watch my back and I theirs."

"Don't worry, Ronin, keeping you safe benefits me, too," she responded "As long as you have my back, I have yours."

She said exactly what I wanted to hear. I had no doubts that she would do what was needed. I relied on that.

We lay in silence as the truck's motor drowned out our conversation. When discomfort lost its charm on her neck, Connor relaxed and rested her head next to mine. But as the truck picked up its pace, the ride became bumpier. I laid on my back and she rested her head on my chest. We endured the bumps on the road in the old truck for hours until we approached the dreaded city of Elonium.

"The smell." She covered her nose.

"That means we are close. Very close," I said. "We don't want to go into the plant where he gathers supplies. The sentinel at the gate might be able to detect us so we can't be back here when they inspect the bed. Get ready to jump out as soon as he slows down. Stay low, stay invisible, and move quickly."

"You may not know this about me but this isn't my first time sneaking in and out of some place."

"Yeah, that's very interesting," I said sarcastically, half-listening.

"You know what, Ronin—"

"Let's go." I loosened my grip on her when the truck slowed.

She wiggled her way down past the objects next to us and maneuvered out. I managed out next to her, searched around, and then we ran in the opposite direction of the two inspectors headed toward the back of the truck. Neither appeared to see us; lucky for us they didn't have the proper head gear on.

We stopped behind a white building by the river's edge. It was caked with dirt and smelled like a cesspit. "We're just on the edge of Elonium so we have a good distance to cover, since it's one of the largest cities on Ether. Plus, we have to get to the wall and weave our way through there. Let's go," I told her, hurrying away.

It was just mid-afternoon and since we had left so early, we made it to the heart of the busy streets in the exhausting heat. Those who did not get to work today were either up to no good or trying to make a hustle. That was both an advantage and a disadvantage to us. On the one hand, we could easily slip into the crowd and blend in, but on the other hand, that left us exposed to public notice.

"Remember to keep your hood up," I reminded her, but she already had it up and observed the intensely packed crowd. Her mood had shifted to stealth mode. "I guess I don't have to ask you if you're ready." Connor took a step forward and I followed. "Keep your head down, try and control your energy, and expect trouble."

"Got it," she said, clearly in her naturally instinctual zone.

We weaved into the crowd with uneasy grace, what with the pushing and shoving. We kept our heads low, our stride in sync. It was brutally hot, the air was sticky, and the stench could be overbearing at times, especially with the rising temperature.

The heat was at its highest but taking off the leather was out of the question. At any time, military androids could arrive and hose the whole blasted area. A mass confusion would erupt. The leather helped as a barrier against sharp objects meant to stab you and the water pressure the robots unleashed on us would force us back.

We had a good way to go and eventually, trouble would find us; it was just a matter of time. There were those who knew who I was and their dislike of the hierarchy didn't help. But, this was the best route to take. The only other way to our destination would be flying and that simply couldn't be done.

I led us down the ancient part of Elonium named Auden—by choice. This part of my world purposely never evolved by the hands of humans that were either forced here and escaped or came here to escape. Auden never wanted to keep up with technology. Its ambiance reflected the nineteenth century. The people here wanted nothing to do with my part of the world. They had an issue with being able to be tracked. To them, advancement meant no freedom. It worked for them, but only because Monlow saw no value in their worth.

We strolled through the flea market, or an area that passed as one. The people were poor and made their living off bartering. Anything they could make with their hands, such as furniture, or grow in the soil, they sold. The food was practically rotten but when you had little to no money, you could not be so choosy.

Their clothes were clearly hand-me-downs. The women's or little girls' clothing consisted of long tattered dresses and the men wore either warn loose-fitted trousers or sacks for pants. Most of their clothes were either torn or too old to be worn.

So here they sat under the weather-beaten sun, with rubbery skin, haggling over a sale, and the seller refusing to budge. Their health was questionable since they used old-fashioned home remedies. It didn't help that their hygiene methods were outdated. The water was scarce and families shared the same source. Mothers bathed their children in the community fountain.

The buildings were old and made of clay that all but crumbled. The lead-filled paint was not healthy. Simply put, it was simply shelter.

But the oddest thing happened—you heard laughter amongst the crowd even after all the bartering. I felt as if we'd stepped into a time warp. I remembered the times Tanikka would bring me here as a child—our little secret. She loved it here and now, as an adult, I understand why.

It was a home away from home. Earth on Ether. Although this was not my time period, being here allowed me to be amongst my kind. She'd given me a part of my history back. In addition, what I saw around me was a time before all the madness and the chaos started to reign in the world I knew. Past the smells, the oddity, and the poorness of it all, it held beauty—one that I'd never really noticed before this day. I had fun as a child here but I never understood its allure before this very moment. Seeing Connor's smile, I realized she felt it too.

I saw her conversing with a woman. She picked up a little toy for a boy whose mom hadn't a clue that he'd even dropped it. They exchanged words and I could only imagine she was thinking of her little brother, Kane.

After a moment of letting her absorb it all in, I came up behind her and observed her interaction with people. She took in this town and the people of Auden. Although we stood out like sore thumbs, no one seemed to care. She enjoyed herself, which made me like this place even more—but enough time had elapsed. "We must go," I finally said. She acknowledged me with a frowned peep, then back at the place, and exhaled a deep sigh. An expression of disappointment crossed her face.

She said her goodbyes to some women and kids and we hurried to leave. I believed in keeping a tight schedule and we didn't have much time to spare. We made it to the edge of civilization again and rushed back into the masses. We took long strides, making our way through, trying to make up lost time until we mingled in like zombies under the unrelenting sun.

I had no idea what time it was but by the sun's positioning, it was mid-afternoon. I wasn't sure since I had no technology on my person for this trip. Like the town of Auden we needed our freedom as well.

Up ahead I spotted a check point. "Connor." I grabbed her arm and pulled her into the closest alley.

"What?"

"Did you see the group of men ahead in black warfare suits?"

"Yea, I spotted that. Who are they?"

"It's a check point to see if any Elonium is carrying an unsanctioned weapon. They have random points but currently they're popping up everywhere and Military Protectants are covering, instead of the typical Ether Enforces." I peered around the corner.

"They will spot you in a minute. We have to find another route," she suggested, which I wholeheartedly agreed with.

"Let's go this way…" I pointed to the end of the backstreet, but it was too late.

"Hey, you two there, in the alleyway. Step out," a Military Protectant ordered.

"Sorry, guy, but that's not going to happen." I kept my head low under my hood and Connor did the same. "I'm just here with my girl, minding my business."

"I don't care about you or your lady. Just step out. Now!" He pointed the gun and I heard it power up. "By the order of Ether military command, you will." His finger gripped the trigger.

"I can't do that," I stressed, keeping my head low.

"I know that voice. You're …"

Before he could squeeze the trigger, I twisted it out of his hand and blasted him with it instead. Another Military Protectant approached and set off an alarm on his wristband, alerting nearby forces about the problem in sector 18. Connor raised her arm and sent him flying back into oncoming the traffic. A glider took care of him.

Her eyes widened, shocked at what she'd done. "It's all right. Remember, no witnesses." I pushed her forward. "Run!" We headed toward the back of the alley that led to an adjacent street.

With one swoop, she leaped over the brick barrier and I followed close behind. Four Protectants were already on our tail as our feet made contact with the street. I didn't normally run from a fight but this was not any ordinary situation. If one of them scanned me through their mainframe lenses, it would alert the main headquarters and that would bring the whole militia down on us. That included hover jets, hounds, droids, and possible druids—just to take me to my father. Having about twenty guards already on our tails was enough.

Connor was amazingly fast but I was faster. I grabbed her hand and pulled her along with me. We leaped over any wall in our path, shoved any person in our way, and plowed through any object blocking us. They were not using Tasers to stop us but actual electrical heart stopping ammo. They didn't know who they were chasing and Monlow had no qualms about permanently stopping a rebel.

As we ran for our lives, every once in a while, I blasted a guard or Connor sent two in a soaring backwards tumble in the direction they came from. None of the protectants were as fast as either of us so we'd stop every so often, let a few get close, and sneak attack. We hit hard and left them unconscious. The damage we caused to their bodies left them paralyzed. They would never recover or be the same from what we did. Connor might not have liked what we did but she was finally getting it. The more I noted her instinct to survive, the more I realized I wouldn't have taken this trip with anyone else.

We stole head gear off a Protectant in order to listen in on their strategy. Acquiring weapons did not hurt, either. Our tactic—dodge getting blasted, shoot back, then sneak attack and after that, keep moving.

We tossed weapons back and forth between us, then ducked behind shelter to retaliate. The Protectants weaved through the alleyways behind us but with Connor's hearing, we were always able to catch them off guard.

We stopped and hid in a granary waiting for four Protectants in search of us. We planted ourselves on opposite ends of the lane.

They're about to pass you, Ronin. She informed me.

The men were paired up, two at a time. We waited for two of them to pass us and it took two shots to take them down, but I quickly motioned for her to get down. I overheard on the earpiece that two more were about to pass the area where Connor was crouched.

When the two outside entered, we had four surrounding us, so we stood back-to-back trapped in place. With gun in hand, I blasted one but my gun jammed with the second guy. Before he could shoot, I knocked the Protectant's gun out of his hand and we tumbled over the ledge.

"Get down!" Connor shouted when continuous blasts came, but it was my gunman who took the blunt of the hits. Over the radio, I heard them announce: "Protectant down!" One went to check on the fallen Protectant, leaving the other vulnerable. We took that opportunity to tag team the one standing. Connor went high, kicking him in the face, while I went low and broke both his legs. Picking him up, I threw him down a shaft.

I heard a blast behind me and turned around. Both Connor and a Protectant were standing face-to-face and for a second time stood still. I had no clue what happened until the man fell backwards. Connor yanked the gun out of his hand and stepped away with the blaster stationed midair. Connor must have forced the blast back through the gun, hitting the man in the chest.

I yanked back unwanted distress. "We need to go." We grabbed the bags we'd dumped and jumped out the window, passing one Protectant who had landed on something sharp.

Our tactic of sneak attacks went on for some time, while we made sure we were headed in the right direction but unfortunately, we hit an impenetrable barrier—a cement divider. We had no choice but to duck behind a building to strategize.

"What's behind that wall? Can we leap over it?" Connor panted trying to catch her breath like me.

"No." I tried to think of an alternate route. "It blocks off liquid waste and it's highly toxic. The kind that will burn off your skin."

"In the middle of a neighborhood?"

"This is Elonium, Monlow's dumping ground." She examined the wall as if to say what I was thinking. *It's a messed-up place.*

"Be ready." She gave no further explanation, only got up and boldly stepped into the middle of the street. She stood there with her head hung low, not allowing anyone to see her face, and allowed the four Protectants searching for us to approach. When they were close enough, she raised her hands up, lifting the guards as high as the buildings next to us. The men yelled all the way over to the next street where I heard cars crash in midair.

I scanned the block and saw two Protectants come up from behind her, pointing their weapons at her. I tackled her to the ground and we tumbled, knocking down onlookers. As we leaped up, I grabbed a metal construction rod and tossed it at their heads. Their weapons blasted into the air as they flew backwards into the unstable electrical cables. Their bodies jerked uncontrollably from the electric surge.

Everyone scattered when the cables crackled on the ground but there were so many that one pinned us against a building. I ripped a piece of wood off the house and moved it out of the way.

"In here." I pointed to the nearest abandoned structure. "We have no other choice but to get over this wall. Connor, there is no way around it."

We slid to the floor as the front door lit up with bullets. It was a four-level apartment complex and we needed to find the stairs to the rooftop to figure out our next move. Keeping low, we crawled our way towards the stairs. As soon as there was a break in the gunfire, we ran towards the back of the place where the stairs had to be. We hit the floor again when the front door flew open and a smoke bomb was released. That time my wound felt the hit but we had to keep going.

"Over here," Connor said, pointing to the sign that said 'Rooftop Entry'. We scrambled up and got to the door but it was locked. I kicked it in and headed up four flights, passing a scared man hovering on the stairs.

We pulled off wooden boards that blocked the rooftop access and kicked out the door. On the roof, we searched to see which way we needed to go. "Over here!" I shouted over more gunfire. "We have to leap on each rooftop in order to go around the dumpsite…"

"Can't you just teleport us?" Connor gasped from the smoke bomb exposure filling our lungs.

"There are times it's just quicker to run and this is one of them. Besides, the distance is only three feet apart. We have to outrun them, then pick them off one by one. Jump!"

"What about you?" She watched me back up to the rooftop door.

"Just keep going. I'm right behind you." I all but pushed her forward and ran back to the door when the guards made it to the landing. I hit the first one in the throat and as he went down, my foot made contact with the next one's masked face. He fell back down the stairs. As the first one got back up, I used his weapon on both men, who were Ether Enforces. The Military Protectants had called in local enforcement for backup.

Damn!

I caught up with Connor on the third rooftop. She refused to go any further without me. We leaped over several more rooftops, working our way around the toxic dump as we avoided getting hit.

"More are coming," Connor yelled over the gunfire as we squatted behind a rooftop unit. "I hear them not too far behind us."

"They'll never stop until they apprehend us."

"Why? They don't even know who we are."

"It's forbidden to run from the law. Runners are used as a deterrent to others and if they don't catch us, they will be punished. Just keep going."

We made it to the last rooftop. "Wait!" She held up a hand. "Ronin, I can't make it." She pointed to the next complex, which was a least twenty feet away. We both looked back at the law coming for us. We'd managed to put some distance between us but it was not enough.

"Yes, you can. We have no other choice." She was right; this jump was by far the farthest.

But then, a hover jet appeared over us and announced, "This is the district 18 patrol guards. Stand down. This is your final warning."

Final warning. There was never a first one.

I had no other choice but the one she wouldn't like. "Hold tight and remember, don't let anyone see your face," I shouted over the loud blades.

"What are you about to do?" Her tone told me she already knew the answer.

"I'm not sure of the distance so I cannot teleport. We may wind up in a rooftop shaft or between walls. I'm going to have to heave you instead. Roll with the throw, Connor." Before she had time to protest, I picked her up and tossed her towards our destination. She soared in the air and somehow, her body angled to where she was upright when she landed and rolled with the momentum. I backed up, trying to avoid the spraying bullets behind me, and leaped into the air, refusing to believe that I would not make it.

Unfortunately, my right arm was hit as soon as I touched down on the rooftop. It was a rough landing but we both made it alive. She dragged me behind a roof air shaft for cover. I examined my bleeding arm but it was only a graze—nothing too serious. "We have to go."

Keeping low, we jumped off the structure down onto the brown grass below. Taking the stairs would've only slowed us down.

"My leg!" Connor hobbled over to the side of the divider.

I threw her over my shoulder and put some made distance between us and the hover jet. Weaving between the community's mini gardens and under trees, we had cover—for now. I laid her down by a tree.

"Connor, I need you to take down that jet or we'll never get away."

"Take down a jet!"

"Yes. It's like the size of a helicopter in your world so you can do it," I knew she could do it. "Remember, your powers are more advanced here."

"You're insane, you know that?" But when I didn't say anything Connor scrunched her face and raised her arms. She concentrated hard on the blades. At first, nothing seemed to happen but then it appeared as if the blades slowed and the aircraft struggled to remain in the air. A loud noise erupted from the jet and it started teetering to its left. One blade broke in half and the jet went spiraling down. A loud crash ensued a few blocks over, followed by an explosion. Red-orange smoke filled the sky. "I did it. I actually did it."

"That will take some heat off us for a while. Stay here," I told her, and went to get rid of our tail.

With purposeful steps I snuck behind an Enforcer and kicked him in the back of the head. He fell forward but held onto his weapon, then rolled over and aimed at me. Dodging his bullet, I tossed a knife in between his eyes.

His partner had to be close by but it was Connor who noticed before I did.

Ronin, about five feet behind you!

This mind telepathy was something to get used to. I looked at her, letting her know I heard, and stepped back into a bush. The guard eased right past me and I snuck up behind him, wrapped the strap of the gun around his neck, and choked him off the ground. He wriggled and kicked but it was only a matter of seconds before he would stop. Connor turned away.

When he no longer moved, I dropped him to the ground. I bent down over him but behind the head camera, took it off him, and smacked it with my boot. I did the same to the other guard's camera, then headed back over to Connor who was attempting to stand. "Here, let me help." I pulled her up.

"Thanks," she said, gaining her footing.

"Can you walk? I got rid of their trackers but we have to keep moving. They know we're in the general area so more will come."

"I can walk." She limped forward.

"Wait, Connor." I blocked her from going any further.

"What?"

"We have two options." She waited for me to continue. "We can stay in this course or …go through the mountains."

"Why are you so hesitant about the mountains?"

"It can be tricky and such; then there are the caves."

"What's the 'such'?" she asked me suspiciously, and with good reason.

I didn't think she would overlook that last part. "If I told you, then most likely you would not want to go, but it's faster, less dangerous, although it can get really wet. Just put it this way. It an enormous maze. Some people go in but they don't ever come out."

"I know I'm going to regret this and I know you're holding back a lot but let's do the mountains. If you're hesitant, then I know the military will be, too."

"Let's go. When we find a safe spot then we can rest for a few. It's getting late."

"Time flies when you're having fun and we're having a blast," she joked, but I was inclined to believe she was being cynical.

I led us into more of a dense area until we approached a large round boulder I was already familiar with. We could have gone farther but we would have to go up so this spot was the best option. I grabbed Connor and she slammed into me, catching her off guard. "Don't let go," I said, and she held onto me.

A warm sensation washed over us both as our cells dissipated together, then reappeared whole again on the other side of the rock.

Letting go of her, I stepped back and saw her wide grin. She actually thought that exciting. Oddly, I somehow never scared her with the things I said or did. She never backed down from me.

"This way." I pointed forward.

The place was as expected and as I remembered—wet, dark and eerily quiet. Splashing on the wet earth, our boots kept our feet dry, our hues naturally lightened, adjusting to the dimly lit passageway the farther in we went, but the cool temperature at night would not be kind.

"How many miles is this cave and its passageways?" Connor asked with her attention straight ahead.

"It covers half of Elonium, the biggest city in all of Ether. It runs in every direction." We continued onward, passing garbage and damp rubbish. Thankfully, it only came up to our ankles. At least this section. "This way." I pointed, making sure we kept on heading north.

"So how do you know this place, from a map?"

"No." I recalled. "There are no maps to these caves. I know them because I used this route many times to weave my way through Elonium. Not everyone knows about them and it's very easy to get lost in here. This place is a maze but I like to have two contingency plans upon escape."

"How long did it take for you to learn the paths?"

"I stumbled in here one day during a break from military school, which is like boarding school from where you come, and when I got older and had more freedom, I'd come here a lot. It took me years." I explained checking familiar markings on the wall making sure we were going in the right direction. "I'm sure you're wondering: 'He went to boarding school.'"

"I kind of pegged that the first time we talked."

"Really?"

"Yes, that and being royalty. Remember the whole joke about going steady?" She waved her hands, making a gesture. "Hee hee, haa haa." She laughed strangely. "Good times."

"Yes, I do remember that. It hadn't been a good time; we'd fought." Then I asked, "What exactly does 'going steady' mean?"

"Huh...what?" She sped up.

"I definitely have to know now. You can't even look at me." I pushed the issue, sensing her discomfort.

"It's nothing, Ronin. It just means we're dating. Like only seeing each other. That's all. Geez, stop making a big deal out of it. All right?" She increased her speed but didn't have a clue what direction we were even headed.

"Wrong way." I pointed to my left and she turned around. "Oh, I'm not 'making a big deal out of it'," I could not let this go. She was always the sarcastic one, the one that pushed my buttons, and for no other reason than to see her rattled, I had to take it up a notch. "Is that what you want us to do, go steady?"

"Ronin!" She stumbled but the wall caught her. "What has gotten into you?"

"I just asked a simple question. You're the one who brought it up. Why do you sound so alarmed?" I was actually enjoying seeing her squirm.

"It was just...a joke, okay, Ronin?" she stuttered.

I stifled a satisfactory smirk. "All right. All right. I was just asking."

"No, you're messing with me. That's what." She threw me a curt glance.

And I was. I let it go silently laughing to myself. We walked on, passing nothing but wall or rock. The water trickled from the direction we headed in but we could walk around it. After a while, we entered a wide section near low water and I figured this would be a good spot. "Let's crash here." I dropped my bag. "You need to rest your leg."

"I'm okay, but I want to look at your arm. It's still bleeding."

She was right. Blood was steadily dripping down to my elbow but I'd forgotten all about it. "I'm fine. I've been hit worse," I said, positioning myself next to her. We both leaned against the bumpy wall and it felt good to sit down. We listened closely to our environment and it seemed safe enough. For now.

"Let me see your arm," Connor said, ripping a piece of cloth from a shirt inside her satchel. She took out the bottled water and wet the rag. "Take off your coat." She yanked on it impatiently and I maneuvered out of it, lending her my arm. She wiped my wound with her a piece of rag, cleaning it off.

"It's but a surface wound. Its fine," I told her. "And before you ask about my side it's not even bothering me." I patted it.

"That's cool, but even surface wounds can get infected," she explained as she took the other half of the rag and wrapped it around my arm. I watched her tend to me like she'd done this so many times. "Yes, I have," she said.

"What?" I asked when she answered the question in my head.

"You were going to ask if I'd done this before and the answer is yes. And no, I can't read minds."

"Then how…"

"Your expression."

"What expression? I've been told that my face is usually stoic. I'm usually expressionless." I felt some kind of way about that.

"Well, I could tell. Was I right?" She finished tying up my arm. "There, good as new."

We both examined her work. "Yes, you were dead on," I finally answered when she looked up at me. After a second, I asked her about her leg again.

"It's better. Honest." She stood up and jumped on it. "See, no ouchy. I just needed to put weight on it."

"Here." I handed her a bag of protein which consisted of nuts, berries, and cocoa to sweeten it. Then some dried fruit. She kneeled down, opened the bag, and we both rested comfortably again.

"You sure know how to treat a girl."

I laughed out loud as we ate. "Yes, the Prince of Ether knows how to show a girl out on the town. Bagged fruit and protein bars in a cave. Just wait until our second date; the possibilities are endless after this."

"Why, Ronin, are you making jokes? I didn't know you had it in you." We both continued to laugh. Probably because of the perilous state we were stuck in.

"I'm sure it's because of you."

She stopped eating to face me. "Whatever do you mean?" she said sweetly with an odd accent. I think it was one of from the southern states of America.

"You're easy, Connor," I said, chucking a nut back into the bag.

"Excuse me? You want to run that by me again?"

"You know—easy. No false pretense, no false tales, and your bluntness is refreshing. You're easy to mesh with. Well, when we're not about ready to kill each other."

"Not everyone would agree with you on that one. Maybe the people here are much more difficult than me. I'm usually not the 'go with the flow' kind of girl."

"I don't have to put on any airs with you is what I mean. You're not impressed by my title or who I am. Trust me, I know you have your opinions." I peered over at her, being a bit more serious. "Plus, you stood up to your Keepers and protected me. I never thanked you for that."

"You don't have to." She gaped into her bag and not me. She must not have been used to sentiment either. That I could relate to.

"Yes, I do. Thank you, Connor, for having my back even when you don't know why." I dug deep for what I was going to say next. "I'm sorry for trying to hurt you."

"Yes, that was messed up," she said jokingly, but with a serious undertone. "I swear, Ronin, if you start to get soft on me, I'm going to puke."

"I thought you earthlings liked that kind of stuff." She shoved me and her smile slowly faded away. With my thumb, I wiped a piece of chocolate from the corner of her mouth and licked my finger. "I'm sorry I shouldn't have done that." I surprised myself. Removing my hand, I shifted over giving her space. "We'd better rest for a while, then head out soon."

"Yea, sure." She half-smiled, half-blushed. We rested on the cool ground, both staring up in silence, and all I could think of was us both safely making it to the professor's. Well, that and of Connor being so close to me.

* * *

"Ronin." Connor nudged me awake.

"Yes," I whispered back still half asleep.

"I hear something in the water."

I eased up to peer over her and the stream of water from before had risen to about where we lay, which would be my waist level, and it was choppy. It could only mean one thing. "Slowly get up. Slowly," I repeated, tapping her arm. "Place your bag on your back and we'll inch our way to higher ground.

"What is it?" she asked, upon standing and grabbing her satchel.

"First, let's get out of here. Remember when I told you the creatures here are different. This is one of them that you don't want to confront."

As soon as she took two steps back, a slimy tentacle reached from out the water and wrapped its limb around her leg, snatching her in. I reached out for her but the creature moved so quickly, she was yanked out of my reach.

I jumped into the murky water and swam after her, following the huge current and the thing that took her around the corner. If it didn't crush her in its snug grip, she'd surely drown.

By the third turn the cave dropped about fifty feet. Seeing the splash where the serpent landed, I dove in but had to come up to the water's surface to catch my breath. Taking in a long swig of air, I went back down in search of Connor. Even though the creature was dark blue, its humungous size and the bubbles it left as it moved made it easier to follow. With my eyes adjusting to the darkness, I swam down further, inching into murkier terrain through the choppiness, and caught up with them both.

Further down was almost still except for the bubbles that escaped Connor's lips. She fought hard to break free from its bone-breaking death grip but it would not let go. Swimming up to her, I gave her breath from my lungs, then pulled away. I gripped my blade to help her fight but Connor pulled a knife from her boot and stabbed her kidnapper between its eyes. The creature wriggled about but ultimately Connor was released. I grabbed her by the arm and pulled her upward out of the entanglement of the monster.

Once above the surface, I held onto her from behind while she coughed up the water she'd swallowed. "Are you all right? Can you swim to the waterfall?" I asked over the noise of the splashing water.

She answered with a nod, still unable to speak and swam in the direction of land, then stopped. "There's another one." She coughed again. "I saw its spiked back swim around us," she gasped.

She was right. Another creature was circling us. "You keep swimming. I will get it!" I shouted.

"No, we will," she managed to say with a full breath.

It bumped us a few times while it circled us. Every so often, it wrapped its tail around one of our legs, pulling us down, then released us—toying with its food.

With two sharp objects in hand we treaded the water waiting for the next hit. As soon as it bumped me, I quickly stabbed it in the center of its head with my vane. It swam away, then soon floated back up dead. Without warning, a third rose out of the water, threatening us with its large mouth of long, yellow, jagged teeth and sharp wide fins. After tossing me across the water with its tail, it took Connor under. I went in chase of the splash and found her stabbing it over and over again in its back, but its grip would not yet loosen until she sliced a limb. Finally, she managed to break free but to make sure I swam around it, wounding it several times. There was so much blood in the water we needed to leave before more predators approached. I yanked her away and we swam to safety.

Swimming over to the wall, we climbed the slick rock as water cascaded down. I was right behind her as she climbed in case she slipped and fell. "I got you, Connor. Keep going." Up we went until we reached the very top and I all but lifted her up on the last step.

She crawled to spot, coughed up more water, then fell over and lay very still. "Connor, are you all right? Is anything broken?" I asked, searching for blood, but there was none.

She faced away and I knew she was in pain. "It's just my shoulder." She held onto her arm.

I moved her hand that gripped her dislocated shoulder. "Connor..."

"I know..." she released a groan from me touching it.

"I'm going to need to...."

"I know," she repeated.

Taking off my belt, I placed it in her mouth and she bit down hard. I positioned her back flat. "This will not feel good at all. Matter of fact, it will feel like I'm tearing your arm off, but trust me."

She shut her lids. "Just do it."

As I held her arm out straight, she jerked her leg. Then, I slowly lowered her arm in an agonizing position but she endured, biting down on the belt while facing away in misery. When I heard the appropriate pop, I put all my strength into setting it back in place. Connor spit out the belt, her whole body shaking.

"Breathe, Connor. I know everything hurts right now but you'll heal quickly. Just hold your arm close to you for now. We don't have a splint."

"It's fine." She lay there, trying to ride out the sensation of too many nerves firing at once.

"I don't even know how you are alive. You should have drowned seeing how long you were underwater; then, you climbed the bank with your shoulder. I have to say I'm impressed with you, for being a girl."

"I don't know either and shut up. You're not funny." She waved her hand in the air as if to suppress her emotions. "Adrenaline."

I looked at her for a minute. She wasn't even aware of how strong she was getting, but everyone has their limits. "I'm not judging if you can't but can you go on?" I asked, hoping she would be able to.

"Yes, I just had a moment." She sat up and I applied my belt after she shook her head at my attempt to wrap it around her arm and neck. "We're in this until the end, right? Monlow must be stopped. He's destroyed too many lives and he wants to cause more damage. Let's go," she said.

With no more bags to haul after being lost in the water, I helped her up and led the way. I knew her body screamed for her to rest but she kept going. Her body would heal a great deal by the time we reached 'behind the wall'. We cut through the rock's opening, which led back to the actual tunnels. She stumbled a few times but I caught her until she regained her stride.

"Are you all right to walk?"

Connor glanced over at me. "Yes," she said, hastening her pace. "Which way? I want to get out of here."

"The good part about the attack was that it gave us a short cut. We're closer to our exit. But expect the police or military to show up again at some point."

"I don't expect anything less from this crazy planet."

We made it to the north side tunnel exit. Grabbing her close like last time and catching her off guard, I teleported us out.

It was already dawn. I had slept longer than I had anticipated but now was glad we did. More people meant more coverage. With our hoods up, we hurried like never before. We were getting closer to the Walldouskin, a.k.a. the wall, but we still were a great distance away. If all went according to plan a boat would escort us past security.

We were headed towards the outskirts of town when I noticed we picked up a tail. Not by the law guards, but an old-time companion. The kind you try to shake but doesn't want to get shaken loose.

"Connor, we have company… No, don't look." I mumbled into the crowd of bumping people and disgruntled *Sodders.* So many upset beings, it's a wonder a fight didn't break out every five minutes. "We're going to have to make a break for it."

"Okay—" She pointed down to the gun pointed at my gut.

"I don't think so, Ronin, Prince of Ether." A *Sodder* by the name of Toukin stopped us. His breath reeked of stale cigars and day old garbage. "This way," he grumbled, shoving the weapon into my side. He looked normal from the front but in the back, his head had green and black spikes and he had a long tail.

We walked three blocks over then stopped by a metal orange door that creaked when he opened it. The entrance led into a dance club. I played along until the time was right to stop being nice. As I glanced over at Connor, I could feel her tension rising. I could almost see her brain calculating as her gaze roamed over the large dance room, the long metal bar, and the four goons holding weapons.

"Ronin, it's so nice to see you," an old acquaintance named Kanton said, buttoning his cheap blue suit upon standing.

"Funny thing, Kanton, I can't really say the same thing." I backed up. "Your breath smells like sh…"

"I'm hurt. Truly hurt." He belted a loud, obnoxious laugh. "We're old cronies and old buddies don't stiff their friends." He strolled over to Connor and scanned her form like an avid window shopper. "How about this." He scratched his hefty belly "You can give me this nice piece of a human." He stopped to sniff her hair but Connor shoved him away. "I like it when they fight." He pretended to bite her then licked his overly swollen lips. "Yes, give me her and we call you and I even." His English was broken but he tried.

"I'm not into the smelly, fish lipped, potbellied kind of guys, but thanks," Connor frowned "What are you anyway?"

"She's ripe. Shugna Ronin, I may even pay you for this one myself." His eyes fixated on Connor like she was his next meal. Problem was, she actually would be his dish. His kind ate humans. Alive.

"No, Kanton, and last I remember, *your* boss stiffed you, not me. You and I never had a deal. And she is not for sale. So, unless you don't want to stay alive,

I suggest you tell your goons to back off." He was too busy leering at Connor to pay me any attention. When his long, bony tail touched Connor, she grabbed it and chopped it off with a stiletto from Kanton's own belt.

That was my cue to not be so nice.

We both went invisible and at first, the goons didn't know what to do so they just shot into the air. While Kanton lay on the floor crying over his flopping tail, Connor snagged his gun and took out two oblivious goons. Meanwhile, I jumped up, wrapped my leg around one thug's neck, and flipped him forward. The last guy became more anxious, seeing his partners being taken down, so he decided to spray bullets across the room, taking his boss's lackey, Toukin, out while he ran to the door. With bloody tail in hand, Kanton headed towards the back of the club. Him I punched in the throat and he somehow managed to shoot his own foot so I left him to the law, which could not be too far away with the racket we were making.

"Let's go!" I shouted to Connor who was rotating her hurt shoulder. We both pulled up our hoods and headed back out the door and down the alley, stopping short as soon as the law blocked the front entrance of the alleyway.

"Stop!" two androids shouted in sync.

We immediately headed in the opposite direction, leaping the fence that brought us to an adjacent street. Once again, we were on the run. We weaved our way between pedestrians who scarcely stirred but would definitely not move for the law. Them, they actually tried to slow down.

We were getting close to the docks but we still had a little way to go. The droids did not just use bullets; they used pothole bombs. That wasn't their real name but the weapons they used made holes in whatever they hit, which was usually people running from them on the street.

Every time their blue laser focused on us, we waited for the piercing sound and we knew one was coming. We waited until that signal, then leaped out of the way, hoping we didn't get hit by a bullet when we dodged. A few times, we didn't leap far enough out of the way and our foot got caught in the hole.

"Why are they trying so hard?" Connor yelled over the spray of bullets when we hurried into a quick spot to take a breath.

We've must have run about five miles already but we still had a few more miles to the docks.

"At this point, they either think we are not from here and or they want to figure out how and why we keep avoiding them. For humans or hominids without abilities, we should not have lasted this long."

She tried to catch her breath. "We need to somehow get the upper hand. Why don't we have weapons of our own?"

"Because Elonium has metal weaponry check points along certain parts of buildings and drones that fly above. We wouldn't have gotten far."

"Monlow and this place are insane." Connor took a long breath. "Well, those droids are going to catch at least one of us soon. We need a better plan other than dodging bullets."

"That's what they're were built for." I peeped out to see the droids and lawmen down the block searching homes. "They were fast and even if they got a glimpse of our faces, they could calculate who we were. I have an idea if we get just a bit farther on."

"You ready?" She nodded and we took off, trying to stay hidden, but it was impossible. We ducked when we could but that proved pointless when we spotted men on the roof. We were getting close and these snippers were just what we needed.

"Stay put," I said as we hid in an old abandoned home. "I've got this."

"Well, whatever you do, hurry up. They're getting closer."

"Yea, I figured that with the bullets and all."

"Really? You choose to be funny now." She retorted.

I took a chance and teleported to the roof while Connor stayed put.

On the roof, some men got spooked with my sudden appearance and fell off but there were those who attempted to fight. When I was able to retrieve grenades, I tossed them right at the droids—the only weapons capable of destroying them.

"You're up, Connor." Even though I was a good distance away, she would be able to hear me. But she was already walking through the smoke of the bombs I had thrown to take down the guards.

In regards to the rest of the police snipers, this time I took pleasure in letting them see my face. They did not wear lenses that scanned back to the main headquarters, so I had no fear my father would find out. When they recognized me, they either froze or wanted to fight.

I fought, without remorse to their welfare. I broke bones with such complacency, I held no regrets. These men would never work again under my father's rule. This was about survival and I would leave no witnesses.

When I was done taking down the twelve rooftop men, I helped Connor in the street. So many came for us and it never seemed to end. The dock was always heavily guarded and there was always a quick turnaround. Side by side, we fought without hesitation against the consequences.

Finally, Connor stopped in the middle of the street with bullets fired at us. Holding up her hands, she stopped the ammunition in midflight. One of her hands lowered as did the bullets to the ground. The droids froze by her will. The Enforcers ducked in fear of what she had just done, getting out of the way. Then, lifting all of these men plus droids, she sent them flying back so far, they landed on a dump site. It was the most miraculous thing to see.

"Connor…" I stopped when I saw blood trickling down her nose. She fell back, passing out, but I rushed to catch her. Throwing her over my shoulder, I ran full speed to the docks that was about a mile away. Behind a net of crates and gears, I went invisible and she did too, along with me. Invisibility remained an odd skill to me; I never really used it, I always went in head first and fought my way out. With this trip, though, that wasn't an option.

No one had gone out on the dock after the gunfire erupted. Getting caught up with the law was not good—not on any planet. On Ether, you could get arrested for no reason other than you looked crooked.

Sneaking on the ship was not a problem; making sure we didn't bump into unwanted attention was quite another. I've stowed away on a few boats in the past for reasons I care not to explain so I knew this type of ship well. It was military—so who would suspect the military of harboring fugitives? Fortunately for us, not everyone who was military rooted for Monlow, one being a companion of mine who made sure the third room on the top deck was unlocked. It was not that large, maybe ten by ten, but big enough for the both of us and there, we would be safe. Even bad guys have associates. Ones that don't ask questions.

On the ship, we made it to safety in the storage room, where I became visible once again. I laid Connor on the floor to try and shake her. "Are you all right?" I asked when her eyes opened.

"Yes," she whispered rubbing her head.

"No, don't get up." I reached over her and grabbed a bag from the corner, which contained the supplies I requested from my mate—water, food, and other important necessities. I pulled out the bottled water and a rag from my back pocket and handed it to her. "Have you ever passed out like that before?"

"No, never. My nose has never bled before. I don't understand it. I actually feel stronger here." She wiped the blood from under her nose and I pointed to a few spots she missed.

I stopped and stared at her for a minute. "Didn't you suffer from body ailments on Earth? Your powers haven't fully developed yet, right?"

"Yeah. Tanzia said it's because of some rite of passage thing. It a suffrage thing that makes me worthy of my abilities or something like that," she explained. "I thought that was over with here."

I got up to double check the door. "You are stronger. Your shoulder is almost healed. What I'm thinking is you're still coming into your abilities and even though you feel better, you're pushing your limits."

"I thought since I feel stronger, lighter … that my abilities were finally fully developed." She sat up and slumped against the wall as if defeated. "So basically, when I go back home, if I survive, my misery will return?"

"Who says your powers won't come in by then or that you have to go back?" I was curious about the afterwards, if there was one. "To Earth, I mean."

"What?" She sounded startled.

"Who says you ever have to go back to Earth?"

"Ronin, I have family, friends, all of whom think I literally fell off the face of the Earth." She said as if pleading for me to understand.

"That I appreciate, but if you feel better here, then you can split your time between both planets." I had no clue what I was asking her. This wasn't even making any sense in my own head.

"Ronin…" She swallowed back words, then got up and broke eye contact with me. She paced for a few moments before continuing. "What about Monlow?" She changed the subject like I often did, which I was grateful for. "If my abilities have not fully developed then how in the world will I be able to defeat your father?"

"You can and you will. Trust me, Connor. You may not like where my messed-up plan is headed, but it will work."

"This plan that I know nothing about?" Her browns cut me a side glance. "Why am I trusting you so much, Ronin?"

"If I wanted to hurt you, Connor, I would not go to such lengths to do so, nor would I turn my world upside down in order to do it. It would have been done two years ago."

She placed a hand on the wall to steady herself when the ship left its docking station. She grabbed her head. "I'm going to sit down." She hugged her knees and said nothing at first. "Things were simpler when we were enemies." She bit her bottom lip revealing her uncertainty.

She could not make eye contact with me as I sat down next to her. "You have no idea how much I wish we still were. You cloud my judgement so much that I ..." It was me who swallowed back words this time. Not too long ago, I'd thought Connor spoiled, pampered and annoying, but recently so much had changed.

Unable to restrain myself, I reached my hand behind her neck and pulled her lips to mine. I did what I'd wanted to do since she'd arrived on Ether. Since that first kiss on Earth.

There, stowed away, uncertain of our wellbeing, I kissed her with all that was within me as if this were to be our last time together. We fell upon the floor and I could think of none else than how she could possibly be my Destiny.

Our lips bonded as one, and I took refuge in its warmth. We kissed—our hands unbound by limits and our imagination running as wild as her untamed hair. With one hand, I grasped tightly to her mane and with my other, I greedily explored her terrain—an expanse of flesh and soul ruled by no master. We were free to do as we pleased, riding the currents of this savage sea, and our actions mimicked such principles.

Then, too soon, although I wanted more time, so much more, Connor stopped us. I deeply exhaled, staring at her now stunning lavender hues and she into my greens. She touched my face with her tiny hands that took on the burden of having to save two worlds, and it all was so unfair. My heavy head fell against hers. "I know," I said. Sitting up, I cleared my throat, trying to find some composure. "We should rest."

We said nothing else—I just stayed awake and watched the door in case someone barged in. Reaching over, I grabbed the gun out of the bag and kept it close while her head rested upon my chest.

* * *

A bang sounded on the door. Clasping a hand over Connor's mouth, I gripped the gun with the free one. But the knock was a code—my mate telling me we were close to our destination.

"Who was that?"

"Our signal out of here. We're about to dock."

"We're past the wall?"

"Yep." I grabbed that bag, cracked open the door, and when the coast was clear, signaled for her to follow. With our heads low, we crept to the catwalk and tucked ourselves low behind the deck stairs. When the boat docked, we rushed off the ship. If anyone saw us, they would not say a word. There was no need to go invisible but we still needed to be cautious. At one time or other, they got paid to stow a person away, too. Nowadays, everyone was desperate for money, especially the working class.

We stepped down onto the manmade beach of Walldouskin, also known as "The Wall". We headed toward the main streets where life was more relaxed. On the outskirts, we found food carts, small shops, and buildings made of glass.

"Turn your jacket inside out, exposing the red. Things are a bit more conservative over here. Anyone wearing all black is seen as an outsider and people are not so welcoming. Brighter is better."

As she turned her reversible jacket inside out, I did the same. "Here, put these on."

"Where did you get these?" she asked as I handed her red flats. She removed her boots and even though she groaned when she used her left shoulder, she was already better.

"Don't worry, just hurry up." I grabbed her boots and tossed them in the bag.

"If brighter is better, then how come you still have on your boots and wearing dark blue, which happens to be my favorite color?"

"This isn't a fashion show, Connor. Besides, blue is a boy's color, not a girl's, and before you comment, because you always do, we need to keep moving."

"I can walk and talk, you know."

"I know, but try not to." I marched off, ignoring her gasp.

We rushed inland to meet my contact as planned at The Wall, a place I favored. It had a lot of greenery, trees, and shops, but mostly, relaxed people. My palace grounds mimic such a calm environment. I never want the ugliness, of what I do outside its walls, to ever cross over into my home.

In the quiet park, we met up with Henrique's assistant. "Good day, sir," Markose said with an exaggerated smile—a show for the onlookers. "One must always be happy and serene here.

Good day, madam." He gave Connor a slight bow.

"Hello," Connor retorted hesitantly. "Is he all right?" she whispered to me right in front of the man.

"Yes, madam, this is The Wall, where a happy pretense is nothing but a must in public." Markose explained to Connor.

"Is this where Tanner was from?"

"If you're referring to that dreadful pale foul monster, then yes," Markose answered again.

"Let us go. We've traveled far and would like to rest our soles," I scanned the area, feeling all too anxious to settle in.

"Of course, sir."

This time we traveled by car to the dwelling I hadn't visited in a while. As a child, this place was more of a home to me, unlike my father's. I wiped my mind of old memories as we hurried along to Henrique's place.

By the back way, through the patio door, we entered Henrique's far from humble, grey stone home, as he was a man of stature. One of many, if not the main one.

"Through the study. You remember, right, Ronin?"

"Yes. It hasn't been that long," I assured him.

Passing shelves of books and two offices, we entered his larger study, where my professor stood. The man who'd been more of a father to me than Monlow could ever be. "Good to see you, professor," I said to Professor Kenrick Henrique.

"I'd for sure thought you two had been caught but I should've known better. Ronin, you never cease to amaze me." He never judged me and I never seemed to have disappointed him. Grabbing me tightly, he gave me a burly hug, securing me to his chest. When he released me, he looked me over as if to make sure I was still in one piece, even though I stood right in front of him. "We'd heard about the great commotions over the scanners and I knew that it was you and your companion here." His gaze roamed over to Connor. "Well, look at you. I could feel your energy as soon as you walked in my house." Connor did not even hear him; she was too focused on something else.

Chapter 5

Connor

"Willow!" My pulse quickened as I saw nothing but red even though my eyes instinctively glowed a different shade. She bashfully stood in the corner, twisting her bottom lip, then walked up to me.

"Connor, it's so nice..."

I don't remember what I was even thinking when my fist made contact with her nose. As if in slow motion, her whole body flew back into a bookshelf. When she looked up at me in shock, her mouth was filled with blood. The red fueled my anger even more and I punched her repeatedly until finally, she fought back.

I bit my tongue when she uppercut me but quickly bounced off the couch and kicked her in the gut. After she went down, I kicked her again, spit in her face, and punched her continually. She barely had time to defend herself. The furniture floated around us but I was too furious to calm down. She was supposed to be dead for what she'd done to us.

"All right! All right!" Ronin grabbed me and Kenrick got a hold of her. "Are you trying to kill her?" Ronin shook me.

"Get off me!" I yelled, squirming out of his arms and shoving him away. He held up his hands and backed off when he saw the rage on my face. After glaring at Ronin for a long second, I slowly turned to Willow. "We mourned you, you back stabbing traitor."

"Life wasn't easy for me either!" Willow cried out. "Look at my scars—"

"Scars! Scars! I don't give a damn about your life here or your scars. You did it to yourself. You betrayed us!" I screamed at her to shut up. "You got the Keepers and the rest of us all but shunned by the council. The San council watches us day and night and the Keepers pay for it. We yougows pay for your betrayal every freaking day. It's hard for them to even trust us anymore." My body trembled with such revulsion for Willow, I clenched my fists, wanting so desperately to fight. "You got people killed, Willow. So many are back home crying over you, wanting to risk their lives to come here to save you and you care about scars. Do you know what we have to put up with because of you?"

"Connor…" She hung her head low, crying.

"Oh, no, don't cry, Willow. Save that act for someone who doesn't know you." I pointed at her. "Save those tears for your mother who hasn't left your house since you went missing in the hopes that her precious daughter will one day walk through the door. Save it for Ron's mom who lives on antidepressants just to get out of bed since her husband went missing, and save it for Selene who lost Kahn, the love of her life. Yes, they both made their own decisions too but you could have warned us. Days, weeks went by and your conscience never once surfaced. Tell me, how did you even get our blood? Did you stop to think what you were doing was wrong or only after you were forced to come here? We could have died." I finally gulped a long breath. "So no, Willow, I don't give a damn about you or your scars. To me, they're just reminders of your actions."

I turned my back on Willow and faced Ronin. "I should have never trusted you. You lied when you said she was dead."

"Yes, in order to prevent you all coming over here and getting yourselves killed."

"You know what?" I raised my hand to prevent him from touching me. "I don't even care anymore." I stormed out of the room and headed out the back door. I heard them calling to me but I couldn't concentrate, let alone understand what they were saying.

I headed over to a stream, and onto the bridge. Water always calmed me but not today. "What?" I asked when I heard Ronin approach.

"I'm not condoning her actions because I don't believe in betrayal but you protected me against The San and hid my visits from the Keepers. Is that not crossing a line?"

"You're right, my actions were questionable with you but I never *intentionally* set out to hurt anyone. My conscience was there pecking at my brain and culpability always ate away at me. My instincts directed me to stay quiet and eventually I came clean. I've known her long enough to know she never once thought that what she did was wrong. It's all about what's best for her. She's only apologizing because she thinks it's the right thing to do not because she's actually sorry. I don't think she even cares about anyone else but her interests."

"I understand that, Connor, but we have to work with her. We all have to work together." He squinted in the light of the sun.

"You better find someone else because I'm not working with her." I couldn't even stand still I was so furious.

"We have to. She is San. We need her."

"You might but I don't," I snapped.

"Think of it this way. She doesn't want to die, either. Her being here proves that, Connor. And the only way for her to survive is to join us."

"You cannot honestly trust her, Ronin?" I tapped the side of the bridge with my nails.

"I never said that but we need her, Connor. Please." He shifted his stance awaiting my answer.

I stared at him for a long time, then took a long, exasperated breath. I didn't want to agree but we needed all the help we could get even if that meant working with Willow. "If this backfires, Ronin, you are the first one I'm coming after."

"Just trust your instincts, Connor. They have never steered you wrong so far."

I started to head off the bridge but stopped short when I noticed Willow watching us from the glass door, just staring. Her face held no expression. Not attempting to join in the conversation but observing like she was examining us. A thought came to mind.

"Ronin." I turned my back to her. "You helped her survive this whole time, didn't you? It was you who taught her how to fight because she never would on Earth…"

"Yes, I taught her because I knew she would serve a purpose in all of this."

"I don't even know what to say or how I feel about that but it's none of my business the company you keep. I just don't trust her."

"You've explained that both physically and mentally. But right now, we all need to get over our own hang-ups if we're going to survive. You never know, she may surprise you."

"Oh, wait." Suppressing my anger, I asked the question I already knew the answer to. "Ron's dad?" Ronin shook his head, his eyes lacking hope. So then I had to ask, "Was it bad?"

"Yes, very. Ripped in half by Monlow himself on day one."

I shut my lids for a brief second at the thought of that loss. I didn't know the man but for Ron's sake. "What about Khan?"

"To be honest, I don't know. Monlow promised to take his powers and let him suffer as a mere human but you never know with him. He could be no longer with us or he could be working as a slave in a mine shaft."

"Is there any way we can search for him?" I hoped for Selene's sake. Maybe if Khan could explain his actions it could at least give her closure if nothing else.

"We'd have to search every inferno of every place on the planet to try and find him. It's impossible."

"I hate your father." I spit the words out with such loathing. "The more I know about him, the more he sickens my stomach."

"You and a lot of others, Connor. That is why we are here, so will you be able to work with Willow or not?"

"I guess if I'm able to work with you then she should be a breeze," I said snidely, walking past him.

"Ouch."

I didn't really mean that. Working with him came naturally easy. I still hated that about myself. It was me resisting my instincts to work with him that made this so hard. I just spoke that way to him because he'd lied about Willow being dead—but I got his point. After what craziness we'd gone through just to get there, how could I have lasted in this place without him? But, what I said held true: if I was able to not only work with Ronin, but also be here with him, trust him as much as I had, then I could work with her.

After taking another long moment, I walked back toward the house, entering through the door where Willow had stood not just five seconds ago. Now, she was nowhere to be found. My face scrunched up when I saw the chaos I'd created with my fit, with books and furniture laying toppled on the floor or out of place. I shamefully apologized to the professor who was straightening up my mess. "I'm sorry for the way I acted in your house. The furniture, books…"

"No apologies needed. I got to see you in action firsthand. I mean I'm sorry over the reasoning, but to be able to look at the person who may be able to bring Monlow down is a historical moment."

"Well, I think a few people helped me survive and I won't be doing this by myself. It's a collaborative effort," I, immediately began helping him clean up. He was a tall man with salt and pepper hair and a scruffy beard. He didn't look old enough to have gray hair yet but maybe people here aged differently. He wore green khakis and a red and tan plaid shirt. No leather at all.

"Yes, but he's your kin, which makes your blood the key to all possibilities."

I turned towards the door when I saw Ronin walk in, then faced the professor again. Being in a strange place made me a bit jumpy. "Yes, but just because we are related doesn't mean I can defeat him." I was still confused on that part. I felt people were putting too much faith in me. *I'm just Connor Esquibel, a simple girl from Earth.*

"Stop and think about it, Connor. If you and he are related, then what he can do…"

"I can do?" I finished his sentence, my tone skeptical.

"Exactly." He held up a finger as if I'd discovered the answer to life's big mystery.

I leaned against the tall mahogany bookshelf and handed off books to the professor. "Wait, are you saying that I carry that same exact genes as him, or that everyone in my biological family is able to do what Monlow is capable of?"

"No, I think it takes a very special person to do what Monlow is capable of. What I'm saying is, since you two are related, your blood carries similar genes. That means you are more capable than anyone else."

Okay, is my brain stuck on stupid or is this man talking in circles?

"Please, can you speak plain English? Are you saying I can do all he does? Because I always assumed he was gifted in the ability to take other's powers, like I'm capable of telepathy, telekinesis, invisibility, and enhanced hearing"

"Are you sure those are all the capabilities you have? From what Ronin has told me, you have yet to fully come into your own."

"Well no but…" I lost all thought when Willow came in with a tray of snacks and drinks, and set them down on the table.

"I brought food after the long trip. I know you must be hungry. After my trip alone, without the help of Ronin, I was starving."

If looks could kill, Willow would have shriveled up to a prune. "What are you saying?" I placed a hand on my hip and all but crushed the book in my other. "What's your point?" Ronin bumped into me, warning me to calm down, and I remembered to breathe again.

Walking over to Ronin, she grabbed his arm and gave me a sheepish grin. "If it were not for Ronin and I working and *sweating* everyday together when I lived with him… Oh, he told you about us living together, right?"

I just had a heart attack brought on by a fit of jealously and the need to kill.

Ronin strode away from her and stood in neutral territory between us. "And I thought I was scary." He cleared his throat. "Listen I can feel the tension between you two and I'm not playing into it. I'm here on a mission so either we do this or we all can call it quits now. Are we in this together or not?"

"Of course, you know that I am, Ronin." Willow batted her lashes up at him, then turned to me.

I wanted to puke over her lame sugary sweet act. "Yeah, whatever. I'm here, aren't I?" Turning away from her, I faced the professor who gave Ronin a raised brow. I didn't exactly know what it meant but Ronin got it when he reciprocated with a head nod. "Anyway, Professor, so say that I either don't fully come into my abilities here or if I do and consuming other's abilities isn't one of them?"

"Then you have your answer."

I looked at Ronin in utter annoyance. "Is he serious?"

"That is why we call him professor all the time because he wants you to come to your own conclusions. What he is trying to say is that we can put a plan in motion but it doesn't mean it will work out exactly as we predict. There will be times we will be on our own and quick decisions will have to be made. Some of which will change us forever. Are you ready for that?"

"So, basically, do what you have to do when the time comes," I said, placing the last book on the shelf. "Yes, I'm ready. Like I said, I am here."

"Exactly," the professor said again.

The doorbell rang right before it opened and voices erupted in the front room. I was actually hungry but would have rather died of famine than eat anything Willow made. I went over to the window and cracked it open to stare out into the enormous backyard, needing to take in some fresh air. "Hey!" I squealed when a plate was shoved into my rib.

"Stop being juvenile and eat. It isn't poisoned if that's what you're worried about." He bit into the sandwich and tossed it back on the plate.

Why was I acting difficult, even for me? Maybe it was all the lies, the secrets and it was just too much. "I'm not being juvenile." I folded my arms. "I'm just not hungry."

"Oh, really, then that must be a bull I hear charging in your belly," he spoke starkly, referring to the ever growing growl my stomach had released ever since I'd seen the food. Ronin relaxed his face. "Eat, please. Your brain needs to function while we devise a plan." His tone was calmer but he sounded very serious.

I took the plate and bit into the sandwich—the best one I'd ever had. After wiping the slobber from my mouth, I thanked him. "I appreciate it." I barely made eye contact with him before shoving more down my throat.

How does he always manage to get under my skin?

I felt so embarrassed by my behavior but I managed to finish eating, down a drink then rushed to the other room. There sat five other men around a long rectangular wooden table while the professor and Ronin stood at the head. Some wore bright leather while others dressed preppy like the professor in either light colors or casual wear. A few acknowledged me when I walked in and sat down but my full attention remained glued to Ronin. His gaze followed me to the couch, then he shifted his attention to the table.

"Glad you're on our team," said an older man with deep set wrinkles and graying hair. I shook his extended hand and smiled politely. "I'm Dr. Pausat."

"I ask that today we all speak the English tongue," the professor began. 'Today it seems like a small group but I assure you there are a lot more of us out there. Unfortunately, we can't all be at the same place at the same time. For safety reasons, you understand." The men agreed with either nods or grunts.

"Hold on, Professor," interrupted a round bellied man with a permanently wrinkled forehead. His scowl made him appear mad at the world. "Before you continue I have to say, by looking at the girl who is supposed to help us, she seems mighty small—not to mention young. I was expecting someone *experienced* or at least grown. What can she possibly do?" A few other men voiced their opinions too but they all agreed with the man.

"Did you just call me a little girl?" I stood from my seat. "Are you afraid of heights?" I asked the man who seemed to be the most outspoken.

"No, why?" he responded, shifting in his seat but his belly did not make it easy.

I slowly lifted my right arm and with it came his seat. The man gripped the arms of his chair and looked down at the floor, which was getting farther away from him. When the man tried to jump out, I pinned him back in his seat. He fidgeted but it was useless; I applied too much pressure. Then I lifted each and every piece of furniture in the room and rearranged the décor. Everybody moved out of the way.

The man maintained a skeptical look upon his face. "You're not convinced?" I asked him when he gave me a deeper scowl and cursed at my antics. The glass door slid open and I flipped the outspoken man upside down before floating him out into the warm air.

"Ok…okay," he finally stuttered.

I followed behind him. "Are you sure?" I sent him higher. "If you'd like, I can send you right over that wall."

"Holy shyte!" the man yelled.

"Connor," the professor said in a warning tone.

"Not yet," I said, unable to figure out what had come over me—but I was enjoying this very much. Maybe too much for I did not stop.

I spun the man around several times, then made him come to an abrupt halt and left him stationary right side up. I uprooted two large trees—one could hear them whine from the unnatural evacuation but I did not stop. Transporting them toward to my captive, I encircled him with the foliage, spinning them incredibly close around him. Whether Mother Nature was angry at me or she wanted to join in, I had no clue, but the wind picked up, reminding me of her presence. The gust whipped the debris around us, even pushing against us, adding to my show. Once satisfied, I turned around and addressed every person who stood and watched in silence.

"Would anyone like to join him?" I asked, but no one said a word. "Does anyone else have any doubts about my abilities or if my age matters?"

"I think we've had enough of the demonstration, Connor," the professor said. He did not sound pleased.

I stopped the spinning trees, broke them in half, and placed them with the rest of his wood pile. Then, I slowly lowered the man back down and he stayed put for a minute, trying to catch his breath. And with that, Mother Nature took her leave.

Walking back in, I didn't miss the sparkle in Ronin eyes. He, at least, had enjoyed the show, if no one else. Everyone followed me back inside and I took my seat. The last one to enter was the potbellied man in the chair.

"Are you all right, Searene?" the professor asked when he took his seat at the table once again.

"Nothing but." He nodded and adjusted in his seat towards me. "Remind me never to doubt you again." He cleared his throat, trying to sound calm, but I'd rattled him. It seemed as if the men here needed to uphold a tough exterior but oddly, he didn't seem mad. "To push my luck, what about the plan?"

"It will be one we all can work on and figure out together." The man sat back, rested his folded arms on his belly, and gestured for the professor to continue. "We all play a part in this because we all somehow have either access to the mountain by way of work or know someone who can get us in. Our objective: to overthrow Monlow one way or another. And if we do this, we all have to trust one another or at least the plan. Plus, we must have a backup design. But know this: not one person can know the plot as a whole. That protects the rest of us if we're ever captured. This is a dangerous game we play but we have to trust in it."

"That's a lot of trust," Searene rubbed his knees.

"Yes, but there is no other way to guarantee everyone's safety," the professor stressed.

"That I understand, and I do trust my fellow man. Our families all but starve. Our lives are threatened every day and with each passing hour, it grows worse. We've suffered long enough. Those like me, I'm not worried about, nor even about a plan because if you're a part of it, Professor, there is no concern. It's the prince here that I don't trust. Everyone present knows of his reputation," Searene voiced.

Ronin stepped forward. "The man you know as Monlow is not my blood. He is not my father." The men exchanged inquisitive looks amongst themselves. From their shocked expressions, no one was expecting that. "Yes, that's right. A very long time ago, he took me from my homeland called Earth and robbed me of my childhood memories. He staked claim on my life and reared me to become what I am today. You may not like me or care for me but rest assured, I'm good at what I do."

"So now that he is no longer your birth father you turn your back on him. So I ask again, why would we trust you? You've done cruelty to this planet and the people on it by letting the people suffer and we're supposed to believe you've had a change of heart? That you will be a better ruler?" Dr. Pausat said.

"Ronin walked closer to the men, removed his dagger from his belt, and placed it in front of them, then rested his palms on the table. All of this was a sign of good faith. "I place my own dagger in front of you as a sign of good faith. Yes, I've done things, heinous things; some I regret but definitely not all. There were things that I had to do in order to survive. Haven't we all?" He searched the faces of every man in the room. "Can you call me a good man? No, but I am far better than that man who resides on that mountain." He pointed upwards.

"Monlow is dying but it may take months or even years and until then, how many of us would he have to hurt? Good men have perished by his hand—many who have served him well. He now executes simply because they know too much or dare to refuse his unreasonable requests. He's even offed two of my most trusted men because they failed in a task that *I* set upon them. No one is safe, not even me. And as of yesterday…" He took a deep breath in preparation of what he needed to say. "He threatens all young boys under the age of sixteen in fear of retaliation…" The men leaped up in an uproar but Ronin continued, "And will forbid procreation in fear of anyone overturning him. This, I cannot sit back and allow."

Every man rose in protest. "You lie!" They spoke about their son's ages and of their expecting wives. "This can't be true," Dr. Pausat said.

"No, I speak the truth but you can walk away with blinders on and continue to live in fear or stand and fight with me."

"But how do we know we can even trust you? You're not one of us. You've never suffered," Searene said.

"Oh, I assure you, good man, I've suffered. Our suffrage may be different but I most certainly have paid a hefty price being the son of Monlow." Ronin exhaled. "So no, you don't know if you can trust me, just like I don't know if I can trust you, but we are all here for a single purpose. I am what's left."

"Not if we kill you as well." Searene stood exceptionally close to Ronin and without hesitation, I rose from my seat. Ronin held up a palm, stopping me.

"I will not take offense to what you just said, Searene. You worry about your family, I get that, but how much worse will life be if I were to suddenly perish after my father? You think that any greedy dictator in this galaxy or the next would hesitate to take over Ether? There will be endless battles from inter-ested parties docking here to claim leadership—and who will be left to stop them?" Ronin stepped closer to Searene, his expression flat. "Me being alive … my fierce reputation would be the only thing saving this planet from utter destruction."

Searene did not step back but no longer stood as straight. "He's right, Searene," said the professor. He touched both his and Ronin's shoulder but it was only the older man who stepped back. Ronin's tough demeanor reminded me of the first time he and I had met. To put it in one word: intimidating. In times like this, he appeared so much older than what he truly was—a teen like me. Yet, at the young age of eighteen he took on men twice his age. Ronin finally backed up and grabbed a glass of water, no doubt to collect himself. Once he drank the full glass, he returned to the group—seemingly more in control.

"Monlow must be stopped!" Searene shouted. "My wife is expecting our third son. All I have are boys. He must be stopped!" He slammed his fist down on the wooden table.

"Yes," Ronin nodded in agreement. "And stopped he will be." He walked over to the first man. "I know all of your jobs and status so here is what I propose. Searene, you bring his meats to the castle every day, right?" The man nodded. "On that day, you need to put something special, something poisonous in his shipment." Then he faced the men next to Searene. "You, Gordmelaan, guard Monlow daily but you will abandon your duties. Just know that you won't be the only sentinel standing down that day." Ronin walked over to the couch I sat on. "You, Roubusk, are a hired gun searching for the very person you are sitting next to, the one you will never find, but instead you will protect her when the time comes." The man faced me with no particular expression, except perhaps acknowledgment. "Last but not least, you, Dr. Pausat, work in the very laboratory at which you're searching for an alternate cure in combatting Monlow's illness. You hold the key to the master plan."

No one said a word at first. All Ronin got were stares for this was all finally hitting home. Things had become surreal. Then, Ronin faced the professor. "And you will have to make a special trip to him on the very day it all comes down. You will make sure he is right where he needs to be—alone. You and he discuss finance matters privately, so he would not dare allow anyone in except the two of you. Problem is, you cannot take him down when he discovers that your meeting is a trap."

"Yes, I know that on the day of our freedom I will meet my demise." The Professor patted Ronin on the back as if to console him. "It is for a good cause."

Observing their closeness, I wondered what Ronin would have been like if the professor were his guardian. What a different person he would have turned out to be. But in some sick and twisted way, I was glad he was here and on our side. "And us?" I asked, referring to Willow and me.

"We outsmart, outmaneuver and outfight. That's what we do. It's the San way," Ronin said, lightly tapping the table with the butt of a dagger.

"What?" Willow spoke for the first time in a while. "He's what?"

"Long story, Willow." She shook her head in disbelief. "I'll explain later."

Somehow, the more Ronin spoke, the more reassured I became, feeling as though we could do anything. His composed demeanor and confident tone calmed me. Plus, the idea of fighting excited me. What was it about an impossible win that ignited my blood? As if I needed it. *Oh God, am I somehow actually like Monlow?*

I noted Ronin staring at me as if he could read my mind. "We will do this and we will prevail." He spoke to everyone but only addressed me. I faced away, confused about my questionable revelation to myself. But I shook it off to listen to the men talk. I needed to focus on what was important and suppress all doubts.

According to the plan, Dr. Pausat would retrieve a vile of Monlow's blood and give to an ally scientist to make a special toxin but the date was to be determined. Getting the blood was not the problem but handing off the vial was. Every tube was watched closely behind a locked room in a special case where cameras kept watch. As Ronin had said earlier, Dr. Pausat held a valuable role but would not say why in front of any of us.

But, they did talk of poisons that would be harmful only to Monlow's unique system. It had to be done in such a manner since Monlow had workers taste his food before he ate it and that way, his taste testers would not get sick from it. Being that Dr. Pausat was a part of Monlow's research team, he knew his genetics well. Then, the when and how would be determined during another private meeting between him and Ronin.

The meeting lasted well into the night with detail after detail being scrutinized and critiqued. The professor held a map to the mountain Monlow called 'Dom', which was short for three words in Latin, 'Domus est unum', meaning the 'home of the one'. Monlow thought highly of himself; after all, he'd overthrown the last ruler and had since ruled for over two hundred years. He had a reason to think highly of himself, which had however soured into paranoia.

When the meeting was over, each man left separately. "Remember men, you know not of each other and you will not speak of what transpired today to anyone or to each other outside these walls. You are never to be seen together and if you find yourselves in the same place at the same time, find a reason to leave. Do not let anyone *think* that you are familiar with one another. Reasonable deniability is the key," the professor added before the men left.

The only ones left behind were just us four again: the professor, Ronin, Willow and I.

We headed to the kitchen where the professor began to prepare a meal. He had made sure the staff was given time off for the whole weekend. The room was massive with dark, multicolored walls, brown wood beams, a long wooden table in the middle that twenty men could fit comfortably at, and all the amenities a kitchen would have.

Retrieving two large bowls from the built-in refrigerator, he threw the contents from one bowel into a pot while adding seasoning to the other before adding the ingredients to an oiled skillet. It already smelled appetizing. He and Ronin spoke softly amongst themselves, making sure we could not hear. Willow and I sat at the table, across from each other, and it was awkward to say the least. Every so often both men glanced back at me, then went back to chatting. It was nerve-wracking but I did my best to ignore it. At least I tried. I could have easily eavesdropped but decided not to. Just because I could hear something didn't mean I should or, in this case, wanted to.

"You're the hot topic," Willow said, spinning the napkin ring between her fingers.

"What?" I asked.

"They keep glancing back at you." She pointed to them. "What are they saying?"

"I don't know. I don't want to listen in." I could not help but sound annoyed. "Why do you care?"

"I don't." She shrugged, tugging on the napkin. "But you could hear them if you wanted to, right?"

"Yes, but if they wanted me to know what they were talking about, they would let me know."

"Suit yourself. Since living here I've learned the more you know, the better off you are."

"Are you kidding me?" I snapped. "That's what I told you back on Earth. You're the one who resisted, not us."

"Yes, but Ronin stressed the importance of that to me. He's better than any teacher I've ever had. Being with him day after day helped my confidence..." There she went on again singing Ronin's praises as if the rest of us were so insignificant back on Earth. "He was the only one who believed in me when no one else did. We'd talk for hours and he'd listen to me vent. If it weren't for him taking care of me and pushing me, I would have never survived out there. *Alone.*"

"What's wrong with you?" I could not help but stay irritated at her ridiculousness. "We all believed in you. It was you who always second guessed yourself. Besides, how can you say that about Ron, you know, your supposed boyfriend, and what about your bestie Cheyenne? Neither one you've asked about, by the way."

"Well, I would have if you'd given me half a chance before attacking me like a wild animal when you first saw me."

"Oh. My. God. Are you serious?" I leaned in real close to her. "Can it with that act, Willow; no one is around but me." I rolled my eyes, then sat back on the bench.

"But I'm not acting, Connor," she said, her voice high-pitched. "You did attack me!" My mouth fell open when she leaped out her seat like I was going to "attack" her again. "I had to survive out there all alone with no one to help me." An actual tear fell down her cheek.

"Wow!" I didn't know if I should laugh or clap. "And the Academy Award for most dramatic actress goes to Willow Montgomery. How long have you practiced that one?" I decided to clap.

"What's going on?" Ronin rushed over. "What now?"

"You know what, Ronin? I'm trying to get along with Connor but she is impossible." She pointed at me. "I've told you before when we were home." She wiped that one pitiful tear away from her cheek. "I'm still trying to get over my terrible ordeal alo…"

"Alone! Yes, Willow, I think we've all heard you the first twelve times you said it." She was working my last nerves. Even now, she kept on playing the victim, trying to manipulate Ronin like she had Ron.

"See, Ronin, she's impossible." She folded her arms and sniffled nothing. Ronin handed her a tissue. I don't know what for. She couldn't manage to squeeze another tear out.

I obnoxiously cocked my head at the guy who was standing there eating this up, and I had to laugh at this tired situation. Ronin flared his nostrils at me. "Willow, I'm sorry you were left all alone but you would have never been ready unless I pushed you. You would have never known what you could do unless your life was at stake."

"You know what? Who cares?" I shook my head and walked away.

"What does that mean?" Ronin asked.

"Nothing, just plain nothing, Ronin." I leaned against the counter.

"Listen, we all—and I mean all—must get along. So, I need you two to get over your past and your hang ups, let go of your egos and work together. If you cannot, then let me know now." Ronin pointed two fingers between the both of us.

"I didn't survive out there and get here just to go home now. I can do this if Connor can just let go of the past. I will not be judged by her every day. The way she looks at me tells me she can't stand me. How can we work with anyone like her, Ronin? Kenrick?"

"You have some nerve. How could *you* call anyone untrustworthy?"

"See!" She unfolded her arms and backed away. "Hang ups. How can you judge me when you're here with Ronin? I'm sure your Keepers and the council would not approve."

"She has a point, Co—"

"Wait, Ronin." I held up a finger, interrupting him. "What do you mean by 'your Keepers'?" I squinted. "They are yours as well, Willow or have you forgotten what you are?"

"I... I just meant that after you all thought that I betrayed you, you disowned me." She stumbled on her words and tried to recover. "That's all I meant by that."

"Yeah, try another one because I don't think that's what you meant." I winked. "I think you slipped up on that one. Firstly, you can't even admit that you did in fact betray us; secondly, you haven't asked about your family or anyone back home; and thirdly, you're standing over there playing the victim again." I wanted to wring her selfish neck. "Just be real for once in your life, Willow!"

"I am..." she whined.

"No, you're not. Did I mess up? Yes, I did. I defied the San, no questions asked, but my instincts told me to trust Ronin so I took a chance and we learned that he was in fact *San. San*, for Christ sake! Even he didn't know and we always protect each other no matter what, or even when we don't know why. But you did it for yourself, not for Ron like you claim." I pushed off the counter wanting nothing more than to leap across the table to beat her for all the crap we'd taken from the Keepers because of her and Khan's betrayal.

"Tell me, did you even think of your family or what could have happened when you did what you did? Did you feel any guilt when you went out of your way to steal a vial of our blood? At any point, did it occur to you that what you were doing was wrong? You could have gotten us seriously hurt or worse."

I exhaled all my pent-up frustration but my body could not stop shaking. "So, stop playing the victim and own up to your crap like the rest of us have to. Oh, just so you know, the Keepers know that I'm here. They may not all trust Ronin wholeheartedly, but he is our best chance for survival."

Willow sat back down, her head in her hands and cried so hard I almost felt remorse. Almost but not quite. "I am so sorry. I did it for me. I went to Khan after I saw him and Ron's dad talking at his house and asked him about what I'd overheard. That's when Khan sucked me in. He was so convincing."

I stared at her for a minute, fists clenched, and even after her confession, it was hard for me to feel sorry for her. I walked away to take some long breaths and thought really hard. Ronin was right; if we were to do this, then we needed to let go of the past.

After I got myself together, I paced back to the table. I listened to her blubbering and noted the jagged scars across her arm. What craziness she must have endured. She was no longer the bubbly sweet girl with uncertainty in her eyes. Her features were now hardened and she'd aged in such a short time. Jagged scars dug into her pretty face, short spiked hair replaced her long, thick, dark tresses, and her body had grown thin and muscular. Life was so unfair and it sure as heck didn't come with a manual. "Willow," I finally said after calming down a little.

"Yes." She raised her head now, wiping away real tears.

"Just be real. Like Ronin said, we have to work together and if no one trusts the other, then this will never work."

"You're right. I just figured you hated me anyway so why try?" She pulled on the haggard tissue in her hand. "I'm so ashamed, Connor." Willow teared up again.

I sat down and squeezed her hand. "Well, we have plenty of time to make up for our mistakes." She squeezed my hand back. Although a part of me remained bitter, I was willing to let it go like others did with me so we could get through this madness alive.

"We're either in it together or not at all," Ronin reiterated, and both Willow and I nodded.

"Now, since that's settled, let's eat," the professor said, then placed two large trays on the table—meat and mixed vegetable platters—then grabbed an assortment of cheeses, fruits and bread with different creamy spreads. It felt like an early Thanksgiving.

"This looks and smells so delicious." I told him, letting go of Willow's hand and eyeing the food. You would have thought I hadn't eaten in a year.

"Thank you. I know you *San* have increased metabolisms and passionate emotions." The professor smirked in jest. "So, I made a lot. Please dig in." He grabbed a chair and sat at the head of the table. Ronin took a seat on my side and Willow was across from us but when it came to food, it was every man for himself.

That night, we had red wine—my first time drinking it without my parent's permission and it actually tasted good. The warm liquid relaxed me and I was able to let everything go. We ate an abundance of food and talked like friends, but in actuality, the only two that knew each other well were the professor and Ronin. We let our guards down knowing this might be the last relaxing night we'd have in a long time. We would never sit, eat, or drink like this again. Actually, none of us might be alive in a month's time, so we relished the moment.

"Willow, tell us, how did you get here alone?" the professor asked, done with his food. He sat back with a glass of wine in his hand.

She tossed a piece of bread on her plate. "I hated Ronin for leaving me at that night club soon after our training had ended." We all listened as our bellies got full. She went on to tell us about waking up to some fat, hairy creature tucked under her the next morning in an alleyway, about her stealing food, how strange Elonium was, and meeting up with two kids from Earth who took her to their hideaway in the sewer. She told us how she was tricked into going to Nede.

"I've heard of that place, which is haunted by the Forest Folk." The professor interrupted. "Nede is a play on letters. It's Eden backwards, as in the garden. When you first arrive, it looks like a dream but when reality hits, it's far from that. Those Forest folk feed off tainted memories and have the power to manipulate minds." He took a swig, then sat back and rubbed his belly. "I'm sorry for interrupting. Keep eating." He gestured. "I don't have a high metabolism like the San."

"Mean and smelly was the thing that took me there." Willow pinched her nose. She explained how Nede was indeed a hoax. "Hence my hair cut," she said, explaining between being yanked out when she first arrived and all the damage it incurred during her time here, she'd gotten her tresses chopped off and how she'd managed to get away. Also, how she'd been forced into the forest behind Nede, as well as her run in with the strange animals including a creature called a gadart. As she looked at Ronin, she actually seemed pissed but soon, her expression went blank. He seemed not to have even have noticed.

"How did you get to the professor's?" Ronin asked, eating a piece of a yellow plant.

"When I got over the wall, I snuck into Henrique University and waited in his office."

"But how did you find the university and get there? It's not like the school is across the street from the wall."

She picked at a piece of bread. "Oh, I got in via the back of a truck that stopped at a market. I got out pretending to be a shopper easing my way into the street and hailed a taxi, which took me to the university."

"After all this time, you still had money?" Ronin asked, sounding suspicious.

"What gives, Ronin? No, but I hopped out that taxi and he couldn't catch me. Why?"

"That's just one remarkable story," he answered.

"Not remarkable. True." She held up a glass took a sip, oblivious to his stare.

I wondered what Ronin was thinking but the professor caught my attention. "So, Connor, what do you think of all of this?" He put his glass on the table. "Meaning the plan?"

"I'm not sure..."

"Do you want Monlow's control? I mean for yourself?" He gestured towards me, sounding ever so sweet.

Now I was suddenly in the hot seat and after a glass of wine that tasted like fruit punch, my mind was not so sharp. "What are you talking about?" I asked with heavy lids. Maybe I was a bit too relaxed.

"Since he's your kin, do you feel entitled to rule? Should Ronin worry about your intentions?" His tone was pleasant but I wasn't so sure about his meaning. Ronin glared at the man and twirled his glass, listening intensely to the conversation.

"What? Kin?" Willow interrupted. "Geez." She giggled. "I seem to have missed a lot."

Guess I wasn't the only one feeling too relaxed.

"I've never known Ronin to trust anyone so quickly. He claims he does not fully trust you but he's resting a lot on your shoulders. So, will you let him down? Let us all down?" The professor sat up in his seat, no longer smiling.

"Where is this coming from? I've never said anything about taking over Ether or wanting the throne," I said, confused.

"You may not have said it but it's in your blood. After you were born, he tortured your mother in unspeakable ways. The memory of your mother bloody and beaten is still etched in my mind and will be forever." He tapped the side of his head and the edges of his lips turned downward. "What was done seventeen years ago feels only like yesterday." He sat silent for a moment, examining his glass as if his mind had retracted back to that awful memory. A memory I didn't own—but thinking of her lying there, beaten, turned my stomach.

I put down my fork, no longer able to eat after he spoke of my biological mother. She'd given her life so I could have one. It was so unfair.

"Back then, Monlow was destined to live forever but he became reckless, too brazen even for him. He pushed his limits thinking that he was invincible. Instead of sticking to his kind, the San, and only robbing them of their abilities, he took to the forest folk, taking the abilities of an enchantress." He leaned closer to me. I wanted to move but stayed where I was, both nervous and intrigued.

"The thing about witches is that they are rather deceiving. The power he took was from what appeared to be a frail enchantress but in truth, she was most gifted. With the help of another sorceress, the one you got rid of on Earth, he took another's power but with it came a price. His body could not withstand the abilities that were not meant for him, so he became deformed, sinking into vileness, and his health rapidly declined. In one way, he is stronger than ever but in another, he is weak; so weak his body is failing him. Death is imminent."

It was I who leaned in closer so our noses almost touched. "I don't want his powers, I don't want to rule and I certainly don't want to harm people to get it," I gritted. Ronin had been right; my mood, strength and temperament were getting the best of me.

"My, my, what a temper," the professor sneered. "This place will do that to you as proven by what you did to Searene earlier. You seemed as if you enjoyed it … a lot."

Getting up, I walked to the sink. I ran my hands under water, which always seemed to sooth me, and noticed my hands shaking. I looked back at the professor, who kept watching me. Shutting the water off, I wiped my hands with a towel. With my back to them, I said simply, "Yes, I can be trusted." Then I turned to him.

"Good, because if this is done right you will be tested in ways you cannot imagine, ways that will make you question your own sanity but most of all, your integrity. You will need to reach deep down inside yourself and find that viciousness, that survival instinct which will help you persist. But the question is, can you come back from it? After this, Connor, you will never be the same. Are you ready for that? Are you ready to give up who you are today to become the person we need tomorrow? This is no easy task we ask of you."

He was making me question my self-preservation. As I went to speak, he held up a finger. "No, don't answer me. I want you to think long and hard and answer yourself. Just know that if we win this battle against Monlow, you, Connor, may lose it all as well, but he will get off easy for he will no longer exist. You, Connor, will have to live with the consequences."

For a long time, I said nothing, unsure what he was asking of me. I figured this would be hard, harder than I could ever imagine, but just assumed we would either win or lose and I would go back to my life either way.

Is that no longer possible?

"Sorry to put a damper on things but that is what I do," he said, picking up his drink again and reclining in his seat. I half-smiled. He gave me a lot to think about. "I see you're deep in thought. Try not to ponder this too much. The answers you seek will only come to you when it's time."

"Yes, Professor, you know how to wreck a mood." Ronin stood to pour more wine.

"And you know how to cause trouble," the professor said to Ronin.

"Willow, are you all right? You're mighty quiet," Ronin asked.

But she looked up at me. "He is right, Connor. You will find yourself doing things you could never imagine in a million years. I am no longer the same. I could not imagine going home again to Earth, as much as I miss it."

I walked over to the table. "Willow, you can go home. So many people miss you."

"But I am no longer me, the Willow they know."

"Does that matter?" I asked.

"It does to me. Can you honestly say you are the same person from the time you walked through that portal from Earth to this very moment; or that you haven't seen or done things you wish you could erase?" She went back to twirling her napkin ring.

What she said was heavy and truthfully, I didn't need to think about it. She was right. I thought about having to use a gun, about having to put my hands on humans and not just against supernaturals. "See," she said, reading my face, making me blush. "This place changes you."

"It's late and you three have to set off tomorrow. My men can fly you to Vonvere and from there, you can travel back safely to the palace."

"True." Ronin checked a square device and when he pressed a button, the time flashed above. It was close to three in the morning. "I need a long, hot shower and a good rest," he said.

"I second that," I said, wanting so desperately to get out of this room and leave the spotlight. I wanted to be alone.

"Willow, you know where your room is. Ronin, you know how to find the room you usually stay in. I left linen for both you and Connor."

"Wait, what?" I asked. He and I had crashed in the same room before but that had been out of pure need since we'd been so close to the mountain.

"Good," Ronin said, grabbing his coat and dagger. "Connor, you go where I go. Just because we're behind the wall doesn't mean you're safe. Monlow has spies everywhere."

"But…" I stopped talking when he left the room. *Guess the conversation's over.*

"Let's go, Connor," Ronin called from up ahead. We walked down a long hall, past the sitting room we had stayed in earlier, and headed down another hallway. The home was as large as it was cozy.

We entered a room to our left and there, in the center, sat one bed. I nearly leaped out of my skin when he shut and locked the door behind us. Even though we'd been in a room overnight together, no one I knew ever found out about it. My cheeks felt warm.

"You can take your shower first. I'll make sure this place is locked up tight," he said throwing his belongings on a chair. I hugged my arms and rubbed the back of my neck. "Are you cold?" he asked.

"I don't know," I answered, unsure of anything. I suddenly felt like I was having an out of body experience but didn't know why. My nerves were getting the best of me.

He made sure the window was shut tight. "If you don't want to go first, then I will," he said, pushing on the window to make sure it didn't budge.

"No, I'll go." I scurried into the bathroom and noted the clothes on the marble countertop.

"The professor acquired clothes for us since we lost our bags earlier." Ronin poked his head in. "Keep this switchblade in the shower with you." He placed it on the edge of the tub, then left without another word. As soon as he did, I locked the door and fell against it. After a moment, I disrobed and hopped into one of the best showers I'd ever had. I scrubbed away all the dirt, grime and muck. I must have looked and smelled horribly, but after a while you don't seem to notice smells, especially when your mind is focused on so many other things.

After what must have been twenty minutes, I was fully clothed. I opened the door to the room and found Ronin's back to me. He turned around as he was eating an apple with a knife. I stood in the doorway unable to stop watching him eat.

"You want a bite?" He broke the silence. "I know the professor interrupted your meal and I've seen you eat." He held out a piece stuck to the end of the knife and I plunked it off the tip.

I needed to go outside to get some fresh air.

"Where are you going?"

"There." I pointed at the patio door adjacent to our room.

"Make sure to keep the lights off so no one can see you. I'm hopping in the shower." He removed his shirt while he spoke.

Gripping the door handle to the patio, I broke it off. "Jesus!" I covered my mouth.

"Are you all right?" he called out.

I held up the handle, embarrassed by what I'd just done. He rushed over, lifted my hand and examined the handle still in my palm. "Connor, you bent the metal." He examined me then the thing again. "This iron is not easy to warp." He stared in wonder before prying it from my hand and innocently gliding his fingers from my wrist down to my fingers. A warm sensation stirred inside me.

"Are you all right? You're acting peculiar," he said, echoing his words.

Shoving a knife in the hole of the balcony door, he twisted it and opened it. "I...I think the professor is right," I swallowed, fidgeting with my hands. "This place is affecting me."

"Ether will do that to you," he responded.

I walked outside but he kept the door open. When he walked away, I closed my eyes while taking in long breaths.

Connor, what has gotten into you? Every sensation feels so heightened. Is it just this place or is it me too?

I decided to purposely forget the last ten minutes of my life and just relax. The area reminded me of what I'd always imagined the United Kingdom would look like. The house had two floors, adorned with light colored stained glass windows, dark wood trimming, and red brick with a chimney off to the side. A lot of land surrounded the place and no other house was visible.

The temperature was a little chilly but I still felt somewhat warm. I sat down in the cushioned lounge chair and pulled my knees up to my chest. Looking up to the stars, I reflected on the day. What a long one it had been.

I woke to Ronin placing a blanket over me then lying next to me on the seat. I hadn't even realized I'd fallen asleep. I must have been more tired than I thought. He pulled me close and my back rested against his chest, his head above mine. His fingers intertwined with mine and we stayed that way until sleep took its toll again.

* * *

The sun was our natural alarm clock as it greeted us with a beaming smile. The pleasant aroma of food cooking wafted our way and woke my belly.

"We need to get going. Our escort will be here in an hour." Ronin got up first and I wriggled the best stretch I'd had in me. When I felt eyes on me, awkwardness set in. I avoided that gaze, remembering last night's oddities.

"Are you all right?" he asked yet again, placing the blanket back on the shelf. "You were acting strange, even for you."

"Real cute." I removed my smile when his face showed seriousness.

"Do you want to talk about last night or what happened on the ship? Shugna, what happened between us on Earth?" I slowly shook my head barely able to face him. "Are you sure?"

"Yes." I hoped he did not want to probe any further. I pointed to the bathroom and he reluctantly stepped aside, letting me pass. In the bathroom I fell against the door again.

Why is it that I can take on creatures twice, hell three times my size, but I can't deal with emotions?

But Ronin is so mature. He's the Prince of Ether and I'm just a girl from Earth. I pushed all that to the back of my mind and cleaned up.

Twenty minutes later, we were back in the kitchen and once again, the professor prepared an abundance of meats and cut up an assortment of fruits, and other things I didn't recognize. Though that would not stop me from eating them.

"You spoil us rotten," I said, ogling the food. "Good morning."

"I hoped you all fared well," he said to all of us but his gaze fixed only on Ronin who was busy checking the outside. He pushed back the curtains to the double glass doors which lead to a walkway in the backyard.

"I've heard from Barreck. Our escort will be here within the hour," Ronin informed him.

Willow marched in carrying her daypack. Walking over to the fridge, she grabbed a drink without saying a word. "Willow," I called wondering what was up with her.

"Hey," she answered examining the contents in the refrigerator.

I walked over to her. "Are you all right?"

"Yup." She moved away.

"What's with the cold shoulder?"

"Nothing. I'm just tired."

Wow, not even eight hours later and she'd become the ice princess again.

When I tried to walk away, her words stopped me cold. "You must feel privileged." She poured herself a glass of water and then looked past me as if I were insignificant.

"Privileged?"

"All this extra attention you're getting?" She smirked. "I mean from Ronin and all."

"It's for protection's sake, Willow." I could not believe her. "You know I didn't ask to be Monlow's direct descendant and all this extra attention doesn't feel like a privilege, believe me. But if you want to swap roles then so be it. Please let's swap. I'm begging you." I cupped my hands together in prayer.

"You're ridiculous, Connor. I'm just making sure that your head is on straight. We all seem to have to rely on you so I don't want to go through all this for nothing." She spoke so nonchalantly but she was very serious.

"Willow, I have a constant mark on my back and every day I think it may be the last one. Monlow wants me dead, not to get to know me. So how would I feel fortunate?"

I waited as she took her time finishing her drink. "I'm just saying, how could a girl not like all the attention a guy like that is giving her?"

"What is wrong with you? This is not about Ronin. This is about taking down a monster that wants to wipe us out of existence. I cannot believe you are actually jealous." I was seething at this point.

"Whatever, Connor. Glad we cleared the air. If you and he are strictly business then there is no problem," she said icily. "Oh, and a word of advice, you really need to learn to control your temper better."

"What..." I began but she walked away, taking our idiotic conversation with her.

I really think that she is trying to drive me insane.

I thought that conversation was a bit odd even for me. Truthfully, I'd never really known her that well, even back on Earth. She was the rich girl who lived in the million-dollar home thirty minutes away from me so we didn't have much in common. Her mood shifted like the wind there but now it was impossible to keep up.

But deep down inside, a part of me felt guilty. As much as I wanted to deny it, Ronin and I were closer than others knew. I just could not figure out if that made me a horrible person, a treacherous one or whatever else. I was so confused. I just needed to stay focused on the mission—that was my priority, no matter what.

Shortly after breakfast, what appeared to be the most advanced flying contraption I'd ever seen touched down on the grassy area in the professor's backward and we headed out. The professor followed us out and we said our goodbyes.

"Thank you for everything," I said to him. He shook my hand but held onto it.

"Remember what I said." He nodded with the utmost seriousness. "Make sure you're ready for this."

"I heard you and I'm ready." I had no clue about what I'd agreed to but I'd come this far so there was no backing down now. With that, he let go and I headed to our transportation. Barreck, the pilot, pointed to what looked like a hoverboard. I stepped on the thing and it lifted me up to the level of the flying machine.

The inside of the flying machine was decorated in mostly black, offset with white and grey. There were eight seats, and two upfront for the pilot and copilot. It wasn't the size of a jet but definitely nice and spacious. When the pilot strapped me in, he stared at me for a long moment and I stared back. I noted a lot of people doing that lately. Once he got an eyeful, he moved on to Willow.

I overheard the professor speak to Ronin. "You know I have always loved you like a son. I've never judged you and never will but remember there is good in you still." Ronin kept his face averted, his expression flat, but I would have sworn he was fighting back tears. "We won't meet again, my son, but promise me you will take Monlow down. Don't let this all be in vain."

"I promise," Ronin assured him and the professor pulled him in for a hug, ignoring the youth's extended hand. They stayed that way for a long moment, then Ronin ripped himself from the man's arms and rushed away. This was their goodbye.

Ronin got inside and strapped himself in. He leaned forward in the seat, resting his elbows on this thighs, his stare was that of one who wanted to rip someone apart. Somehow, though, he managed to stay composed. Years of practice, I guessed.

As the machine lifted off, Ronin stared out the window and watched the professor until he was out of sight. None of us sat next to the other. Maybe it was the stress and we all needed room to breathe. I laid my head back on the black plush seats, expecting to feel the change in altitude but felt nothing. The ride was smooth. The main lights shut off and the smaller lights lit up.

"What is this thing called?" I asked Ronin.

He looked at me for a moment before answering. "It's a rodaane. It's like a helicopter on Earth but more advanced." His view returned to the floor as if he sank in deep thought. I said nothing else to him but gave him his space. He kept his fingers clasped and his jaws clenched, no doubt trying to keep his emotions together. He was already mourning the loss of the professor.

Thirty minutes later, we entered the outskirts of Vonvere and soon after touched down on top of an all-white building. Actually, all the buildings where white. Ronin unbuckled first and jumped out into the hot sun, followed by Willow, then me. It was sweltering, the sun's glare blinding.

With Ronin as the leader, we rushed past two armed sentinels accompanying a man who appeared to not only look just like Ronin, but also dressed exactly like him. The pair exchanged a glance but nothing else. The three of them headed away toward the rodaane.

A doorway led into a long cool antechamber, which eventually opened up into an extravagant suite. The walls were charcoal grey marble, while black concrete pillars lined the room. Blackout curtains covered large windows, with artifacts on white stands stationed in front of each pillar, and paintings of obscurity, the value of which had to be mind-blowing, were strung up high.

This place was far different from his palace and the colors matched the ambiance. The energy was gloomy and brooding, if a home could possess feelings. Something told me the artifacts in glass cases were more than pretty, shiny objects to admire. They had to be of great importance.

When we took a left, entering another hallway, I remembered his twin. "Why did that man look just like you?"

"He's my hired identical. His sole purpose in life is to look like me when I need him to and keep his face hidden when he's not me." Ronin started to unbutton his long leather jacket as we walked down another lengthy hall, passing numerous closed doors.

"And the white buildings?" I continued.

"So it's harder for the droids to distinguish one structure from the next. The reflection has been known to blind their red eye. It messes with their perception and memory chip." He removed his jacket.

Reaching the end of the hallway, he opened the double doors and a roomful of windows greeted us. The view was spectacular. The place overlooked a clear blue ocean—nothing but an endless sea. I walked outside the glass doors to the balcony built over a cliff.

"Is this your other home?" I asked right when two females walked in and my breakfast threatened to come back up. Unfortunately, I knew them both. Back on Earth, one had pretended to be Ron's grandfather's nurse but she wore no uniform this time. Instead, her outfit consisted of a short leather shirt over tight leather pants. She actually had gorgeous features and her dark hair brought out her crystal blue eyes, especially when the sun reflected on them. One would think she was normal but I remember her fire-breathing threats well. Standing next to her was the menacing Goth chick Cheyenne and I had fought. Nothing had changed about her at all. She still wore the same leathers with spiked hair and tattoos that could come to life.

Them being here reminded me again how cruel Ronin could be and that he had been our enemy not too long ago. I was not naïve enough to believe he had turned over a new leaf and would suddenly walk the righteous path after discovering his true roots. I'd already seen firsthand on this trip that he would do what needed to be done in order to survive.

"Relax, everyone." Ronin held up a palm and I released my tightened jaw, realizing I'd clenched my fists. "It is way too intense in here."

After a second, I relaxed my grip and blinked back my rage, as did the others. But my glower remained intense.

After the Goth chick gave me a once over, she turned her attention to Willow. "So." Her hard gaze rolled over every inch of her. "You're still alive, eh? I'd thought you'd be dead by now." Her accent was thick and harsh.

"No thanks to you. Yes, I'm still alive," Willow barked. I'd never seen her so brave before.

"It's not my job to babysit simple little human girls." She sucked her tooth at me and Willow.

"Simple?" I marched towards her and we met halfway in the room, standing extremely close. "You want to try that one again?" I challenged her. "Last I heard you need us simple humans or you can figure this out yourself."

She laughed. "You think you are so tough, little human girl?" She stepped closer and our noses touched. We were exactly eyelevel.

"Do we really need her?" I asked Ronin, my attention still on her.

Ronin stepped in and pried us apart. "I see it will never be a dull moment with you two around." He looked between me and her. "Right now, we will need all the help we can get."

I walked away towards the window, barely able to breathe in that suffocating room. I peered out keeping my back to everyone. If someone had told me months ago that there were supernaturals and I would be on another planet, siding with the enemy, I would have thought they were crazy. I felt like I was being tested. How was I to be sure that after this was all done, Ronin wouldn't still come after us? My mind was getting jumbled with all the chaos and confusion. I put so much faith in him and that might all backfire on me one day.

"Connor." Ronin's voice shook me out of my heated thoughts.

"Yes," I said, still not facing him. How do you fight alongside people you can hardly stand, let alone be in the same room with?

"Everybody out. Connor and I need to talk," he told the others.

"No." I spun around and a levitating sword, pointed at the Goth chick's heart, dropped. She growled at me.

"Out," he said, opposing me. Once they left, he kept his distance. "You're picking up on the vibe here and everyone else's energy."

He was right. I could breathe a little better once the room had cleared. I shut my eyes trying to regroup, then opened them to see he was still giving me space. He was being cautious. "Not only them but this whole place, including the strange artifacts we passed."

"Being on Ether makes you more powerful but it also means you will pick up on others' vitality as well. Soon you will be able to distinguish each individual being—humans, aka hominids, or abnormals, aka nunans, as your kind calls them. So much is getting thrown at you at once but you need to learn how to desensitize the weight of the energy."

"I know, Ronin, I know," I answered rubbing my face. It was hard to stand still.

"When we get back to the palace, you, Willow, and I will need to learn how to work as one and the best way to do that is to train. I don't know if you've noticed but your shoulder is healed."

I rotated my arm and he was right.

"I know you don't trust me, Connor." His serious tone held strong. "You have no reason to. You may even think I will betray you after this is done. That is what I would think. But this cannot work if you and I cannot trust each other."

I walked up to him. "You were able to defy the San before, something we should not be able to do. So, if you end me there will be no resistance, and you will be free to do as you want with no ties to anyone."

"I've had years of cruelty drilled into me and that's allowed me to do the things I have done," he reminded me. "But speaking of trust, why didn't you tell me about this so-called Destiny? Why did Tanikka have to explain it?" He squinted as if trying to read me. I tried to walk away but he grabbed my arm, stopping me. "Answer the question, Connor." He sounded angry.

"I don't know." I yanked my arm away. "I wanted you to make your own decisions without prejudice and I'm glad I kept my mouth shut. The professor already thinks I want the throne and if I told you, you might've thought the same thing." I stepped away but my attention stayed focused on him. "Does it really matter, Ronin as long as it works to our advantage?"

He wiped his mouth with the back of his hand. "How do I know you won't use this to rid *me* afterwards?" he asked, and the look in his eyes showed serious caution. He'd changed the subject, something he did so easily. Maybe to ponder what we said before he spoke about it again.

"I think if there is anyone who has proven he will do anything to survive I think that is you." I gritted my teeth. How dare he accuse me after all he'd done to our kind?

"You don't trust me at all, do you?" he asked.

"No more than you trust me," I quickly responded now in his face. "Anyway, I thought you studied the San way? Shouldn't you know about this Destiny?" I asked him.

"So, this is a San way?" he asked but I didn't answer, only glared in his direction. He took a long breath before continuing after hearing no response. "Yes, I have studied, but you know as well as I that they tend to scratch things from the book. Like Monlow is nowhere to be mentioned."

"How do you know they remove history from the books?"

"I may not have Keepers but I have my resources." He walked away.

There came a knock on the door, interrupting the conversation I never wanted to have with him.

"Come in," he ordered.

"Your transportation is here, sir." A man in a black suit bowed.

Ronin glanced back at me for a moment as if to contemplate something, then addressed the disturber. "We'll be right out." The man slightly bowed once again, then shut the door behind him.

Without words, Ronin entered his walk-in and put on another jacket—this one black with gold trim. Somewhat observing him, I ventured in and was immediately in awe over the multitude of clothing. Ronin positioned himself in front of the mirror, making sure he looked presentable as a royal. After all, he had a role to play. I just wondered if he was playing a role for me as well.

Turning my attention away, I noted the most bizarre thing.

In the corner, next to all his suits, jewels, and other clothing sat an open vault. Inside lay the very article that had saved my life—the bracelet Ronin had placed on my wrist long before I even had any suspicion of who he was. The once shiny chain sat frail and blackened on the sides for it no longer held power. Reaching in, I took it into my hands.

A hand reached over and touched it and I looked up at its owner. "I had it sent over." Ronin stared at it as he spoke.

It hit me. This place was more than just another home; it was a getaway. A sacred place to him. This was where he kept all the things that were important to him since he could never show that side of himself to the public. This whole building seemed to be a vault of sorts where his most treasured possessions stayed hidden. And I was among his most memorable—yet, before two days earlier, he'd had no clue as to why.

Taking the tattered bracelet, which no longer held value, he placed it back in the vault. He waved his hand over the opening and a solid door appeared. He squeezed my hand and my breath caught in my throat. As much as I wanted to be angry at him, to hate him, I was seeing an actual humane side of him that he kept hidden from the world.

He headed to the closet door and shut out the lights. It was time to leave. After one last look at the vault, I hurriedly turned to leave but Ronin blocked my exit with a raised arm. I stopped. Slowly wrapping his arm around my waist, he placed his forehead against the side of mine. I shut my eyes and gripped his arm. We stood there for a brief moment, letting our feelings collide. In that moment, he all but told me I could trust him and in my way, I told him the same.

We got swept away in forbidden territory. My body soared from the elation and with it came a wave of fear from such a joining. I wanted to run but he held me even tighter, as if he knew I wanted to run. For two people who didn't know how to express themselves, we understood each other more than most others could ever fathom. We needed to learn to trust one another and get off this ride of constant struggle for control—or this mission would never work.

There came another knock on the door and as it opened, our walls rebuilt themselves.

I walked ahead without looking back.

Chapter 6

Connor

The ride back to his palace was a silent one with just the three of us—Ronin, Willow, and I. His hardened expression returned and I could understand why. Ether was poisonous.

The closer we went, I could feel the constant pull of Monlow's energy, like a dark cloud that blanketed this planet from the man they called 'monster'. Was he truly as hideous as they said? I guessed I would soon find out.

We hovered over Ronin's palace and lowered onto his garage roof. Once we touched down and the vehicle door opened up, Ronin did not jump out like he usually did. He hesitated, then rushed out after a moment. We followed suit.

I'd never seen this side of the palace before but it was just as stunning. I could feel us rising up in the air and the scent of sea salt soared through the opened windows. The breeze lifted the sheer yellow curtains and the sky was a partly cloudy red blue hue. The rooms were as roomy and colorful in shades of turquoise and Arabian orange with mahogany wood paneling. Numerous people were lounging there or straightening up when we walked in.

The place seemed more like a sanctuary—warm, serene and utterly peaceful. There wasn't the hum of technology or much advanced equipment.

"How do you know you can trust this many people, Ronin?" I whispered as we traveled past various rooms.

"I have gotten rid of most who seemed untrustworthy but some I had to keep or it would have looked suspicious. Most have been with me since my youth. They came over with me from the Dom and are grateful to me to be out of that…" He bit his tongue and didn't say what he wanted to say. "Anyway, they've learned not to question my guests and to turn a blind eye to what I do."

"Judging from the first time I came here, there seem to be definitely fewer people," Willow said.

"But it's still a lot of them, even the transporters." I could never be comfortable with this many people always around me, especially now. "Did we need to take the transporter?" I asked when he headed down stairs.

"We had to head to Vonvere to be seen traveling from there. My men can be trusted."

"But what about mind readers?" I asked

"There are ways around that," Ronin confirmed what I'd hoped.

"Please tell me you don't have a lot of technology here so…"

"We can't get spied on?" Ronin finished my sentence. "On it, Connor." After that, I quit with the interrogation but needed to make sure this place was safe.

We seemed to be in a more secluded area of the palace when we entered a sitting room. Immediately, two women came in, carrying two trays of food. They placed them on a round glass table next to a glass wall, then poured drinks in three glasses.

Ronin walked over to two large computer screens. "Don't worry, Connor, everything is encrypted," he said, staring at the screen. He appeared troubled but I didn't question it and just left it alone. As soon as the women left, I grabbed a drink while sitting on the couch.

Willow's mouth fell open. "Hey, that's not fair. I'm tired too." I rolled my eyes and sent her over a glass. It felt good not to move and a nap was on my immediate to do list. Curling up on the couch, I shut my eyes, wishing I were in my own bed.

"Don't get too comfortable, Connor. We have our first battle session soon, so make sure you fill up on nutrients. I've seen you both fight and I'm not impressed."

I shot up. Ronin toyed with some gadget I'd never seen before. "Excuse me? I'm going to ignore that jab. I thought you meant that when we got back we were going to train—as in starting tomorrow." Ronin did not respond, only focused on the computers. My head fell back on the couch.

"Get used to it." Willow dragged her feet over to the table.

"What do you mean?" I asked, watching Ronin hurry out the room without a word.

"Make a plate, expect the worst kind of pain and believe me, don't ask for mercy," Willow advised me, slapping meat on her plate.

Sucking my teeth, I shoved a piece of meat in my mouth, then quickly grabbed more as it tasted delicious. Being alone with her was kind of awkward. Who was I kidding? Being around her and Ronin was more than strange. I brushed the feeling off and wondered about Willow's time here. How did she ever survive or wind up here at the palace? "Willow."

"Yeah." She turned around.

"What happened to you when you first got to Ether? I mean, how did you wind up here with Ronin?"

She placed her plate down on the table. "I was so scared." She moved her head from side to side and water instantly rolled down her barely tanned cheeks. "Ronin's minions took us straight to Monlow after we portal jumped. Stupid me, thought that if I could just explain my story, he would send me back." She swallowed the rest of the food in her mouth. "Connor, he is hideous. You cannot imagine how ugly and scary he is. I was afraid just being in a room with him but when he ripped Ron's dad apart, right in front of us, that's when I knew the meaning of horror."

"That's awful. Poor Ron. He doesn't even know." I pictured what she said in my head and placed down the food in my hand.

"That's terrible!" she suddenly sounded angry.

"Well, yea..." I was confused. *What just happened?*

"That was the easiest part. After leaving Monlow's chamber, I sat rotting away in a cell next to this hideous monster, a gadart, who used me as an incubator." She touched her rough face and scarred arm.

"That's how you got..." I touched my own cheek. Her skin reddened and she turned away from me.

"That ... that thing was pregnant and when I fell into the dark side of the cell, she'd inject me with her unborn. They used my warmth like ... like parasites." She spat and kept her back to me while she spoke, but by the glass wall's refection, I could see the scowl upon her face. "I sat in the only light my cell provided, begging to die, but death never came. I pissed myself I was so scared and purposely starved, refusing to eat the food they gave me—at first because it was still alive but after a while I'd hoped my life would end."

I was sickened by what she told me. "Willow, I'm so sorry..."

She spun on her heels and held up a finger for me to hush.

"Finally, Ronin rescued me from the fresh hell Monlow had put me in, got those things out of me—those gadarts—and brought me here." She exhaled. "This place is where he trained me, worked me, and he would not give up on me until I became what I am today—part freak, part mortal."

"Part what?" I wanted to hug her out of pity or punch her for being so stupid in thinking that, but something told me not get too close. "No, Willow, you're all human. Like me."

"No!" she shouted at me and I stepped back. She shut her lids for a few seconds then reopened them exposing her big brown hues that no longer held innocence. She inhaled, then wiped her tears and got a hold of herself. "Ronin helped me when no one else cared…"

"That's not true…"

"Yes, it is." She shut me up. "Ronin is tough, misunderstood, but he is good. He saved me, Connor. Don't you get it?" Her arms were bent and she held her hands tight. I just nodded, not wanting to interrupt. "He's just as important as you, if not more. One day he will be ruler of this planet and if something—anything—happens to him for protecting you, I will not hesitate to come after you." She pointed at me.

It took me a minute to digest what she said and her threat threw me off. We stared at each other for a long while. I just could not figure her out. One minute she was this naïve victim and the next, she was bone chilling. Had she always been like this or did Ether morph her?

Finally, when I was about to speak, the door opened and Mindalous entered. "Willow," she said in a flat tone.

"Mindalous." Willow glowered. "I bet you never expected to see me again, huh?"

"I had my reservations," the woman said and neither spoke pleasantries. "Willow, your room is down this hall and…"

"I don't need your help. I can find my way," Willow cut her short and stormed out the room.

We both watched Willow's abrupt exit. "Glad that you are well, Connor."

"Thank you." I half smiled through the tension Willow had left behind.

"Will you follow me?"

"Um … yea sure," I said, still half dazed by Willow's behavior. She took me back to Ronin's room to change. "There, in the closet, I made a place for you. You will wear these combat clothes during battle sessions."

"Thank you," I said with a smile, then let it fade as soon as she left and plopped down on the bed. God, I missed my own room, my own space. What I would give for a simple nap. Letting that thought go, I hurried up and put on the clothes given to me. They were not my style, or my size, for that matter. After examining my reflection in the mirror, I began tugging on the top.

Who are these clothes made for? A Barbie doll? Why is everything so tight around here?

Out in the hallway, I met up with Mindalous and we remained quiet while waiting for Willow. My stomach flipped thinking of how much stress I needed to release. Then it dawned on me: Ronin and I had already fought and I barely survived that. He was gifted in enhanced combat.

Ronin is going to kick my butt.

Soon after Willow came out, I didn't even face her, only followed Mindalous. We entered a large room with a soft wood floor and long windows from which hung tan sheer curtains that shifted when the breeze drifted through from the beach. In the middle of the floor, Ronin sat shirtless and shoeless, his dark hair falling whimsically upon his shoulders. Ripple after ripple of muscle traveled up his arms and down his chest into a well-toned abdomen.

Damn!

I blushed and quickly looked away. Three fighting sticks were positioned in front of him and his serious demeanor. After entering the room, I actually looked forward to a good fight. Keeping active kept my mind and energy flowing.

"Pick up the Kali sticks and stand in front of one another." Ronin stood and began to slowly pace around us with his arms behind his back. "This is just the beginning of however long it will take for our plan and all parties to become symbiotic. That could mean weeks, but plan on it taking months." My stomach dropped. *That long.* "I want to see what you each are made of. Do not hold back because I assure you that your skills need developing. I will push your limits to the extreme, then push even harder. Do not take strikes personally. We are on the same team and will continue day after day well into the night and sometimes early morning—battling, strategizing, and working to become as one. Expect broken bones, bruises, pain beyond measure, but we will *not* miss a day of battle." He paused. "Are you ready?"

"Yes..." I said in the prone position but instead of Willow answering him, she struck me across my face with her stick. I jumped back but she kept charging, backing me up to the wall, then pressed her stick to my throat. She actually appeared to be angry.

"What are you waiting on, Connor?" She winked but no smile followed.

I shoved her off me. "Just didn't expect such eagerness." I touched my face, feeling for blood. I had to admit she'd stepped up her game, a lot.

Her stick came for my leg but I jumped up and smacked her in the face. She skipped back, also checking for blood, but I didn't hit her that hard.

"This isn't a beauty contest. Fight!" Ronin shouted.

And that was exactly what we did. Willow was vicious, angry, and brutal. She used her stick well; I had totally underestimated her. This was clearly not the same Willow who refused to fight back on Earth. She went for my hand but I evaded her strike. Then, I aimed for her legs but she leaped out the way; when she came down, though, I managed to hit the side of her head. She roundhouse kicked me in the gut and I completed the roll, kicking her in the throat. Back-flipping, she struck my jaw with her foot. I fell back to the floor, knocking her legs from under her. She fell face forward and rolled over; I leaped on top of her but she punched me in my face as I pinned her arms down, then bucked up with her hips. We rolled over to where she pinned my arms with her legs and delivered two punches to my face. I used my legs, wrapping them around her neck, and pulled her back to the floor. Rolling over again, we grabbed our sticks again and swung on each other. None of us gave the other a chance to recuperate.

We swung, jabbed, hit, punched, and kicked any part of the body we could reach, but I noticed she kept going for my face. As much as I didn't want to make this personal, she was doing just that. After she struck my face one too many times, leaving a gash across it, I dropped my stick and grabbed hers. I yanked it out of her hand and tossed it across the room. Grabbing a fistful of her hair, I pulled up, lifting her, and swung her across the room. She barely had time to recoup when I levitated her up into the air and slammed her back down.

Electricity flew across the room, knocking me back. I slid to the back wall, but I got up when she ran towards me and we collided in the middle. We took to the floor, punching each other repeatedly in the face; blood spewed, until we tumbled over, hitting the side wall. Yanking down the curtain, I tied it around her neck and tossed her again across the room. She hit me in my back with another bolt. Face forward I fell, spinning over when I heard her come for me. She jumped on top of me but I squeezed her sides tightly with my thighs. She lifted me up off the floor by her hips, trying to get away, but I refused to let go. I clawed at her face, drawing blood. Her eyes wide, she started choking me. I squeezed my legs tighter around her ribs and unraveled her fingers from my throat. Holding her arms wide, I snapped two of her ribs on her left side. She yelled aloud when I refused to let her go.

"I could kill you!" she shouted, unable to move.

Suddenly, she was lifted off me. Sitting up, I saw Willow scramble up and head for me. Ronin pointed his stick at her. "Stand down." She stopped and punched the wall, seething. When her adrenaline subsided, she grabbed at her side. The pain finally struck. I said nothing, only stared at the hatred towards me, clearly in her eyes, but it felt good getting back at her for hitting me in the face repeatedly.

"Are you two done?" he roared. The scowl he gave me deflated my ego. I slid back and stood. "Which part of "not personal" did you not understand?" He stood directly in the middle, between Willow and me. "That was poor at best. Do you think your individual agendas trump our mission? Do you think we have time to waste on both your issues?" After he wiped his face with his free hand, he faced the floor. "If either of you want out there is the door." He pointed the stick at our option. "If not, then don't waste my time." Neither Willow nor I moved. He walked over to a cabinet imbedded in the wall, grabbed two towels, and tossed one to each of us.

We wiped the blood from our faces then tossed them in a bin. "There is a time for emotions, there is a time for passion, but this is not it. I am not asking you to be best friends outside this room but in here, in my damn room," he pointed to the surrounding area, "you *will* work as one." He finally was able to face us and the heat radiating off of him meant that he was beyond pissed.

With a long inhale, I walked to the middle of the room, mentally chastising myself for losing control. At first, Willow did not budge, only frowned over at me. She stared at the door and after a second of contemplation, looked over at Ronin, then walked over to me. "Fine."

"You need to wrap your ribs," I advised her, but she ignored me.

"Grab your sticks and begin," Ronin ordered, stepping back. Once again we fought, but this time without passion, without feelings; as a matter of fact, we were completely detached. The session was—in a word—ruthless.

This training continued for hours, during which we struck any body part with as much force as our bodies would allow. We evaded, blocked, deflected just about anything to avoid a hit and we only cared about the punishment we inflicted. The floor was slippery from both sweat and blood. My body ignited, rising to the occasion as my adrenaline kicked up with the contact attacks.

As soon as we took our first break, I walked over to the cabinet, grabbed a towel and a bottle of water, and headed outside. I stood with my bare feet in the sand, inhaling the fresh air, in no mood to speak to anyone. Whatever was up with Willow, she made her anger clear.

She and Ronin talked about something but I didn't care enough to eavesdrop. Rather, I stare out at the beach. The sea smelled like it did back home but one distinctive odor wasn't familiar—one that did not affect my approaching serenity.

"Connor," Willow called to me. "You need to eat." She seemed to be in a much better mood and her abdomen was now wrapped.

I turned my head in her direction like I was having an out of body experience. "I'm not hungry." I actually wasn't. For the first time in what seemed like forever, my stomach didn't rumble.

"You need to keep your strength up."

"Willow, I am fine." I wasn't the least bit upset. "I just need a minute."

"Okay." She shrugged, walking away. "I'll leave you to yourself."

I walked closer to the water and stuck my feet in. Shutting my eyes, I let the sound of the ocean engulf me. My mind drifted up to the sky and my body relaxed. The stiffness in my joints loosened and the ache in my muscles subsided a little. In and out, my breathing steadied, taking in the breeze that came off the salty sea. It was peaceful.

I thought of back home and of my mother. I'd gotten no word on whether she was even still alive. I had no clue how my family coped and what had become of them, just like they had no clue of my whereabouts. I didn't know what the Keepers had told them. My parents either thought I'd run away or that I'd possibly died. Those thoughts broke my heart. God, I missed them so much, even the Keepers and their sessions. What I would give to be an average teenage girl again, living a normal, boring life, oblivious to the world's dark side. I didn't pity myself, only worried about my family. They have suffered so much because of me, because of what I am. My dad was trying to help me, when they adopted me, and all it did was backfire on him.

Sorry, Dad.

I opened my eyes and took in more of the scenery, allowing the sea to help me find inner peace for a little time. But the longer I stayed, the more my mind would not fully relax. Right then, my body needed—craved—the adrenaline. I gave into it. Battle helped me release all my pent-up frustrations.

I turned around when I'd had enough and headed back inside, walking past them both standing off to the side. Emotion played no part in my mood, only the thought of battle. My life had become so screwed up, I needed to let it out. Picking up the Kali, I stared at Willow. "Are you ready?"

She sneered at Ronin and sauntered over to me. "It looks like the San taught you a thing or two back on Earth."

"It seems the same thing here," I replied.

Without Ronin's approval, our session began but this time it was worse than the first. When I lunged and made contact, it wasn't about hurting her or getting even for the things I thought she'd done. This was strictly business.

This time, when we fought, Ronin stood in the middle of the room telling us what moves to make, how to avoid getting struck, how to take the blow, how to twist our bodies. It was virtually impossible to mimic the positions he asked us to take and most of our attempts sucked.

He challenged us to try different moves, to counteract each other, and to push each other's limits. We stayed in position for a certain length of time to strengthen our core and our overall muscle tone. Ronin wanted us as fit as possible and he wanted it last week. In his mind, we were already behind schedule and needed to be ready to fight anyone or anything who set out to find me.

The time sometimes passed quickly and in other instances, lasted forever but all of the ordeal felt excruciating. When the night had turned mostly purple and the stars shined brightly, we called it quits.

"That was a good day one. Tomorrow we will meet again," Ronin informed us.

So that was day one of many dreaded ones yet to come. "Can't wait," I said, heading back outside to the water.

This time, I walked into the clear ocean until the water was up to my knees and fell backwards into it. It felt so good to be weightless and free. I should have worried about what was in the water but my body aches subsided enough to make me not care about anything at this point. The next day, my body would feel like it wanted to die. If the battle today represented our regimen, then there would never be a time for me to heal and not suffer. Right now, it felt like it had back on Earth when my body was going through the change.

As I floated in the water my muscles screamed at me for pushing so hard, especially without any food to fuel it

A splash sounded next to me and I leaped up. Someone grabbed my arm and I pushed them back. *Ronin.* "Oh, I didn't know it was you."

"What was that crap in there?" he barked at me.

"What are you talking about?" I had no clue.

"By now you should be able to run circles around Willow and me but she was not far behind you," he snapped. "I just wanted to see where your skills were at but Shugna, Connor."

I was confused. "You're the one with enhanced combat skills. I guess you taught her well." I shrugged, completely lost over his annoyance.

"Bull, Connor! Even on your worse day you should be able to take her down. Easy. I know the Keepers trained you and I know for a fact Bynder is one of my best adversaries. You are stronger, smarter, and quicker than what you're feeding me. You're not doing yourself or us any favors by half-assing. You're either here or you're not but if you're not don't waste my time." And then he stormed off.

"I'm not half anything, you jerk!" I ran after him and kicked him in the back. When he hit the sand, my goal was to pin him down but he rolled over and grabbed my foot. He threw me over his head but I landed on my feet. Kicking sand in his face, I spun around, elbowed him in the nose, and jumped on him to take him down. He flipped me off him and jabbed my side with his fingers.

When I went to punch him, fingers jabbed me again but from behind. He'd teleported behind me. I spun around and was thrown into the ocean. I splashed up, pissed, but was shoved back down under and held there. I struggled to get up but the only thing I managed was to swallow water. Ronin had his whole body on me and he would not let up. He was killing me.

Every nerve in my body surged from both fear and hatred so I stopped fighting and gave in. I lay there very still, removed all fear, and quieted every sound around me, setting my mind free. My body lifted up out of the water and into the air, taking Ronin with me. I don't know how but somehow, I manipulated the air under me. When we were about six feet in the air, Ronin fell back but I grabbed his arm but he yanked loose and disappeared.

I dropped back down on land, not very gracefully, and he was nowhere to be seen. I could see him if he went invisible so he must have teleported elsewhere. Shutting my eyes, I listened for any movement other than the natural current of the ocean. When the air altered slightly to the left instead of going right, my arm instinctively reached up, caught his leg and sent him soaring over the ocean, much farther than where he'd tossed me. I left him suspended.

He held a smug expression. "Now that was session one," he said with such satisfaction I could have killed him but instead, I dropped him in the water and walked off.

He teleported in front of me and blocked my path.

"I hate you, Ronin." I foamed. "You tried to kill me."

"Kill you! Don't be so dramatic, Connor. I needed to bring out your survival instincts so you would fight. For some reason, you hold back. I don't know why but you do."

"I don't know, Ronin, maybe because when you battle people you know a part of you holds back so you won't hurt them." I waved my arms in the air like a lunatic, anger eating at me. "It's called humanity!"

"Screw humanity. I need you to live. You have to survive. Forget me or Willow. Don't you get it? If you die we all die so hate me all you want but you have to stop holding back and fight. Tap into that carnal nature of yours and bring with you tomorrow what you just did in that water. Connor, you are a natural fighter. But it's like you restrain yourself until you're forced to get mean. In that room, we are mortal enemies." He pointed to the place that made my body miserable. "Remember that."

"Fine." I heard him loud and clear. Nothing else mattered, not even feelings. I sent him flying back out to the water again and it brought a smile to my face.

Then, I headed towards his room. Willow was nowhere to be found. By now she must have been in bed. She was the lucky one.

Ronin sloshed up behind me, sounding just like me. "Hey, since we're all going to be roomies for a while, am I going to get a separate room like Willow?" I thought this a reasonable question, plus, a girl needs time to herself.

"I thought it was understood that you are to be with me at all times. I meant what I said about guarding you with my life. You don't leave something valuable to someone else to care for when you can take care of it yourself," he explained, opening the door.

"I'm not precious cargo."

"Monlow would never inform us that he knows you're here or that I've betrayed him. He would storm this palace in the dead of night when we're most vulnerable. If we are together then we can flee at once through the tunnels. The very tunnel that leads from *my* secret room. Mindalous knows how to get Willow safely away. We also need to strategize as much as possible."

"Oh," I said, feeling stupid. "I forgot about the tunnels."

"I don't know who all I can trust and your death means the end to so many, including me. This is why I don't really trust anyone else with your life. You think I'm overzealous but we've come so close and we can't leave anything to chance. Can you understand that?"

He'd just said a mouthful and he was right. My shoulders slumped and released the tension. "Yes. I just…"

"Had to ask." He finished my sentence. "I expect you to ask questions. When don't you ask questions?" He headed to the sitting area of his room.

"Now, wait a minute." I felt some kind of way about that. "I don't always…" I started, then had to stop myself. *When don't I challenge someone?* His face told me to stop getting defensive. "Shower?" I let it go.

"You know where it is."

I headed straight to the facilities and, within three minutes, stood under the hottest water one's body could tolerate. It felt heavenly. I drenched every part of me from head to toe. As soon as I got out, I realized there was nothing for me to change into.

The door opened up and Mindalous entered, carrying clothes and a basket filled with scented lotions and oils. "I would have brought them in sooner but I was busy tending to another matter." She smiled showcasing her perfectly white teeth.

"Thank you," I said. As I reached for them, she gently pushed my hands away.

"I will take care of you." She reached for the lotion.

"I can lotion myself," I quickly said.

"Very well then. Put your dress ware on over there." She handed me the basket and pointed to a partition in the far corner.

I dressed behind a screen after applying lotion. I really didn't need much. Ether had a lot of moisture so my skin was far from dry.

"When you are done, you can come sit and I will untangle your hair."

I felt embarrassed but my hair was a wild and curly mess. Even in my previous life, I could never control it without my sister's help. I would have objected but in truth, I needed the assistance.

I walked over, tugging on my clothes. I felt awkward wearing tight black pants and a top that could fit a toddler. It was too snug. Back home it was sci-fi t-shirts and loose jeans. But it was a necessity to stay dressed in case we needed to flee during the night, as Ronin put it; and tight was good so during a chase, nothing or no one could grab onto us. What an awful way to live. I'd never worn tight clothes before. I missed my geeky outfits so bad.

I pulled on my shirt, trying to make sure my stomach was fully covered. "Quit yanking on your shirt. Everything is covered. You have a very attractive shape." Mindalous commented and I blushed, tugging even harder. I wasn't the attractive one; my sister was. I was the plain, tomboyish geek.

"I don't normally wear clothes like this," I said, sitting down on the cushioned bench in front of her.

"There is nothing wrong with what you have on. You're just not comfortable with your body yet." She looked at me through the mirror across from us.

She removed my hair band, freeing my everyday ponytail, and my hair fell in a messy heap. "You have a lot of hair." She studied the mass for a few seconds then attempted to hack through the tangled mess with a comb. All of a sudden, we burst into laughter. "Let's try something new," she suggested.

Mindalous took some cream, rubbed it in between her hands and applied it to my hair. It smelled like sweet heaven. As soon as she did, my hair decided to behave, turning soft and shiny, the curls coiling as they should. Her hands in my hair reminded me of how my sister Ebony would always help tame my wild curls. My smile faded and I looked away as a wave of nausea hit me.

"What is it?"

I looked up at her through the mirror and pointed to my hair. "My sister used to help me." Tears stung my eyes.

She grabbed my shoulders and squeezed them. "You will see them again. Just believe and hold strong to that." I touched her hand and nodded. "Now look at yourself."

I turned my head from side to side, checking my hair. Long silky, curls flowed down my back. It looked amazing. "Thank you."

"Now go. Ronin has very little patience and he is always working. I'm sure he's waiting on you." Standing, I hugged her so hard, she nearly fell back. We both laughed again. "Sorry, San strength and all."

"Go before he storms in here. He can be impatient and demanding."

"Impatient" and "demanding" would not be the words I'd use.

I rushed out the bathroom and saw him leaning over a table reading some brown documents that appeared aged, an electronic tablet near him. Eventually, he noticed me standing there, waiting. "Your hair," he said. "What happened to it?"

"Nothing happened to it." I frowned.

"No, I mean it looks nice." He pointed the now rolled-up documents at me. "You look nice." Clearing his throat, he gestured toward the table. "Please come eat. I know you're hungry."

"Maybe I will have just a little something." I headed straight to the cushioned sitting area, and wanted to shovel the whole spread down my throat. But, instead, I acted civilized and used a plate. I kneeled down next to the low sitting table and grabbed rolls, meats, anything within reach. Everything tasted so good and my stomach did leaps and bounds, overjoyed that it no longer starved.

After my first few bites, I felt eyes on me. Ronin was watching me in awe, so I covered my full mouth and apologized. "Sorry, but I'm so hungry." His jaw stayed dropped. "You can relax, you know. It's not like I'm going to eat you." I huffed.

Well, as long as we don't run out of food. I do like legs.

The corners of Ronin's mouth curved upward. "Are you laughing at me?" I asked. I didn't really care what he thought. My body was dying. My only priority was sustenance. "You did this to me."

"No, you did that to yourself. You're the one who refused to eat earlier," he said, staring between my plate and my mouth.

"Well I've learned my lesson, okay, Dad?" He raised a brow at me and mumbled something under his breath. Unable to hear what he said, I tossed a roll at him.

"As soon as you finish gorging yourself, we can start working on your role in all of this."

"What do you mean, *start*? Don't you ever stop? We have to get up in a few hours. I'm beat, man!"

"Do you think the war will wait until after you've rested? No one cares about your spirits or your qualms."

"Dang, don't hold back now. Say how you *really* feel," I mumbled. "Do things always happen so fast here?" I shoveled something that seemed sweet down my throat. I don't think I really tasted it. "Or are you always in this take charge role?"

"Yes, life here is much faster than on Earth. Anyway, I like to always be ten steps ahead." He leaned forward over some paperwork. "But sometimes, I would visit Earth just to take a breather. I watched a baseball game once."

Just then, he reminded me of how young he was—eighteen, just a teenager, like me. Most teens I knew were hanging out or going on dates but his pastime was saving his planet from his father. Most of the time he seemed so put to-gether, so adult, but only because he had to grow up so fast. I thought I had it bad but he was only a year older than me and he'd done so much more than any other guy I knew. It wasn't so much that he *wanted* to stay ahead; he *had* to.

I placed down the food and wiped my hands on a cloth. "Let's do this. Is Willow supposed to be here?"

"We each have a role to play. I just want us to go over ours."

I stood to my feet. "You know what? Forget this role for now. I want to know more about Monlow, the *real* father you know. I want to know him like you do. His weaknesses, his triggers, but most of all, his way of thinking."

He fiddled with a tablet for a second as if to consider my request along with everything on the table. "Okay then." He strolled over to the bay window and tucked his hands under his arms. I got the impression he dreaded having this conversation.

And as if a black cloud ascended upon us, Ronin finally spoke of the person he detested the most. "There are those who talk of evil and there are those who fear it but many have not truly faced it. People say the word without really knowing its meaning. They don't know because they have never lived it. I'm not using him as an excuse for the horrible things I have done but I learned to favor atrocity to keep my father appeased. No one knows him like I do. Oh, they've seen the man, others have spoken to him, but they have no clue who he truly is."

He slowly turned around and this was the first time I could see not fear but a mixture of apprehension and loathsome. The light of hope faded from his eyes and he looked like the Ronin I met for the very first time, the one who could have killed me. And as I sat in the room with him listening, his mind drifted away to a place I almost feared to imagine.

"When I was a child, he was mostly human. He hadn't warped into the atrocity he's become today. He used to watch me while I slept as if fixated with me, like I was a mystery to him. When I cried over anything, he would have me beaten incessantly. The punisher, he was called, would literally bind my wrists, strip me of my clothes, and whip me, a child of such a young age. At first he did it to discipline me but then my father enjoyed seeing how long it took for my lashes to heal. If I wept during my chastisement, it seemed to last what felt like hours, but as I think back, it was no longer than a few minutes. So, I fought back the tears and bore his so-called love.

"He made me learn the art of battle from the time I could walk and as I progressed in age, he had me fight grown men who gave me no pardon from anguish. If I withstood the battle for a certain length of time, then I could eat that night. My body grew tired from the constant beatings, the never-ending teachings, and the heartless mental torment—as well as the fact I literally had to fight to eat. All the while, he would yell that no son of his would be weak. A lot of nights, I went hungry.

"When I was old enough, he sent me away to school but regrettably, I came home on the weekends. It seemed like a night of rest was almost forbidden at the Dom. I learned at an early age to live without much sleep. There were nights when he condemned me to the tunnels if I disobeyed him, regardless of whether my behavior was intentional or not. He figured his son should be stronger than what I had become but in all honesty, he would have never been satisfied with any of my developments. Even though I excelled in my studies and battle, I was never good enough, never strong enough." Ronin turned away from me, his hands formed into fists. I could have sworn he fought back tears so I held mine back, too. "There, in the cold tunnels with next to no light or clothes, I served my punishment as a disappointing child."

I was mortified, almost sick to my stomach at what he told me. "No wonder you slept so hard at my house. You still think he will creep into your room at night. Kids fear monsters attacking them at night but not their father being the monster. You can't let go."

Ronin faced me once again and I could see the protruding veins in his neck. "I can't, for reasons I'm about to tell you." He swallowed hard and took a moment to gather his thoughts.

"On my thirteenth birthday, I woke to a guttural growl after being thrown in the tunnels for another senseless reason. I froze for a brief second but my heart skipped uncontrollably. If I died where I lay, he, my father, would let my body rot in that damp passageway like the other bones I'd discovered that first time I was to serve my penance for being human. Back then was when I learned to stay fully dressed and keep a weapon on me at all times.

"As the unknown assailment approached, I withdrew from the light and listened for the feet that drew close to me. My hand tightened on my stiletto and when it came into the light, I saw that it was a Vuzen, Ether's most barbaric creature. I knew it then that my father wanted me dead. My father must have grown tired of me but I refused to die that day."

Ronin opened the window and gripped the windowsill tight, as he exhaled anger. "As the creature methodically crept closer, I stood on my two legs as it did its hind legs towering over me a good two feet. It lunged at me with its wings but I dove under it and stabbed it in the gut. When it came down on all fours, I jumped on its back, pulling back it wings and slicing at the attaching muscles and tendons. It wildly shook me off but then I scrambled into a corner where it could not fit."

Ronin took a minute to breathe while rehashing the life-altering moment. "The animal was vicious but not too bright, so I outsmarted it. It was the only way to win. Every time it lunged at the corner where I'd taken refuge, I jabbed it in its throat. It squawked, making this horrible sound, then growled in fury, determined to end me. But I had other plans—surviving. I kept jabbing but every once in a while, it managed to slice into me. It took more than thirty jabs to take that thing down. I watched the life withdraw from its eyes and it was then that I'd come to realize that brutality from a dagger was my savior and protector, not my father, the one who detested me so. After all, he'd taught me that. There, huddled in the corner, I waited until the doors opened the next morning. The sentinels stormed in with their battle gear on and an iron cage in hand, which told me they had not expected a battered and bruised boy to exit that tomb. But when they approached me, it was the first time they bowed before me. I stopped in wonder, finally feeling I'd accomplished something.

"My father stood there with amazement on his face and instead of me bowing to him like I'd always done, I swore to never bow to him again as I walked past him with not so much as a glance his way. He placed a cold hand on my shoulder and stopped me. 'You finally earned the title of being my son.' He could not comprehend the hate I felt for him. It was then that he promised to bless me with gifts at sixteen if I continued to prove my worth."

"But the San powers always come to us at sixteen," I interjected.

"I didn't know I was San," Ronin explained, and he was right. How was he to know?

"After that night, I no longer slept in the tunnels, only endured combats. At a young age, I was the cruelest, meanest, and most ruthless in battle. I loved gifting punishment. It meant I'd proven my worth to my father and soon would get further away from him. Finally, at sixteen, he kept his word and bestowed me with abilities. Before I was just mean but now, with gifts, I became sadistic. I'd built a crew of nonconformists and we'd traveled off world to represent my so-called father. I established a name beyond cruelty, one of pure evil. I lived in the black.

"Then, I traveled to Earth and could not understand why my heart wouldn't turn completely black after all that I'd done. I encountered the San and hated myself for the mixed emotions they caused me. Out of all my enemies I despised them the most because they caused me to question my actions. They made me want to second guess myself. Seeing how they were, I realized that Monlow's depiction of the San in books was not comprehensive. After dealing with them, I'd always go into reclusion."

"Then I found you under my father's order; at first you seemed like a normal human but then you developed your abilities." He sat down on the ledge, unable to face me, and continued the heart-wrenching tale that was his childhood. "I followed you the night you all planned on breaking into the Caring House, your adoption agency."

"Yes, the night at the carnival when Tony and I were waiting on the others. You were there, weren't you?" I asked. "But how did you know to follow me?"

"You forget I had spies at Mr. Conway's house and they heard everything in the basement that night. The arguing, the lightning bolts from Willow, but more importantly, your plans. Even though you all said you would investigate the place first, I had a feeling one if not more of you could not wait. So, I had each one of you watched. You and Tony led us straight to a San hideout. I thought you spotted me that night even though you'd never seen me before."

"But I've always sensed you, long before I even knew who you were." I recalled that sensation well of Ronin being near but suppressed it for now. "Did you send those wolers in after us? One followed me upstairs in the room."

"Yes, but only to watch you and see what you discovered, then one went rogue."

"I didn't even know what it was; I couldn't even see it, but I sensed it and it scared me to death." That sudden feeling of dread washed over me as if it were yesterday.

"What you don't know is that I was unable to retrieve the books because your elder, Ridgemont, returned to the house as soon as you five ran out the back door—but she saw you. She immediately had anything San related removed from the house after your break in."

"And to think I thought it a scary time. That was nothing compared to this new reality."

We just sat there a long while, allowing time and space to swallow us up. Even though I'd been scared to death the night he had us followed, it had been a smart move. We five were so clueless and that incident seemed like it happened a thousand years ago. As heavy as that night was, I could not shake what he'd just told me about his childhood. What little of one he'd had. We just faced each other as I absorbed what he'd told me so far. It was a lot to take in. So, he was a product of his environment after all. I wanted to cry for him, tell him I was sorry but somehow, I knew that would not comfort him.

"I don't want your pity, Connor. I can read it on your face."

"I'm angry at you and yet..."

"I may just be a year older than you but I grew up a very long time ago. I've done things that would turn your stomach and the twisted part of it is, I don't regret a thing because I did what I had to do to get away from the man I thought was my father. And if you asked me if I'd do it again, my answer would be yes."

I wiped a sudden tear away. My mouth parted but words would not form. I hated him and yet, I didn't. I wanted to hate him. Should I? But then there was the pity he asked me not to feel for him, filling me to the core.

"There are times I hate you so much, Ronin. Actually, we are enemies but we need each other." As I calmly spoke, the waterworks continued to flow down my cheeks, so there was no point in wiping them away. "Finding out that you are San and the fact you hesitate in hurting me—is that enough for us to ever truly be allies? What I know is, you would not be this way if you were never kidnapped and forced to live with that monster. You ask me not to feel pity for you..." Ronin looked down at his hands but I continued. "But I do feel for you. Maybe I'm stupid. Maybe I'm naïve. Hell, maybe that makes me a traitor to my own kind but I can only follow what I feel—and I know you were not born a monster, only made into one. Once your father is gone, then your life will be better and you can finally live as you were meant to."

I stood and Ronin looked up at me.

"And what is that, Connor? Cruelty is all I know." Suddenly, he sounded so irritated with me. "Don't you get it? The only reason why I have not crossed over completely to the darkness is because of the San pull, but if we succeed in this, I don't ever have to deal with them again." What he said stung but his next words hurt even more. "And this so-called connection you and I have—I don't like it. I don't want to be bonded to you or anyone else."

I felt like a fool standing there, tearing up over a person who could be so cruel. "Why? Because it makes you human? It makes you accountable?"

"Yes. I don't like to be governed," he barked.

"But everyone needs to be policed. It prevents us from being psychotic or, in your case one day, a vicious dictator."

"And is that what you are, my consciousness when I go to that dark place? Are you to be my ruler?" He squinted as he leaned forward, placing his arms on his thighs.

"What?" I was shocked at his accusation. "No, I don't want to rule anyone. I'm just saying we all need someone to pull us back when we go too far. You say you don't want to be like Monlow but will you? That's what's he taught you. And stop saying 'they' when you are referring to San. You are one, too."

After a long pause of him suspiciously eyeing me, I gave him space. I could feel the tension rise off his shoulders. He rubbed the back of his neck in an attempt to calm his mood but the scowl on his face would not fade.

After some time, Ronin turned his back to me and peered out into the night. "Monlow…" And just like that, he changed the subject. I wanted to scream, yell, or throw something at him. It felt like he shut the door in my face and it hurt, but he gave me no choice so I had to let it go and allow him continue. "A few months ago, he let me see his true form and although heinous in nature, I did express my surprise. He stood over ten feet tall and his skin thinned, stretching so much his veins were all but visible. I'm not sure if he still had legs; if so, they moved gawkily, unlike a human's. He is weak in certain ways but stronger in others. No matter though, he preserves his strength." He peered back at me. "He appears tired but I know of no known weaknesses, Connor. I fear even in his weakened state he is stronger than twenty men and I know of no weapon on Ether that can take him down."

"So, am I supposed to take on a being that has no known weakness?" I fell into a chair and rubbed my temples at what he'd just said. I needed to think. "What about a hoard of people?"

"There is no way that many people can get to him at once. He is too paranoid. That is why we have to do this under sneak attack. Even though you have thousands of people backing you, there may be a time when you are alone with him and you must seize an opportunity. Whatever it may be, Connor."

"What are you asking, Ronin?"

"Connor, you are stronger than you think, more so than a lot of people I know. And like I told you before, you are a survivor and you will do what is needed to save the ones you love. But you will need to let go of the idea that you are a good person, and rid yourself of every hang up you hold onto—especially any idea that you will return to the life you left back on Earth—in order for there to be a possibility of succeeding."

"You mean I have to be ready to die. I've said it numerous times before but never have expected it to be true until this very moment."

Ronin sat down on the table in front of me. "I'm not abandoning you. Remember, I said I know of no weapon on *Ether* that can take him down..."

"So, there is a weapon?"

"Possibly. It's on an adversary planet. I've sent both Erena and Nodac on a mission to acquire it. They may not care for the San but Monlow ended the lives of my men, their comrades too, and that is hard to come by. While in Vonvere, they informed me that a contact located the device so I gave them my approval to go. It's a suicide job but we have no other choice."

"Suicide?" I whispered. So is that what you've been doing, trying to find weapons for a while now? That's the energy I felt at your home in Vonvere."

"Yes, some of the artifacts there were acquired for this reason but we need to collect as many as possible to attack him in multiple ways. Unfortunately, we've tested most and some hardly cause enough damage to hurt what you would call a mammoth, but this one is supposed to be lethal or at least damaging to him. Like I said though, retrieving it will not be easy."

"This is insane, Ronin."

"Yes, it is, but what war is not? It's not just Monlow we have to battle but his military, as well as a sorceress. You defeated one on Earth but don't think she's the only one. So yes, Connor, be ready for insanity, multiply that by one hundred, then sprinkle it with death."

I rubbed on my temples again. "I said I wanted to know more, right?" I fought back the impending fear that tried to surface and bit down on my bottom lip. In this very moment, I realized why Ronin would change the subject so quickly. Some things are hard to measure, others are too scary to face at a certain time but either way, if you don't move on, then you will get lost in your emotions, which can cloud your thoughts. So, like Ronin, I changed the subject, not allowing his stinging words or the fear to swaddle me. So much was being thrown at me but I had to move on. "Tell me about the palace. It is inevitable that I will wind up there so…"

"Not wind up there, Connor; you will simply walk through the front door, invited."

"What? Monlow will know that I'm coming? How is that a sneak attack?"

"I need you to trust me, Connor. Can you do that?"

I did not answer him, only sat there letting this all sink in. So much to digest.

Eventually he got up, grabbed the rolled-up papers, and unraveled them across the long table in the room. "Come." He waved me over. "These are the blueprints to the Dom."

I walked over to him and we began to strategize. That night, he discussed the Dom, aka the mountain, some of its secrets passageways, as well as more of the plan. He was right: we needed months for this all to take effect.

We stopped hours later with unfinished answers and uncompleted plans but it was a start. I wanted to scream, cry, run away from this madness—but I stayed put. No matter my fate, I had to grow up even though I wanted to be curled up on my bed back home with my parents down the hall. But now it was my turn to take care of them for all the years they'd taken care of me. I had to swallow my anxiety and hold strong.

I managed to shut my brain down in order to sleep but I had no idea how. Then again, I was both mentally and physically tired after all the battle sessions we endured. To add insult to injury, anguish fit on my body like a glove.

Chapter 7

Ronin

Connor and Willow's fighting techniques were very strategic but they held back. Was it something within them that they didn't want to battle each other or did they not realize the seriousness of this task? I needed progression every day and they were not giving me that.

"Stop!" I pushed off the wall and ignored their glares of exasperation. "Connor, you will battle both Willow and me. You obviously need to be challenged more." Connor did not protest, so maybe she agreed.

"Us against her?" Willow scoffed. "Ronin, you seem to have forgotten I survived the Elonium."

"By sheer luck, I'm sure, and that accomplishment has made you carelessly lazy."

"Connor, you know what we need and you're not giving it to me. We talked about this just yesterday. Remember, Willow and I are not your allies right now." Connor just listened and her eyes followed my every movement. "Willow, you keep bragging about surviving Ether, taking both man and beast, and this slop is what you give me? Are you sure you survived alone or did someone actually help you?"

Willow's jaw dropped but she shut it when I held up a hand. I walked over to a music drone, blasted the sound as loud as it could go, and tossed it in air. "Cover your eyes." I handed Connor an eye cover and she applied it. She needed to learn to use her instincts and not rely on sight and sound.

Without warning, I knocked them both off their feet with my stick and went for Connor's head next. She rolled out of the way to evade my strike. As Willow sat up to watch us battle, I whacked her in the side and she fell over. The look she gave me reflected what I was looking for: Anger.

"Battle, Willow. Get up! I'd think this would be your chance to finally get the upper hand on Connor." I was pissed that she didn't even seize this opportunity.

Relying only on her senses and with two attackers, Connor was perfectly positioned to block. She side-kicked Willow back as soon as she stood to her feet and knocked my legs from under me. I back flipped and when my foot hit her jaw, I heard it crack. She stumbled back and stopped to listen but she needed to pick up the pace. I slapped her shoulder with the Kali and she rolled with it, striking my gut with both her right foot and fist. Connor yanked my stick away and bashed me into the back partition. When I bounced off, she mentally pointed the Kali at Willow, keeping her at bay. She fought but the stick would not budge.

Still, every time Connor reacted, she had to stop and listen. That gave me the advantage and I used it. She quickly found herself on the floor. "Listen without stopping, Connor. Stay in motion."

Connor lunged but I blocked. When I attacked, she maneuvered by twisting her body at an angle. Immediately, she aimed her right leg at my face but I bent backwards and she only grazed my neck. She completed the twist, went to the floor, and with one leg extended, bumped my left side. I felt my organs shift but recovered, flipping as she twirled her body, going for my lower extremities. We completed three sessions of attempts with me on the defense until she palmed my chin; my head jerked back and she kicked me in the trunk. I slipped backwards and she sat on top of me. She reached out with one of her arms; the stick collided with her hand and she aimed the baton at my throat.

Wrapping my thighs around her waist, I rolled her over, sitting atop her, took her weapon away and now jabbed it in her chest. As Willow approached us, Connor levitated her against the wall again while she attempted to wiggle from under me, but I tightened my thighs and squeezed her arms at her sides.

"Come on, get me off you!" I shouted while bearing down on her. She tried everything from attempting to free her arms to raising her hips to buck me off but she could not throw me off. "Think, Connor. Do I really have you pinned? Think!" Connor then draped her legs around my neck and yanked me back, finally getting me off her. But instead of her being able to pin me down, we both scrambled up and away.

When Willow's oppressor fell to the floor, a pop was heard in the air. Connor went flying through the glass window and landed on the deck, taking out the glass table on her landing. Willow ran up to her and crunched on the shards of glass that spewed everywhere. But as she approached, Connor was already up and elbowed in her mouth. Willow toppled back and tried to electrocute her again but Connor diverted the bolt out towards the sea. I leapt through the broken window and landed on Connor's back but surprisingly, Willow electrocuted me this time. It hit Connor too but I took the blunt of the blow.

Willow stood over me. "I didn't appreciate what you said. I busted my butt out there..."

"You're like a broken record, Willow." My body involuntarily shuddered. "I've survived for years here. Don't let these pretty walls fool you. This was not easy to obtain." I jumped up, shaking off the surge that ran through me. *Damn!* I'd forgotten how electricity felt.

"I know, but..."

"So then you know my life is not, nor has it ever been, a storybook tale. I really don't care what you did then; it's about now. Let me clarify this for you, Willow. This is about saving the only planet I've ever known, in addition to yours."

"Why do you even care about Earth, or is this some attempt to gain more power?" Willow asked. By now, Connor had gone back into the room and watched us as she drank water.

"Do you want power?" I asked, wondering where these questions were coming from. Her moods were all over the place. *Is she scared, angry, what?*

"What?" She stepped back on the glass that crackled underneath her feet. "I don't gain anything from this?" Her voice went up.

"Are you sure?"

"Yes!" She held up her arms to shoot me again but once was enough. I held down her arms, twisted her body around, and backed her into the room. Letting her go, she tried again but was unable to strike me. She put up a good fight but I could anticipate her movements.

Willow aimed her fist at me but I blocked and stepped back, letting her frustration of not getting the best of me build. Every time she attacked, I dodged, then brought her to the floor. She'd get back up but never on the defense. She could not get the upper hand until she electrocuted me from the floor. My body locked up in the air until I landed on my stomach.

I cursed under my breath. I hated being electrocuted. "Now, if you'd only show that anger every time you fought." My mouth twisted.

"You're sadistic. You know that," Connor said, extending her hand to help me up, but her goal was to send me hurtling back. Instead, I used her energy, spun my body horizontally and landed on my feet. When I landed, my elbow connected with her back and she smashed into the divider. I flipped her upside down and hammered down on her neck. Her bones cracked. Her body went limp and instead of retaliating, she tried to sit up but I would not let her.

I flung her against the wall.

"Recover faster! Stop thinking and just act."

Connor managed to get to her feet but swayed as she stood. When Willow lunged, however, Connor punched her in the gut and kicked me in the back. I bent forward and struck her chin with my heel. "Follow through! Block!" I shouted. "Come on, stop letting me get the upper hand!"

Training went like this for a while, with me constantly attacking, Connor's lack of follow through, and Willow seemingly hesitant to participate. We maneuvered, twisted, and contorted; it was, as Connor said, 'sadistic'—she could not have been more accurate. I was hard on them both and they returned the favor. The Kali was no longer used, only fists, abilities, and anger. We needed to win and time was limited, so I sought perfection.

Over and over we battled, bruises already developed on all of us but the hurt and the need to breathe slowed them down. They had to understand that the only thing they needed during a battle was the mental capacity to live. Nothing else mattered.

Connor pushed away and removed her blindfold. "I think you expect too much, Ronin. I am so tired from yesterday!" Connor barked.

"Are you whining?" I was not even in inch away from her face. "I want more. Now I want to feel your hurt, your passion, your rage. Have your lives been so easy up to now you harbor no ill will towards anything? People are trying to kill you. We need to all be on the same page. We are as one in here but we battle like mortal enemies so when the time comes to face them out there, we will fear nothing."

"Well, it's not working!" Connor panted, bent over with her hands on her knees, trying to catch her breath. "I think Willow is dead."

I looked back at Willow who just lay on the floor, staring up at the ceiling, and gritted my teeth. "After hours of fighting yesterday, Connor, you handed my ass to the sea and there are times you can use your abilities and you don't. There is so much you can do; you have no idea because you second guess yourself. You are not consistent. Do you realize we can get a call any day that this is it but until then, we battle, fight, and try to kill one another until one of us is half dead? Then, we fight more. That is the only way to learn." My hands were clenched, I was so serious—but I could not understand why they didn't get it.

"You make it seem as if we are incompetent," Connor protested. "We've fought before and lived, so why—?"

"Not incompetent, but from what I've seen, just not well enough. Your Keepers are not here to protect you. One day you're good and the next not so much. You need to stop giving into the what-ifs, the hurt, even the need to breathe. Your mind has to be one with your body, flow like one single thread of energy. You have to tell yourself that nothing else matters but this very moment and give it your all." I watched them both staring at me with blank expressions. They didn't understand, and never really would. I would have to show them. "You won't get it unless I show you what you could be facing." I shook my head at them. "Battle lesson over today. Go get cleaned up. We have a trip to take." Releasing my fists, I stormed out of the room.

* * *

After resting for two hours, we were up in the aero-glider with me steering. I did not want my location being tracked. They'd already seen Elonium, a few creatures but no real monsters or our enemies. They'd yet to see Ether's true viciousness.

"Where are we going?" Connor asked.

"To a place you would call the Underworld, where you come from. A place where ugliness breeds and the monsters are not governed." With that answer, she sat back and asked no other questions.

We glided down to the deepest, darkest trenches of perversity. Here it was every man for himself. No one cared who you were or where you came from. We were all equal and fair game. This was where the vilest came to be free, to never be judged. I used to venture here a lot when I didn't care if I lived or died. That might have been only two years in the past but it seemed like a lifetime ago. *I would do just about anything now to survive.*

We exited the vehicle and stepped down onto wet shiny ground that appeared to be made of stone. No one asked what it was mixed with but over the years, I'd learned it was a combination of blood and bones on top of stone.

"Keep your head low and ask no questions," I ordered as we hurried down the street.

We walked past the nastiest of Ether. This trip could have been the worst mistake but if it worked, then they would understand just how ugly this place could get. With me in the lead, the three of us headed toward the cupola of mayhem and muck. There were those who lingered outside for reasons one cared not to question.

I stopped by the warped metal door where bullet holes were jammed with spikes. A large black Glutton stepped out the door. The creature was enormous in size, its nose long, and lips red and wide. It smelled as if it didn't know what a bath was.

"Three may enter but all may not leave," I uttered, handing him a wad of currency.

The beast scanned us first with its eyes but lingered a tad much over Connor and Willow. "Hey," I pulled back my long coat and showed him my blade. The beast might have been large but it still had vertebrae to sever. Snorting at me, it pulled out a wand to scan us better. It wasn't looking for weapons but for scanners from the inner city radar. That is a tracker to give away our location. This place was so secretive that it did not feature on any map.

He opened the door for us to enter and as we did, he sniffed Connor's hair. I held a knife to his throat in warning. He backed up. I put my knife away and we entered Perdition.

"Welcome to Metadonia," I said, sniffing the stench and feeling my old self resurface. "This is where everyone has a method to their madness. Ugliness in its purest form." We stood at the top of the metal stairs overlooking the balcony where the mixture of musk and sweat lingered around us like a second skin. I investigated the large room of various mistrustful characters who were up to no good like me. In the middle stood an electrical barbed wire fence which, when shut, did not reopen unless an opponent did not stir.

"This is not like Scott's cage fight back home at all." Willow covered her nose. I still could not pinpoint her mood and that was disturbing to me; I was normally good at reading people.

"No, it is not, but I have a feeling he would love this place even more," Connor said. "It's wall to wall chaos." A sly smile crept across her face. So, there was a bit of dark and twisted inside her, after all.

"Be careful, Connor," I faced her. "You may come to like it here." I began to descend the stairs to enter a world of bedlam.

"Ronin, your idea of taking a girl out is both frightening and thrilling." Connor walked ahead of me when we reached the floor and pushed her way through.

"Yeah, thanks, but I will stick with a movie and dinner," Willow said. "Why are we here anyway?"

"For this." I waved my hand in a sweeping gesture to encompass the whole scene.

The lights dimmed and the fence shut two opponents in. "Hurry," Connor said, shoving her way ahead. When one male creature with extremely large, round red eyes touched her, Connor twisted his arm behind its back. Willow backed her up, standing in front of the nunan with a knife.

"Are we going to have trouble here?" Connor asked.

The thing spoke something in a broken Elonium language and cocked its head towards me.

"He concedes, Connor." A leer crossed my face. "We're barely here five minutes and you two are already causing trouble."

Connor stared at me for a few seconds, then let go and headed to the main event.

After making sure the thing didn't follow us, I caught up and warned them to stay close. "Just remember this is no ordinary event. A lot of hominids here are far superior to most out there." They both nodded and Connor even curtseyed. I chuckled at her warped sense of humor.

We managed to get to the cage, passing both man and beast. Some knew me as the Prince of Ether and faced downward, while others only knew me by my reputation. I had to worry about personal grudges. Being the prince on this planet gave me few allowances but a lot of enemies. My past history gave me no pardons.

"Why is everyone staring at us?" Connor asked.

"Because your faces are new. Most beings don't care for each other, but new faces are never to be trusted." I searched the crowd and discovered the ones who found my companions interesting. Some turned away and others did not waiver. I grabbed onto Connor's coat. She was getting seriously close to the fight. "There is a second barrier around the cage. There's the electrical cage we see and the invisible one we don't," I warned her. She stepped back.

"What are they?" Willow's face showed disgust.

"Relax your face," I told her. "If you show an ounce of judgment they will challenge you." I adjusted my belt, making sure my knife was easily accessible. She did as I asked. "One's a human and the other is a flappezt."

"A what?"

"Relax your face, Willow," Connor reminded her.

"Just watch," I said, amazed that a human would take on such an opponent. A flappezt was not the most vicious being but it was far from the kindest. The human got in two strikes before he was done. The flappezt grew twelve feet, picked the man up by the top of his head, and threw him into the fence. Burned flesh sizzled and the stench added to the already-pungent aroma.

The crowd here did not place bets; they only waited for the next unpleasant end. That was just the beginning of the evening, which would go on well into the night. Fight after fight erupted inside the invisible confines. One living being entered but only one left. Sometimes, neither walked out. Fights erupted outside the cage as well and there, the real battle began.

Walking away from the main event, we headed toward the real fight. A decouas was taking on a wettle. That was a long history of distrust and hate between the two closely related species. Stolen territory had ended their long-lived union. But the decouas was far more vicious, even though they stood equally in height of eight feet and a size of three hundred pounds. Four arms the both of them had and bodies made of stone. Each time, the ground shook when one of them fell. Each blow cracked the other's chest cavity but not enough to keep them down. If you happened to be behind one when it fell, you would be sure not to get back up.

The crowd howled and whistled around us, the energy amped at the match up. They wanted to see the massive battle that had been long awaited. I myself wanted a closer look but kept scanning the crowd for degenerates that might have wanted to cause harm to us. When I usually came to this place, it had been with my faithful four, which was now down to two. Here had been where we met. They were used to a world where you had to constantly watch your back. A world where you would not survive if the other did not keep a close, protective eye on it.

"Ronin." I pulled out my weapon, confronting the person who touched me. Connor quickly removed her hand. I relaxed with an exhale.

"Yes," I answered, searching my surroundings.

"You faded out."

"I'm fine." This palace brought back bad memories. The environment was getting to me and I tittered on the verge of unadulterated rage and insanity.

"Ro…nin!" Willow struggled to say my name. A wide green creature with long arms, one I knew all too well, had its eight fingers wrapped around her throat.

"What do you want, Vantex?" I asked the old, backstabbing mate of mine. He was harmless. Maybe not to Willow right now but in the big scheme of things, he was.

"Where is Nordac?" he asked while sniffing Willow. He was no more than a whiny rodent in my book. "She owes me. Is she no longer in your crew? These two seem too…" his nostrils expanded as he smelled the air around them, "…clean." Whilst frowning, he exposed his long, yellowish brown, rotten teeth.

My stomach churned, "Please don't smile. Ever," I spit out a disgusting taste in my mouth. "You will have to take whatever deal you two had up with Nordac. Now let the girl go." I noted a burn mark on his hand, "You should really put something on that burnt flesh. It still smells bad." It most likely was just his own body odor.

Vantex gripped her tighter, now possessing her like a child refusing to give up its toy, "Let me have it?" Before I could answer, she punched him in his pencil-thin nose. He dropped her to stop his nose bleed, but unfortunately, she bumped into Connor, who tripped over a tail that belonged to a massive being five times her size.

This will not be good.

With its back to us, the being slowly raised its head but remained seated by the makeshift bar. It turned around and the grimace on its face expressed its frustration. I yanked Connor away while everyone, except Willow and me, stepped back—including Vantax. I mumbled something under my breath, not very happy with what was about to happen. I'd known we'd be challenged when we showed up but not this. Anything but this.

The huge creature's eyes glowed red, matching its dry skin. It had a silver ring looped through its bottom lip and the head would have been bald were it not for the long black, beautiful ponytail. That was a deception. Its hair was not just hair, but a serpent that spat toxin at anyone who got too close. It was a moondar.

Moondars were not known for their small talk and anyone who knew anything did not take one on. Ever. They came here for those dense enough to challenge them or try to prove their worth against one. Very few survived and by 'very few', I meant next to no one. It stood ten feet tall, its body built like a truck, and his fists were bigger than my head. This thing was one of the meanest and crudest that roamed Ether and our allied planets.

Shoving Willow aside, I pulled Connor along, hoping the moondar would barely notice. "Who dares challenge me?" It rumbled.

Shugna! I closed my eyes for a second, then turned back around. "No one. Just moving through."

"That one there." He pointed his hefty fingers at Connor. "The dark-haired female. She challenges me."

"No, I ..." Connor began, but I cupped her mouth with my hand. Once a challenge is set, you don't ever back out. It means you forfeit the combat and they can do as they please to you.

"No. It was me who challenged you." I took her place instead. I had no other choice.

The thing looked between me and her, contemplating its decision. "No, Ronin, you will not win." Connor's eyes bugged.

"What would you have me do, Connor?" I whispered as he kept examining us.

"Doesn't he know who you are? Does that mean nothing?" Willow asked, sounding scared.

"No, it does not. Out there, my status may account for something but in here, we are all equal."

"Then let Connor challenge him."

I glared in her direction, "Are you insane, Willow?"

"Yes, Ronin, let me do it," Connor protested.

"No, Connor, not you. Anyone else but you," I pulled her closer to whisper in her ear. "If you win, they will know what you are and a San is not welcomed, not even here. Monlow made sure of that and if you lose, then there goes our plan. I have to do this for us."

"I have decided to choose the man!" The moondar spoke. "She would not give me a tickle of a contest but this one here looks stimulating enough."

"I accept," I said. It had been a while since I'd been in a match I actually looked forward to. Just as quickly, the sadist in me was back.

"You had better win, Ronin," Connor tugged on my arm. I stared at her, then hiked through the crowd, picking up on her apprehension. "Do it out here so I can help. We will be ready to leave as soon as…"

The concern on Connor's face alone should have brought some sense to me but my blood was churning. Sensibility took no part in my judgment when I readied for a fight. "No, I will have to challenge him in the enclosure. If you interfere, this whole place would rain down on us. It's every being for themselves." I walked ahead again.

"Why don't I sense any hesitation from you?" Connor grabbed my arm again. "You actually seem eager to do this. That thing is massive, Ronin."

Without thought, the corners of my mouth turned upward when I addressed her. My heart raced at the thought of taunting death in an enclosed ring, uncaring if I died. "Not pleased but…" I had no words but she was right. I could not explain this in a way she would understand. To cheat death always brought a high. "If I do win, this will work in our favor. I planned on fighting tonight, just not with a moondar." I watched my opponent shove its way past the crowd, plowing through anyone dumb enough not to move out of its way.

"This is crazy, Ronin." Connor would not let go. "We have too much going on for this."

"I have to do this, Connor, or we will not make it out of here tonight. Better it just be me alone and not you two." I had to pry her hand away. "If I don't make it, get back to the aero and order it back to the palace. It will get you there safely. Mindalous will know what to do next, she will get you back to Earth." Standing by the cage, I removed my jacket and then moved towards the ring.

"I cannot believe we could lose everything over a fight!" Connor's mouth unhinged and she glowered at the moondar as if she wanted to hurt it herself.

"Not just any fight. Like I said, this can work in our favor. Trust me, Connor. This is what I want."

"We should just leave," Willow said, searching the crowd. Connor's face scrunched up at her. I cut Connor a glare that told her to leave it alone.

I and my adversary gave our false names to the announcer and he told us the rules—or rather, the one rule, which was simply: only one leaves. But this was not new to either of us. I stood in front of the entryway. *You either do or die, Ronin.* Taking a long breath, I entered the Deathmatch. The crowd cheered at the commencement of the match. It was clearly an unfair fight, but I never liked fair odds.

The moondar stood massive, already sweating as it watched me from across the 25x25 ring with such intensity. I should have been intimidated but if I managed to make it out alive, this could not have been a better match to aid our cause.

After the presenter announced our names, sparks flew off the enclosure when the electricity ignited and the outer barrier went invisible. There were only two ways out: I die or he does.

The floor shook when my opponent stomped and I was surprised the unsteady floor didn't cave in. The beast rushed. Ready for me to meet my maker, I backed up dangerously close to the cage and waited. When it swung at me, I ducked, rolled in between its legs and instead, it hit the electrical fence. Its body shook from the surge and growled loudly. The crowd cheered.

Big does not always mean dumb. The moondar would not fall for that trick again so I stayed in continuous motion. My opponent only had one weakness—its weapon, meaning its hair, from what I'd gathered before but intel wasn't always correct.

The thing charged and I jumped up, using both feet to kick it in the chest and although it stepped back, the hit didn't really affect it. In retaliation, it smacked me into the fence and my body shook violently. I pushed off and landed face down. I needed a minute to shake it off but he didn't give me one. The moondar raced towards me but I rolled out of the way and escaped its raised foot.

Sluggishly, I got up and stepped back, still in a bit of a daze. Every nerve inside me had ignited on fire. My hands were trembling. I balled them into fists and suppressed the sensation. *No matter what happens in the end... what a rush!*

The moondar swung at me several times but each time, I dodged its hit. On the last swing, I spun horizontally, hitting its side and it fell to one knee. Landing on my feet, I punched it in the back, cracking his vertebrae. The moondar bellowed. I'd just found a soft spot. But as I stood behind him, its long ponytail rose and dove at me. I lunged back, stopping myself right before hitting the fence and realized it was not only one black serpent's head, but three. The main crown split itself.

This just keeps getting better.

The moondar quickly spun around but I jumped over its head and all three snakes hissed at me separately. I accidentally landed on my wrists, giving the moondar the advantage. When I tried to get out of its way, a serpent's fangs dug into my shoulder, leaving its lethal toxin.

Within seconds, I could already feel its effects. My time was limited. Keeping my balance, I snuck around to its back and kicked it in the same spot but out of the serpent's reach. Running full circles around the slower moving creature, I kicked him once again, avoiding the poisonous bites. He fell to both his knees after two hits in the same area.

On my third attempt, his arm came around and whacked me into the barrier. My body shook uncontrollably and it felt like my eyes were going to pop out of my head. I had to force myself off the fence and it proved much harder to recoup this time. When I landed on the floor, my body hardly moved. I began to choke on the toxin and that was when my body instinctively flipped over and coughed up yellow venom. The electricity was accelerating the poison in my bloodstream. My insides burned.

Suddenly, I was lifted up in the air and slammed back down on my face. My jaw cracked slightly out of its socket. My opponent did it again and this time, my left shoulder dislodged. The animal could have easily killed me but it was toying with me. If I didn't get away, this thing would get the best of me but everything within me was shutting down.

When it lifted me for the third time, I used the momentum to kick my leg up and hit his hand, and it dropped me. I had barely moved out of its way when I saw Connor in my line of view. Against my will, she helped me sit up and popped my arm back in place. I managed to remove my shirt and gripped it in my hand. My body went flying in the air when the moondar grabbed my leg but with Connor's help, I landed on the moondar's shoulders. I wrapped my free leg around its neck, enduring yet another snake bite, but before the other two could sting me, I wrapped my shirt around all three serpents and pulled on them, trying to rip them from their home. He thundered and let go of my leg, trying to reach the top of its head—but its arms were too short.

The snakes shrieked atrociously, as did the moondar. The slithering villains tore from its head, leaving a trail of yellow puss and blood when I tossed them into the fence. Their bodies sizzled, releasing a foul odor. The mob near that area backed up. Quickly, I jumped off his shoulders and the moondar fell to its knees. With the last of my strength, I kicked him in the back - his weak spot - and my foot went all the way through my opponent's chest.

I stepped back when its limp body fell over. Half-dazed, I stumbled back, barely able to walk or see, and fell next to my challenger. We both lay there facing one another, neither of us moving. After all of this, the venom was going to be the winner.

In order to win, you had to walk out of the ring, but my body would not budge. I desperately wanted to surrender to the burning inside my lungs so I closed my eyes to rest.

Get up, Ronin! Get up! My eyes popped open at the sound of Connor's voice inside my head. It was mind-shattering.

There she waited, by the open doorway which led to my freedom. With her help, my arms moved underneath me and I lifted myself up. But it was she who guided my steps to the door. I stared at her the whole time. She so desperately wanted to enter the ring but if she did, that meant I forfeited. I would have to challenge another moondar.

Coughing up yellowish-bloody phlegm, I stumbled my way on shaky legs and a battered body, inching closer to victory all along with her encouraging words in my head. I took in a deep, solid breath and eased my way down the steps and into her arms.

I could hear the room cheer and rant, some contented with me winning and some angered. I was just grateful to be alive. Barely, but alive.

She all but levitated my body to a secluded area and I slid to the floor with Connor and Willow squatting in front of me. "Hold him still while I pop his jaw back into its proper place," Connor told Willow.

Willow placed her hands where she advised and Connor maneuvered my jaw.

"How's that?" Connor asked, examining her work.

I didn't ask how she knew what to do; I was just grateful she was here. "Good as new." *I joked but that killed.*

"Now we need an antidote for the poison," Connor said.

"Find…" I began.

"I thought sure you would be the one to kick the bucket, you stupid hetcha." It was my comrade. "But she'll be right soon enough."

"Aiden, you look as ugly as ever." I coughed up more mucus. He handed me exactly what I needed; a vial with the antidote to the moondar's toxin. Here in Metadonia, one could find just about any drug, antidote or weapon for a hefty price. Connor placed the ampoule up to my lips and I drank it all in between choking on its nasty taste. With each drop, it brought me closer to life. I swished and spat with water afterwards. "You just made history. No known human has ever taken down a moondar; creatures at times, but no human."

"Why do you sound Australian?" Willow spoke for the first time since the fight.

"That's because he's from your planet," I answered for him and thankfully slapped him across the face. "I've never been so happy to see such a dreadful sight."

Aiden winked at Willow but she turned away, placing a hand over her scars. He chuckled. Being older than us, he most likely found her reaction cute. He turned back to me, "Well, get ready to see more ugly mugs like me, my good friend. I have some guys who want to make your acquaintance, but outside only. Get yourself together and meet me by the starlight." He slapped me on the shoulder and I nodded.

"Ripper," he said, then left.

"Shouldn't we take you home?" Willow asked.

"No, we have work to do." I faced Connor who had not said a word in a whole minute, which was rare for her, "Don't look so serious. I'm alive. Besides, you work best under pressure, Connor." I tried to make light of the situation but the desperate stare ripped the jovial smile off my face. Eventually, she rested her head against my shoulder and gripped my neck tight with both her hands. I wrapped one of mine around her nape. She was truly petrified.

After a long moment, she lifted her head. She'd thought I was going to die and I would have if she hadn't been with me. "I know," I said. "I know."

"You know what?" Willow asked. "What do you know, Ronin? What am I missing?" she whined.

"Nothing. I was just worried that's all," Connor explained but Willow scowled at her answer.

"Fine," Willow snapped but Connor paid it no mind.

"We need to go," I slid up the wall and put on my jacket. I felt better now that the anecdote was in my body but I still felt off. "Please watch your step. Let's not challenge anyone else."

"I'm confused," Connor started. "How is it okay for you to fight the moondar in that crazy cage and they still think you're human but I couldn't do the same?"

"For one, my face is not new and I'm known to fight all kinds of creatures; two—you are new, much smaller than me and although you are strong, multiply your blows ten times. That's how hard those things hit. In order for you to have won, you'd have to use your abilities, therefore, exposing yourself and causing a riot. There is a bounty on any San's head. I'm sure there are a few who wonder how I survived but they won't dare approach me."

"Who are you, Ronin?" Connor glanced at me as we weaved through the crowd of endless gazes. I glanced back at her, offering no answers. "Fine," she threw up her hands and left it at that. "I will be careful, I promise." Connor walked ahead and Willow slid in between us.

Outside, where the fresh air helped my headache, we met up with Aiden and his men; some I knew and others I'd never laid eyes on.

"At first, I thought your message regarding Monlow was a bit iffy." If I didn't know Aiden as well as I did then, I'd be put off by his bluntness. "Got your message to meet you here and after that madness, my men are convinced. They will back any bloke who will take on death head on, no matter how young. Besides, he keeps overreaching into our ships."

I searched the faces of the men who looked directly into my eyes. Always a good sign. "Good to hear. We could use all the help we can get. Your boats will be most resourceful. Expect another conversation from me soon and I will tell you more then."

"Good," we shook forearm to forearm. "Where is your crew?" his gaze roamed over Connor and Willow. "Are they not still with you?"

"Monlow," was the only answer I gave and he understood. "Expect a call soon, brother." We hugged tightly, then we three set off.

"He looks like a pirate with that hat and pants outfit," Willow whispered after we turned to leave.

"That's because he is," I answered. "That's still an acceptable way of living here."

"How do you know Aiden?" Willow asked.

"Why, are you interested?"

"Of course not." Her cheeks turned red. "My only concern is you and this mission. You know that."

"After this war, I could always set something up," I teased.

"Forget I asked." She seemed pissed and separated herself from us.

"Willow, lighten up," Connor said but was quickly ignored. "So, you winning the fight actually was a good thing in convincing others to follow?"

"You mean we won," I corrected her. "I just didn't expect it to be a moondar."

"Sorry you had to fight, Ronin." Connor fidgeted with her hands. It was something I noticed she did when she was upset or nervous.

"It's not any fault of yours, Connor."

Willow stopped in her tracks, "Well, it's not my fault either. If that ugly thing hadn't grabbed me, then I would have never bumped into Connor in the first place."

"I don't blame anyone," I explained. "Like I said, I expected to fight tonight."

"Ronin, I would just die if anything happened to you." Willow stared up at me. "It's not just Connor who cares. If I could have used my electricity, I would have."

Her gaze was so intense it startled me. Willow had carried a world of guilt on her shoulders ever since what she'd done back on Earth. Would it affect her role in this overthrow? She needed to let it go. She needed closure. "I don't want anyone to die for me, nor did I expect either of you to help," I answered and walked around her, then led us out of the lunacy.

* * *

Connor and I had just walked through my bedroom door close to the witching hours when I got word from Mindalous that I'd received yet again another telegram.

"What is it, Mindalous?" I asked her, placing my things on the bed. A warm shower was what my achy bones needed after the night I'd had.

"Your father sent word for you, my lord." She bowed her head. I froze at her words and tightly shut my lids, knowing what it was about.

"The two people who escaped the law in Elonium?" Connor asked.

I squeezed my jacket in both hands, taking my anger out on it. "Yes. He suspects me as I expected." I contemplated taking a shower depending on when he'd sent for me. "How long ago?"

"Right after you left, several of his men came for you themselves."

There went the time for me to clean up. "How long did they stay?"

"Hours. They searched your whole palace. Not too long ago, we finished cleaning up after them."

I nodded, squeezing my jacket even tighter. "Send word that I just arrived and should be there shortly."

"Ronin, no," Connor protested.

"You may go, Mindalous."

"Yes, my lord." She bowed.

I waited for her to leave before addressing Connor. As soon as the door closed, I spoke, "What reason would I have not to go? His men came here unannounced in the hopes of catching me off guard. If you had been here, then everything would have been blown. You and I would've had to immediately flee but who is to say there wouldn't be guards stationed through the woods?"

"But he could have footage of you, me, or us together. You cannot walk right into a possible trap. Let's just go back to Earth now—you, Willow, and I."

"No, this is nothing new. I've done this dance so many times with him." I sat on the edge of the bed, dreading yet another confrontation with that man. "I must go or they will just come for me. If I appear willingly, then it appears less suspicious."

She sat next to me on the bed, neither of us looking out at anything in particular. "Is it like this every day?"

"What do you mean?" I asked, thinking of how my home felt more like a prison, it could be overtaken at any minute.

"Is your life on the line every day?" I felt her yes bore into me and pity was written all over her face.

"Yes," I whispered.

"You must be so tired."

"I am but I'm used to it. Although on days like this I could just end him myself—but it's not so easy."

"Ronin, I've been here for only a few days and I'm exhausted. We should run away. Right now."

"You mean go to another planet and live happily ever after? Isn't that what your storybooks say?" I asked. "We should."

"A planet that is warm, where no one knows us, and where we don't have to look over our shoulders."

"A place where the people aren't cruel, where it isn't bleak and our lives are safe," I continued on with her fairytale.

"You could fish and I could cook, even though I don't know how to do either," Connor confessed.

"Not fish—hunt." I softly chuckled.

"I'm so tired," she said no longer playing along.

"Yes, you are, and I'm the root cause of it."

"No, Ronin…" I looked over at her and kissed a fallen tear on her cheek. What I would have given to stay here with her. We had the most peculiar relationship. One minute we fought zealously and the next we connected as if our existence depended upon it.

I pushed a curl behind her ear. "It will be fine," I lied through a half smile.

Standing, I headed to the facilities. I cleaned my face and rinsed my mouth to rid myself of the taste of the snake's toxins, only to replace it with the stench of my father's demands. Afterwards, I grabbed a different coat.

"No, Ronin; he is the root of our problem." She followed me into the closet. "You didn't know who you were then."

I was furious at how upset she was, at this whole wretched situation and at how Monlow used me like a dupe. "But I've always known there was something different about the San. I just never dug deep enough to figure out why. It's still hard for me to accept."

When I reached for my sword, she grabbed hold of it. "Don't do anything foolish." She paused, then added, "Ronin, we will win but we cannot do this without you. I see the resentment on your face every time you have to go to him but we all need to play our parts, right? And right now, you are the dutiful son. Just tell him what he wants to hear."

I clenched my jaw tight, contemplating what she said and what I truly wanted to do. It would be recklessness if I tried to take him down by myself. I would only be leaving people behind and for what? My ill temper?

I relinquished the sword to her. "You are right." I headed for the door but stopped in the doorway. "When this is over, I will take you to another planet and teach you how to hunt." With that, I walked out the door, not looking back. This might have been the very last time I ever saw her but the word 'goodbye' would not leave my lips.

* * *

It took all of twenty minutes for me to arrive at the Dom. I had my two sentinels with me this time for no other reason than to appear as normal as possible.

We walked down the long white corridor towards his main hall, but he was not there. Instead, he was in his private quarters. Not a norm for him. Even though he called me his son, he was very formal, businesslike. He'd already lost his humanity years ago so formality was all he knew.

"This way, my lord," said one of his sentinels, who opened both doors to Monlow's quarters.

I entered his large chamber but stopped at the threshold. The stench of his black tar for blood loitered in the air, even from where I stood in the sitting area. Unconsciously, my hand covered my nose; the smell was overwhelming.

A loud crash sounded in the adjacent back room, followed by a guttural roar. I rushed there to see him with both his doctor and confidant. "Get out!" he shouted to them both. As they approached, they hurriedly bowed at me, then scurried along. His private study was in disarray. Ledgers and files from his desk, and even decorative objects lay scattered or toppled over across the room.

I picked up a vase when he called to me. "Ronin." He came out of the room then, gliding past me with a menacing sneer. His movements were becoming more foreign to me, less human. His mood now blended in with the bleakness.

"Father," I acknowledged him as he settled in a shadowy part of the room, his dark cape draped over his head. I could not get a very good look at his face. All I could see were his glassy hues reflecting from the light that shined behind me. "You sent for me?" I asked cautiously.

"That was hours ago."

"I was out." He was in a most foul disposition.

"Exactly where? I could not track you."

"Sporting," I answered, and his response was a rumble. He did not believe me. I removed my jacket to show him the numerous burns and scars on my back and down my arms. I turned my back to him and felt the air shift when he approached. His cold bony fingers touched my wounds and I cringed as he dug into them.

"What was the creature that did this?"

"A moondar."

"And you survived the attack?"

"It was more of a challenge than an attack."

He whispered something I could not decipher. I attempted to pull up my jacket but he held it down. "I need to know where you are at all times." He dug his brown nails farther into my injuries. I recoiled but he held on to my shoulder, keeping me near. "We are under attack, after all." He kept digging.

"Enough." I forced his hand away.

Grabbing me by my throat, he carried me to the darkest part of the room. "You are trying to deceive me." He exhaled his foul breath in my face but I had no room to free myself.

"In what way?" I remained calm under his tight grip as he held me up in the air.

"Where were you a few days ago when Elonium military hunted two foes, a male and female, down in the streets? They were both great fighters."

"In Vonvere, as you well know. I'm aware that you had men tracking me. Am I not allowed to live the life of a prince?"

"You forget that I own you." His voice was raspy like that of a person morphing into something hideous. "I gave you not only life but the powers you behold. If I so choose, I can take not only them but your life," He breathed in deeply. "You live only because I allow it, remember that."

This whole conversation was a lie. I was not of his blood, nor did he give me abilities—but I played along. Supposedly, I had no clue about the truth. "How can I forget? You remind me every chance you get." He dropped me to my feet.

"Don't try me, Ronin. Your rebelliousness grows tiresome." He slithered away. "Now I will ask you again where you were and don't lie. I've already questioned your twin and there is no reaching your two female cohorts. Where are they?"

I adjusted my jacket and walked towards the door. He appeared in front of me after a few steps. "You dare walk out on me?" He tossed the settee across the room.

This time it was I who got brazenly close to him. "You seem to forget that I am the prince and I do not have to answer each and every one of your questions."

His body began to swell in size. "I knew it was you. My own blood."

"Really, if you knew it to be me, then why do I still draw breath? Why is it that you have not stormed my castle? If you don't trust me, then strip me of my rank and be done with me," I bluffed.

In a flash, he tore from the room and returned with the severed head of my lookalike, Kalin, the one who'd covered for me in Vonvere and countless other times. Time slowed as I swallowed down all that attempted to rise in my throat. He dropped the head to the floor and came over to me. "The mind reader told me all, Ronin." My father's face was now visible, his skin paper thin, almost clear, and his veins black as the darkness that ruled him. And his eyes were none but black glass orbs.

I stared death in the face but showed it no fear, refusing to give in. "Kalin was a good man. The only one I had to give me an alibi against your very own enemies."

"You still protest even though I show you proof?"

"You give me no proof; only the head of a silenced man. What did he tell you? Nothing!" I shouted at him. "I grow tired of this constant inquisition. How can I do my part if you need to be at my side at all times? Did it ever occur to you that if you can track me, then others can as well? You taught me to cover my tracks but since your paranoia is ravenous, I cannot do my job."

"Your job?"

"Yes, my job. That thing you entrust me with." I tugged on my jacket out of frustration. "Nordac and Erena are searching for the culprits as we speak. They tracked them off world and will be back with the very two that you seek. Or do you not want to know the real truth, Father, and just blame me?" Like Connor said, I was playing the part of his devoted son. I stood there now, turning the tables on him. Were it not for his paranoia, then he would see right through me. It made him question not only others, but his own sanity, too.

He sauntered away, not content but somewhat intrigued. In the darkness, he hovered once again with his back to me. "You have until the end of the planetary alignment to show me these two culprits. If I don't believe them, then it is you who will suffer." He pointed his grey finger at me.

"It's always me, Father." I beat my chest ferociously with a balled fist. "If the wealth does not pour down, it's always me. If the ones you order do not obey, it's always me. If the world turns against you, IT. IS. ALWAYS. *ME*," I growled.

Ironically, the last part just so happened to be true.

"You are the only one who talks so brazenly to me and I'd advise you to watch your detestable glare. Your position will only go so far, Ronin. Do not test the limits of your place in my world."

"Position? You mean your son. I never knew I was one for hire. I thought to be what I am was supposed to be an honor."

"Sadly for you, being my son was never a blessing but more of a burden."

"You never spoke truer words, Father." And with that, I took my leave.

In the hallway, I allowed myself breathe once again. He had taken the life of a good man, my lookalike. My father had bluffed as much as I had. Kalin would not have been able to tell Monlow anything because after every session in my wake, his memory was erased and replaced with false ones. A mind reader cannot tell the difference between a false memory and a real one. He can only go by what the mind perceived as real.

Chapter 8

Willow

I'd been here for months, working with Ronin and the professor, preparing to defeat Monlow. I'd proven my worth to Ronin time after time but didn't feel appreciated.

I understood why Connor was here but her presence irritated me. We could have used all the help that we could get but there were times when I could have kicked her all the way back to Earth. She kept getting in my way. I truly didn't think Ronin and I needed her.

I could not put my finger on it but she seemed too involved with Ronin. I've seen the two of them together and she kept inserting herself in our arrangement, one we'd had long before she arrived.

Today, I decided to approach Ronin regarding her. My belief was they offered more of a distraction than anything else. He was under the impression she needed to be protected but she alone could not take on Monlow. I'd felt his power and Connor wasn't strong enough. She'd get killed.

So, once again, escorted by my help, Mindalous, I walked into the room for another tiresome session and saw the two to them huddled by the doors, talking. They hadn't even heard me enter, and their conversation seemed serious. I wanted to talk to Ronin alone but she was always around. When did she even get there anyway?

Go away, Connor.

I interrupted their conversation. "Ronin, I need to talk to you about something important."

"What is it?" He glanced at me, then back at Connor.

"Privately." I eyed Connor quickly so she would get the hint and leave. I really didn't trust her for some reason. She was hiding something.

Ronin hesitated but just before he said anything, Connor spoke up. "It's okay. I'll go stretch out on the beach." She jogged off.

"What is it, Willow?" Ronin went to retrieve something from the cabinet, avoiding eye contact with me.

"Long before *she* even got here..."

" 'She' meaning Connor?" he stopped to ask, seeming irritated somehow.

"Yes, her." I pointed towards the beach and although very upset, I kept a cool tone, mimicking his. "I've put in my time here on Ether while she had it easy on Earth. I've done what you've asked so why is she here? I never questioned why you even left me that night because now I realize you wanted to push me. I needed to come into my own strength."

"Glad you understand and you are right, but we need Connor. For reasons you know and others you don't need to know."

"You act as if she's the whole plan. You know, the one I don't even fully know."

"Willow, you seem to forget that you made it to the professor's, without whom there would be no plot. I trusted you with that." He pointed at me.

I'd never thought about it that way and had to suppress a smile. "Yes, if it were not for me, would there even be a plan? But you act like she's precious cargo. Like the rest of us don't matter."

He gave me his full attention. "You're different, Willow. Your tongue is far more liberal now than before. You think just because you've accomplished one task, that gives you just cause to question me? You were always spoiled but never so demanding."

"It was a *large* task and I'm not spoiled. I just expect certain things as anybody should."

"Oh, really? You live in a palace where you get doted on. What more do you want?"

"Doted on!" I laughed. "No, I don't get doted on and yes I live in a palace but still, you treat her differently than you do me."

"Because you and she are not the same person. Sometimes your approach is condescending, snide, and just plain rude. You are at times ungrateful and expect a lot."

"Well, I guess I'm just a godawful person." His words stung.

"No, you are not, Willow. You have come a long way but you are hard to peg, hard to get. Normally, I wouldn't care to, but we three have to work together." He squatted down to fiddle with the drone.

"What are you saying?"

"It means we all have a role to play."

"But you're the only one who knows all our roles. Why is she here anyway? What makes her so important?"

He stopped to look up at me. "Because she is the only one who can save him. Were you not at the same meeting as Connor and me, the one where the professor said no one person is to know the whole plot?"

"Yes," I said still not happy with that answer. He knew more than he was letting on and I deserved to know what that was. "Wait, what!" I got confused. "Save him?"

"Yes, him, Monlow. She and he are kin. Her blood, her death is the key to his survival."

"Yeah, I got that, but how does that help us? And if we are being honest, I agree with the professor—can we just trust her? How do we know Monlow doesn't have some mind control over her?"

"What is this *we* versus *her* mindset, Willow? We are supposed to be working together. No matter what we've each done to get here, we all need to work as one in order for this to succeed."

I chose to ignore his unity speech, then something registered. "If Monlow is looking for Connor, then is it smart for her to be this close to him?" I slapped my hand against the wall. "Her being here makes no logical sense. Now it's easier for him to capture her." I tapped my foot waiting for a response. "What?" I asked when he had not responded. I was annoyed that he could not see my point.

"I know my father and he would never think she is here. It's too bold of a move on anyone's part. I know what I am doing, Willow." He hesitated for a long moment, then asked, "What's truly bothering you?"

"I told you, Ronin."

"No, I don't think you have."

He patiently waited.

"Fine, I just think her being here is a distraction. And if we need so much help, why aren't the Keepers or anyone else here, for that matter?" I folded my arms.

"You really want them all here. Are you sure you're ready to face them just yet?"

"Don't think for one second that I'm afraid to face the Keepers and the rest of the pack that left me behind to rot," I protested now, furious about him dismissing my accomplishments. "I've paid the price and proven I'm trustworthy."

He grabbed the sticks and threw them against the wall, then got so close to my face, towering over me. "Don't boast too brazenly. Everyone here has had to suffer and pay their dues so don't think you're any better than the next."

"Funny, you make it obvious that Connor is important."

"The link between them makes her priority, but she is not better, Willow. Don't you get it? If she is captured then he will use her blood, all of it. Then, once stronger, he will rid everyone he feels has betrayed him in the slightest. I, myself, would be first on his agenda. Right now, I still serve a purpose so my life is spared."

"But your life is important too, Ronin." I softened my voice. "One day you will need to rule. We need to protect you, too." He walked away from me. "Ronin … what?"

"Yes, but if she dies, then there is no hope for us. If I die, you all can still prevail."

"All I'm saying is that your life is valuable, too. You need to focus on your safety as well and not Connor's alone. I just think she is too physically close to Monlow and she's a distraction to you who is important…"

"I don't know what game you're playing but it seems to me you just want to get rid of Connor."

"With good reason!" I squealed, losing my cool. What wasn't he getting?

"I focus on all our safety and, like I've said before, that is why no one person knows the entire strategy. Not even me." He pointed to himself but stared at me like I was losing my mind—but I wasn't. My mind was clear.

"Ronin…"

"No, Willow." He cut me off. His nostrils flared and my heart raced, the closer he got. "I've appeased you long enough. Hear me; this is the last time we will have this conversation. This was your one chance."

I watched him walk away again, furious for numerous reasons but one specifically: that he still thought Connor was top priority.

* * *

"What's the problem, Connor, are you tired?" I taunted after I flipped her over for the third time today.

She frowned up at me, then rolled over. "No, not tired, just feeling off my game." She tugged on her top drenched with sweat.

"You look like crap."

"You don't look that great, either. Besides, you're the only one of us bleeding."

"And you've lived on the floor today," I retorted, wiping away the blood from my upper lip. It irritated me that even in her off day, she still got the best of me.

"Break!" Ronin said, and we parted.

"What's with you today, Connor?" I overheard Ronin ask when she went to get some water.

"I don't know. I just feel off." She rounded her shoulders, trying to loosen them up.

I wiped the sweat away while they went off to huddle again, talking and whispering like they always did. What was it that he didn't see? Her distracting him was going to be the end of us. He was too close. Plus, she could be in danger. Monlow's sentinels had just stormed this place the other day.

"Aching?" Ronin asked her, loud enough to be heard.

"No, but something is off," she answered.

"Maybe you being here is messing with you." I suggested, interrupting their conversation from the center of the room. I just didn't trust her. How could we when she was related to that evil bastard on the throne?

"What do you mean?" Connor asked, taking a sip of water.

I reneged when Ronin shot me a warning glance, so I changed to another topic I felt she needed to hear about. "You being here can get Ronin killed."

"What? According to Ronin, me being here is the last place Monlow would look." She stood there, appearing innocent. "Why are you so worried about Ronin? If anyone can take care of themselves, it's him."

"He was the only one who gave a crap about me when I was stuck here in this godforsaken place and not on Earth, safe and warm." I hurried over to her. "Tell me, did any of you ever think about me? Was I even an afterthought?"

"Are you serious? This again?" She threw her hands in the air. "Yes, we cared, Willow, but you betrayed all of us, even yourself."

What she said was unnecessary. I turned away for a second then faced her again, refusing into give into it. "I've paid my dues and have proven myself."

"No one says you haven't but it's you who won't let this go. I think you will feel better when you see everyone again."

"Don't try and psychoanalyze me when it is you that needs to be examined. How do we even know we can trust you?" I looked at Ronin for reinforcement but received none, only a pissed expression.

"Can't trust me?"

"Enough..." Ronin protested.

"No, Ronin, you're too close to see this possibility. Maybe it's the pull of Monlow's power and that's why she's off."

"I'm not under Monlow's thrall and I'm not sending him telepathic messages if that's what you're thinking, too. That's crazy. I think your guilt is not letting you trust me."

"Whatever. When you're under someone's thrall, you don't know it," I shot back, slapping my towel against my leg.

"Yes, Willow, what exactly are you getting at?" Ronin asked.

Hallelujah—he was finally listening.

"I may be a backstabber, a traitor or a spoiled brat, but you are already aware of that. How about Connor? She follows her oh, so great instincts but how do we know said instincts are not telling her to follow Monlow? How do we know that them being related is not a far greater pull than doing what's right? His power is ridiculous, I felt it first hand, so how do we know he is not controlling her right now? Maybe the longer she's here, the greater his attraction."

"You're nuts," Connor scoffed.

"You can stare at me like I'm crazy all you want but did you even stop to question that, Ronin? No, I bet not. Everyone is so quick to distrust me that *we* could be walking right into a trap with her at our side."

"Okay, Willow I hear you. Has she done or said anything to lead you to believe she is untrustworthy?" Ronin asked.

"Not yet, but give her time."

"I'm not dismissing it because you made an excellent point, but for now until anyone shows a sign of distrust it will be then and only then that we can move forward with this conversation."

"Fine." I tossed down my towel. "I will be watching you, Connor."

"And I you," Connor shot back.

Ronin stepped between us. "Now that we've cleared the air, let's battle. We keep wasting time."

"No, I think that's you and Connor," I spat, then stormed off to get in position.

"No sticks, just use your bodies." Ronin ignored my comment.

"Gladly." I got ready but my elated feeling didn't last long when her foot made contact with my nose.

I backed up. "Good one," I said, wiping away more blood. Hand to hand combat was what he wanted and that was what we gave him.

After hours of heated fighting, I returned to my room to go through the usual routine: shower, dinner, and sleep. As I lay in bed, my stomach churned. No matter how angry I was at Connor, she always did the right things and that included having my back. We might not be the best of friends but I could count on her even if it disgusted me to think that. Maybe I was still bitter because ever since she came into my life, it had changed drastically. Who knows, it might have anyway.

Truthfully, the only two people who'd showed concern for me were Ronin and Connor. The ones I originally disliked the most turned out to be my biggest supporters. The only reason why I was willing to fight was because Ronin was set to rule Ether, my new home. If I had it my way, I would be right at his side when that happened. But I saw the way Connor looked at him and he her. Still, knowing Connor, she'd rather go back to Earth than stay here. Maybe there was a reason he'd kept me around this long after all. He'd made it clear the only reason he acted so protective of her was because of Monlow. He's never led me astray so far, so why not believe him? He was the most upfront and honest person I knew.

Chapter 9

Ronin

That night, Connor had become deathly ill. She had a high fever and her shakes seemed to be worse than those she got when getting electrocuted.

I had a mountain of blankets on her but she kept shivering. "Hang on, Connor. I called Tanikka and she's on her way. Can you hear me?" I sat next to her on the bed and her skin color was tomblike pale.

"More…more…blan…kets," she stuttered.

"Take those blankets off her." Mindalous rushed into the room with a bucket of ice.

"But she freezing!" I yelled, watching her hurry over.

"Move, boy." She shoved me away and took my place next to Connor. "All those fevers you had as a child and you still don't get it." She yanked back the blankets, exposing Connor's skin.

"No, pleeeeze." Connor gritted quivering teeth. "It hurts so badly. Everything … hurtsss."

"I know. Poor thing." I have to do this or the fever will kill you. You're already at 105.6F." Connor cried out when Mindalous dumped the whole bucket of ice on her. Connor's lids enlarged and she went to hit Mindalous. "Hold her!" she ordered me. I did as instructed but felt rotten about it. "Keep holding her down." She applied ice under her arms, her groin, and on the bottoms of her feet.

"Why are you doing that?" I asked.

"They are the body's cooling spots. We need to keep her temperature down to prevent brain damage."

I held her down as best I could to stop her from pushing Mindalous away and to keep the ice from falling off, but she kept fighting. She screamed at Mindalous and accused her of attempting to kill her. Shortly after all the ice was applied, Tanikka snuck in through my secret entrance.

"Etsna," Tanikka said when she rushed over to the bed. I held her upper body down while Mindalous sat on her bottom half. It was becoming useless. She was lifting us both up. Connor's screams had become incoherent howls. "Keep holding her," she said to us both.

Tanikka took a thermometer and waved it across her forehead. It read 108. And as if time stopped, so did Connor. Tanikka pulled back her lids and there were no pupils. Her body started convulsing uncontrollably. "Get her into a cold bath," Tanikka ordered but Mindalous was already running to the lavatory. Scooping Connor up, I hurried after her and stepped down in the cold running water Mindalous had started. With Connor on my lap, I let the water submerge us both.

"I'll get more ice." Mindalous ran out.

"What's wrong with her?" I asked Tanikka, staring between her and Connor, whose convulsions had not subsided. "Help her."

"Ronin, this is not the time for you to lose it," she said, fidgeting with her concoctions. "I can't believe you can take creatures three times your size but one little fever and you're losing your mind."

"She's going to have brain damage. Her fever is too high."

"Remember, we're San. Her body can take on a lot. Now here." She handed me a glass with warm liquid. "She needs to drink this, all of it."

I looked at the murky, leafy substance and choked on the smell. "What is this, a cup of death?"

"Boy, just give it to her. All of it." I placed it to her lips but she would not swallow. It eased out the side of Connor's mouth. "She's not..." Tanikka handed me a dropper.

"Give her few drops at a time but hurry," she ordered, sitting next to the tub. She tried to sound calm but I detected distress in her voice. When Tanikka, the calmest person I knew, lost her cool, something was wrong. I squeezed a little at a time in Connor's mouth as she still convulsed. Between my shaking hands from the cold water and her convulsions, it was hard to do, but I made sure not to spill any of it. Mindalous added two buckets of ice on top of the already cold water. I wanted to scream but after looking at Connor and what she was going through, I couldn't complain.

Mindalous placed a lukewarm cloth on her head. "It smells funny. What's in it?"

"An old remedy," she answered, sitting next to us as well.

When all the medication was given, Connor's convulsions finally subsided to tremors. "Come on, Connor, wake up," I begged.

"Give her time. There is nothing else we can do. If this doesn't work…" Tanikka didn't finish but we knew what she meant. So, with me holding Connor's limp body in freezing water and them sitting next to us, their long colorful dresses soaking up the splashed water, we waited for what seemed like hours.

"Ronin, do you want to switch out with one of us? Your lips are turning blue."

I hugged Connor tighter. "No," I said out of fury, refusing to let go. "Why couldn't this be me?" I asked no one in particular and stared at Connor, pleading her to wake up, to say something, anything, to annoy me.

Tanikka checked her temperature and it was down to 102F. "Okay, Ronin, you can take her out. Her fever is subsiding."

"But she hasn't woken up yet."

"I know." She gave me one of her appeasing smiles. "Ronin, it's been a long time. She may not wake." They both stood up.

"No." I shook my head. "She'll wake up." I lifted Connor out of the tub and carried her out of the room, laying her down on the bed but this time I didn't cover her. I just sat there and waited next to her while Mindalous and Tanikka stood off to the side.

"Why is this happening?" When no answer came, I looked at them both. "Why?" I repeated.

Tanikka walked over. "I don't know. She could have picked up a virus here. Something her immunity hasn't built a resistance to. You were a sickly child too, Ronin."

"Well, if I survived, then Connor will. She's stronger than all of us," I told them. "She'll survive. She's just tired that's all." I moved her wet hair from her face and saw a drop of water hit the blanket, then realized that it was me, crying.

* * *

I woke to someone shaking me awake. Tanikka stood over me. I had fallen asleep on the chair next to the bed. "Someone wants to see you." She smiled down at me.

"Connor." I rose to see her sitting up in bed and I was settled next to her. "You're awake." I looked her over in disbelief. "You were so sick..." The words caught in my throat. "Um... how do you feel?"

"I actually feel really, really good," she said, resting her head against the headboard.

"See, I told you she just needed rest." I half smiled, wondering if this could happen again. "Do you know what happened?" I asked her.

"I have no idea." She shrugged.

"Connor do me a favor. Lift everything in the sitting room," Tanikka said.

"What?" She glanced at me and I shrugged not understanding. Connor could already do that.

When Connor lifted her hands, Tanikka interrupted her. "Do it *without* your hands." She stared at Tanikka. "Lift everything in that room." She pointed to the adjacent room.

"But I always use my hands," she said to Tanikka.

"Not anymore."

I turned around and stood to see the sight. Every piece of furniture, decoration, and even the paintings floated in the air. Connor got up and walked into the room. She touched the couch and the table. "I can't believe it," she said, covering her gaping mouth. "It's never been that easy before."

"Last night was your rite of passage." Tanikka said with a beaming smile.

"Tanzia said in order for me to succeed it's imperative that I endure this journey so we can be successful in our mission against those who want us harmed." Connor lowered the furniture and faced us. "My journey is over. That's why I was so tired yesterday. I've finally come into my abilities." Her hands cupped her face and her smile was radiant.

"I agree," Tanikka said. "You are the strongest of us all and that is why your journey was the hardest. You have survived, both mentally and physically. Remember all the pain you've endured, remember last night's turmoil and what you've lost in order to get this far. Will you be worthy of these powers, Connor?"

"You sound just like someone we know back home," Connor said and the saddened expression upon Tanikka's face told me she knew who Connor was referring to. "Tanzia would have asked the same thing." She bit her bottom lip. "Yes, I am worthy."

"I trust that you are. I have to get back to my abode. I believe you two have more sparring ahead," Tanikka gathered her things. She gave Connor a long hug, then snuck out through my room's secret door.

"You ready to battle?" I asked.

"Yes. I've rested long enough." And battle was exactly what we did.

* * *

Day after day, well into the night, we studied the art of combat. The bickering had settled down to almost none. Rather than me leading, Connor gave the orders and we—even Willow—listened. Connor excelled and for the first time, I felt we had a chance to win against Monlow.

Both Willow and I battled Connor and there was no denying her strength, especially when she used her abilities. To date invisibility, enhanced hearing, telepathy, and telekinesis had been Connor's gifts but these were now enhanced. Mine was enhanced combat, which included superhuman strength along with agility, dexterity, reflexes, coordination, balance, and endurance—besides teleportation and invisibility. Willow was gifted with electrokinesis and invisibility.

"We need to push our limits if we stand a chance against Monlow," Connor said just a few days later during a break.

"I agree. We should expect the worst so we need to do the impossible."

"Easy for you two to say. I'm able to levitate things with steady electricity but I don't know how to control it yet."

"You need to expand your mind, Willow. Every time you fight, you need to kick that negativity out of your head. You can win any match," Connor said, taking a swig of water from her third refilled bottle. "Again!" she shouted.

We battled ceaselessly and Connor challenged us both. Around and around we went with Connor countering every block, kick, and strike. She kept Willow at bay by levitating the Kali stick and Willow took beatings all the while Connor and I fought. Her speed had increased incredibly. Connor stayed in the zone and when we clashed, we were officially her enemy. Her punches had become more damaging, her side spins surpassed mine, and she anticipated most of my moves like I used to do her. I dodged her levitation strikes only half of the time and she had no problem sending us out the window, past the deck and into the ocean. It was I who bled more and she kept coming. Nothing stopped her, not even the loud drone or the blindfold, or the skilled fighters I hired to test her abilities. There was no stopping this new found Connor and she wanted even more.

Even outside the room we brawled and Connor never once held back. By using her telekinesis, she used—anything and everything to take me down.

In the living room, she moved furniture to hinder our movement, toppled tables to block our exit, broke glass to attack us. And in the kitchen, she used knives in between her physical combat. She was a force to be reckoned with.

"Come on, Willow!" Connor yelled. "You're better than this. I swear you're holding back."

"Oh, yeah," Willow panted against the wall of the living room. "Then why is it that I never win against you?" She struggled for the umpteenth time Connor had her pinned.

"Because you don't believe you can defeat me. Expand your mind. Believe that you can beat me and you just might." Connor pushed off her. "Again!"

We went at it again, Connor against us. Whenever we went down, Connor went up. It was as if she could read Willow's every move and mine most of the time—even though she wore the blindfold and ear plugs.

"Come on, Willow. You're bringing down my high," Connor barked taking off her blindfold. "I can see you thinking about your next move and I'm wearing this." She waved her mask around. "I know you're better than this. What's with you?"

Willow shot her with electricity and pinned her against the pole but instead of cringing, Connor laughed. "Now this is what I mean." Connor thrust back her bolt and turned it on her, yet the electricity caused Willow no harm.

"But that's when you're caught completely off guard. Maybe I'm just not as good as she is," Willow whined sliding to the floor.

I stood and walked away to retrieve water. "And I'm supposed to believe you survived all on your own through Elonium with what you're showing us?" Even I was surprised at Willow's lack of enthusiasm.

She lifted herself up onto her elbows and forearms. "I most certainly did." Her voice squeaked.

"Then show me, show Connor, show someone!" I was past the point of frustration.

"You can survive far better than me in Elonium so what makes you think I can ever defeat you, Ronin, let alone Connor? You're from here and Connor is *special.*" She poked out her bottom lip.

"But, Willow, you should have defeated me at least once, but not even once have you won."

"You're just a skilled warrior, that's all, Ronin."

I took a long breath. "Your insistent flattery gets you nowhere." I rubbed my chin. "Let's go again." I twirled my finger, insinuating we needed to rewind.

"Let just me and Willow fight," I told Connor, and she took a seat.

Although Willow appeared to have tried harder this time, I pinned her easily. "Dammit! I'm starting to think you don't want to win against me."

"I'm trying but you're better than me. Maybe you and I could have one-on-one sessions then."

"I bet you do." Connor chuckled then covered her mouth. "Sorry, that slipped."

"I obviously need help, Connor. I don't like losing all the time, ya' know."

"But what you *do* like is getting *pinned* all the time."

"What is that supposed to mean?"

"Nothing, Willow, just fight so we can get this over with. I'm ready to head back to Earth."

"Maybe she's right." I held up a finger to stop their annoying bickering. "Willow, you and I will work a few sessions alone." Knowing Willow like I did, she needed to be appeased and if that was what she needed, then that would be what I would give. Anything to get this done and over with. To add to this, I'd heard from the professor that our plan was coming into effect so we had very little time left to play with.

For the next two weeks, I started sessions with Willow, then Connor came later, which she actually preferred so she could sleep in. Before long, Willow started showing progress, not to the level I expected or hoped, but she'd improved, nonetheless.

Eventually more time passed and we were all able to work together again. Soon, our bodies moved as one, in cohesive motion with our hands, torso, legs, and feet. We flowed with the ease of our momentum. When one went up, the other went down. Our timing was on point and our minds became as one when it came to battle. But Connor still kept the advantage.

It had been three months of verbal altercations and physical combat. We three were finally as ready as we'd ever be and it was time to go back to Earth. And especially for Willow—time to face all those we left behind. It was not so much that I cared she'd left on bad terms, but more so that her mind was burdened and it blocked her when it came to succeeding in our task.

People like me, Nordac or Erena cared not for the simple man but Willow needed closure. She could not put things behind her to do what was needed.

Furthermore, we had to go to Earth to convince the Keepers and the San council what the plan involved and bring them back to Ether.

So, on our last day of practice I said the words that surprisingly amazed Willow. "We have no more time for sessions. I've received a call from the professor and the plans are a go."

"Yes, about time." Connor jumped up in a cheer. "Hot dogs and hamburgers, here I come. Sorry, Ronin, but all this healthy food you've been feeding us is not good for the soul."

"Wait, what?" Willow backed away from us. "No, I'm not ready."

"What do you mean, no? We get to see our families. You get to see yours, Willow; they are missing you like crazy. Your mom can finally live again. Now she can leave the house knowing you're alive."

"I know but … I can't." She continued to back away, staring at me as if I'd stabbed her in the gut. Droplets of sweat settled on her forehead and her eyes widened. Eventually, her mind faded, no doubt thinking of the dreaded possibilities like the council banishment.

"Willow you knew this was coming. You need this and it's not up for debate. Tomorrow we leave. Get a good night's rest…" But, as I spoke, she ran from the room and slammed the door against the wall leaving it ajar.

I grabbed Connor's arm, stopping her from running after her. "Leave her be."

"I don't understand. She should be happy to return home even if it's for a little while at least."

"Connor, not everyone is so eager to face their demons."

She faced the door again but let a sigh of defeat escape. "All right but…"

"Just let it go," I said.

Back in my room, I secured our arrangements for tomorrow via a safe phone line, but Connor hardly spoke. Her eyes twinkled.

"Tomorrow, huh?" She asked after I hung up. Her lips had not left their permanent turned up position since she'd found out about Earth. "I'll finally know what happened to my mother. I'll get to see my family or what's left of them." Her smile faded as she felt the impact of reality. Her adoptive mother might not have survived the attack months earlier. She slowly paced the room, tugging on her hands as she dealt with mixed emotions. "…even Selene. I can't believe not too long ago she was the irritating, nosey neighbor I ran from and now she's permanently a part of my life. Heck, I even miss Cheyenne." She looked at me when she spoke of my twin sister, the one I never knew I had, then giggled to herself. "Crazy Scott, Ron and … Tony." She whispered Tony's name then looked away from me. Sitting down on the window seat, she gazed out.

I gathered supplies for the trip tomorrow from my chest. "Just as long as you know that this is a business trip. We cannot stay long. The objective is to tell our plan and, if we have time and the San allow it, you and Willow can both see your families. After that, we have to head back immediately.

"Oh, I have to see my family, I may not be able to tell them everything but they need to know that I'm alive," she said, then focused on me. "We will bring everyone back, right?"

"That's the plan—well, at least mine but I'm not sure if they'll agree. The main one to convince is Bynder. He's not my biggest fan even though he accepted me as San first."

"No, he is not." She agreed with me having dealt with him far more than I.

"Tomorrow we head out early in the morning," I said before we crashed for the night.

* * *

Connor, Willow, and I headed down the dark tunnel before the second sun rose. The first belonged to Cravezty, our ally planet. Not that they had a choice; Monlow gave them none. It was a beautiful world although far less advanced than ours, pretty much like Earth. The people there were not human by any means—more barbaric, but they did not harm their planet. Monlow always said to me as a child that they were far too dense to develop a thought to build technology or anything advanced like us. It was not until years later I learned that Monlow had a hand in that.

I tossed a boun into the darkness and it lit up the passageway ahead. As soon as we reached the door, the metal bolt swung open.

"I could smell the human," Erena grunted, her piercing and ever-changing colored eyes rolled over Willow. I told both her and Nordac what time to expect us at the door. "You reek." She didn't care for traitors and in her eyes that was all Willow would ever be.

"Yeah, well, you're ugly," Willow retorted.

Erena sucked her teeth and bumped into Willow as she passed. She only gave Connor a look. She had no problem with her other than the fact she was an Earthling. She found them to be weak.

Willow's mood swung again and I know it had to do with this impending trip but there was something else I could not quite put my finger on. I caught up with her when she made it obvious she did not want to walk next to any of us. "What gives?" I asked, not really caring about her temper; babysitting was not my job. I was concerned that this trip would go without glitches.

"I'm fine, Ronin." She didn't stop, just kept going. I yanked her back. "Hey!" she squealed and that got everyone's attention.

"Go on ahead," I ordered, "we will catch up." When they were far enough away, I warned her, "I don't know what your deal is or why you're acting like this but it's starting to resemble the old Willow."

"Why are they even here?" She pointed to Erena and Nordac.

"For safety measures. Just because I may be San does not make me a true believer in them or them a believer in me."

"Exactly, so I don't see why we all have to go. I could stay here. They don't want to see me anyway."

"This isn't just about you or your issues. This is bigger than all of us so snap out of it and don't mess this up," I leaned in real close to her, "or you will regret it." I stormed off even after she called after me. I did not have time for little girls' games and their pouty antics.

At the right spot in the woods, my fingers interlaced the eighteen clawed medallion and I held the golden key up in the air. I shook it up and down twice, igniting electricity from the middle, opening a portal to their world. On the other side was a hazy version of the docks hidden by trees. I could already smell the ocean.

We hurried through the whirlpool and shook the key again, shutting the door to my world. The air here was much thicker and although it was easier to breathe, I was used to Ether's altitude.

"Why did we come here and not in the park?" Connor's eyes scanned beyond the trees.

"Because it's too hot there." I marched ahead, cutting through the bushes. I had already sent word to the Keepers that we were coming and to meet us at an old abandoned warehouse on neutral territory.

Nordac shot out each light post with just a pulsating glare before we stepped out from the brush, which left us in the black as we headed towards the warehouse. We kept an ear out for anything suspicious.

Connor stopped for a split second. "I hear them in the warehouse," she gasped but I grabbed her arm before she darted off. I shook my head and did a sweeping motion of the area with two fingers. This was supposed to be a safe location but truthfully, there was no such thing.

With a constant lookout, we made it safely to the entrance. I banged the instructed code and Shak opened the door. With his chest out and tight lips, we stared at each other for a long moment before he stepped back. Shak, the protector of the group and now head of interplanetary relations, let me know he was allowing me to be there. Not everyone was a believer in me yet; some might never be but I was fine with that as long as we could work together. I've worked alongside many a foe when our goals paralleled. But it was Bynder who walked over and shook my hand. I glanced over at Cheyenne, my twin. She crossed an arm across her body, clasping her other one. She had her reservations about me and with good reason—I did try to kill her once.

Connor rushed into the warehouse and hugged Selene tightly. I overheard Selene tell her that her mother was alive and safe.

Eventually, she made her rounds hugging her Keepers—Tanzia, Toschia, Shak, and even Bynder—then moved on to the yougows Ron, Cheyenne, and Tony as we four stood by the door, receiving untrustworthy frowns.

"You will never guess who is here," Connor said, stepping aside. "Where is she?"

I pulled Willow from behind us and she huddled by the doorway. Although she said that she wasn't afraid to face them, she stood hushed with her ankles crossed not moving forward. She began to tug on her spiked short hair when no one else said a word.

"You're alive!" Ron broke the deafening silence but did not move.

I had told them she was dead. Willow stepped back and attempted to cover the right side of her face with a hand but Ron sprinted over to her and pried her fingers away. "You're still beautiful to me," he whispered. He hugged her but Willow's shoulders drooped and she did not hug him back. Ron pulled back and reached up to her scars, but she pushed his hand away.

"I don't need your pity," she snapped, her tone cold.

Ron's eyes widened and he stepped back. Cheyenne came over and hugged Willow as well, but her body language was reserved. Eventually, everyone acknowledged her but only Ron, Cheyenne, and Tony had shown any warmth towards her. The Keepers observed her with either a narrowed gaze or pursed lips, reserving what they truly wanted to say.

"How?" Tanzia asked flatly.

After stepping away from Ron, she answered her assigned Keeper, "Ronin took me in." Willow waved a hand towards me but faced the floor as she spoke. How do you face the one who protected you all your life after you betrayed them?

"You had her this whole time?" Tanzia addressed me.

"Yes, most of it," I responded. "And before you ask why, I never told you it was because we were not allies until my last visit here. And I use the term 'allies' loosely." I flipped over a large crate and sat down, finally loosening my hold to my dagger. Both Erena and Nordac stepped beside me. "Besides, she was a part of the plan that you knew nothing about. The plan I need to discuss with you before we five head back today." As I spoke, Willow positioned herself behind me.

"Like hell they will go back with you," Tony barked.

Bynder placed a hand on his shoulder, "We allowed you to come, Tony. Don't make me regret it. You know Connor has to go back into hiding on Ether." He pointed in my direction, "And Willow has made her decision clear."

"It seems like he has enough females. Why does he need a fourth?" He took note of my entourage.

"Tony…"

"It's okay, Bynder," I said. "Monlow has already taken two of my mates but foolishly, he doesn't see women as a threat—only Connor." I gestured towards her.

"Willow, why are you on Ronin's side?" Ron asked.

"Are we not on the same side? Isn't that why you are here?" I gripped my dagger, immediately thinking of this being a trap.

"He is right," Bynder said, taking note of my slight movement. "We have but one side and one duty - to save Earth. We've discussed this."

"So you spoke with the council, I assume?" I was ready to get this over with. Being around so many San was unsettling as there was just too much bad blood and one mere trip could not fix that.

The Keepers faced each other before they spoke which I always felt was an exasperating habit. "Yes, we spoke with them at numerous and very lengthy meetings but they want to meet with you," Bynder informed me.

"That will never happen. If I ever met with them they would bring an army of supernaturals just to make sure I didn't escape. They would use mind readers to retrieve my knowledge and storm Ether alone. I shall pass."

"We figured as much and that is why we never agreed to that." Bynder rubbed his hands together. "They don't even know we are meeting you tonight."

"So they are on board?" I asked with a raised brow.

"Yes, in the agreement that you fully accept your San heritage and wish they would make you an ally, the fact that you've always protected Connor but mostly because these times call for drastic measures." He glanced back at the rest of the Keepers who always stood strategically spaced. "Plus, seeing Willow standing here in this room is a testament to your word. Although when all is said and done, Willow will have to answer for her actions."

"Answer for my actions! I think I've suffered enough. Look at me!" She raised her right pant leg and touched the scars on her face. "It was you who left me there on an alien planet to die."

"You made your choice, Willow," Bynder seethed. "You chose to side with them..."

"Oh, like you right now?"

"Not when they were our enemies! Make sure you know that distinction, little girl." He stepped forward. It was not like him to lose his composure but Willow showed no remorse. "You could have gotten us all killed and Connor would have been forced over there to give Monlow maybe another five centuries on that planet, giving him the ability and longevity to take over Earth. What you did was reckless and yet you stand there, showing no remorse."

"Well, like I said, I feel I've suffered enough when none of you cared to try and rescue me," Willow folded her arms.

"We did try." Ron stepped forward but she backed up and shot him a scowl. "What's gotten into you?" He stopped advancing.

"Trust me, you don't want to know." And with that, she walked outside with another Keeper, Tochia, behind her. They were keeping a close watch over her.

"Ronin, we are here and ready to listen. We will inform the council of everything with you there and if they like what they hear, then they will back you."

"Well, they won't like it because you all need to come back with us," I told them.

"We would have it no other way but you have to give us some details," Bynder closed the distance between us.

"We have one opportunity and one only. My father's…" I stood up and cleared my throat. "Monlow's patience with me is wearing thin so our window is limited. A comrade of mine has set up a meeting with him tomorrow to set things in motion but a sentinel of Monlow's is our ally and he will get us in. There will be entertainment and a lot of people there, which means a lot of distractions. It's his yearly celebration of rich conglomerates who come to bow at his feet and pay him much respect with a lot of money. His guard will be down. I have ships, allies already on Ether and our nearby planet, Cravezty will be there at a moment's notice. They have waited centuries to retaliate. San, I know you to be kind folk but fiends when the situation calls for it and now is the time. We can defeat him and take the throne. This gala is an opportunity we cannot pass up and to be honest, the only opportunity we have," I spoke only to Bynder, seemingly the only one who believed me.

"And in regards to the throne, we can assume you want it for yourself, right?" Bynder asked.

"It can be no other way." I expected this question.

"Then how do we know we can trust you? How do we know you won't betray us or that you will be a worthy ruler?" Bynder sidestepped when he asked his question.

"I guess you will have to wait and see but would I go to such lengths with Connor and Willow just to betray you in the end?" I brushed a hand over my mouth before continuing on. "Although I have never ruled on my own, I have learned much under his thumb."

"That's what concerns us," Bynder retorted.

"His allies are my allies," I closed the gap between us. "I am a familiar face and this, along with my status, will keep away those who want to compete for the throne," I searched the faces and read doubt. "You still hesitate after I've kept my word and brought back not only one San but two?" I asked.

"With good reason, Ronin. Not three months ago we were mortal enemies. You've caused us much hardship and now, out of desperation, we need each other. No one likes to make such harsh decisions under those circumstances," Bynder explained.

"Understood, but do you really have much choice? He is coming for your planet next. Even if we do not become allies after this, Earth is of no interest to me," I unconsciously turned in the direction of a gasp and noted Cheyenne's tense stare. For some treacherous reason, that sound tugged on my chest. "I was only referring to the planet not the people on it," I pointed to the floor, then quickly addressed Bynder again. "I will make sure this vastly unexplored planet remains safe," I announced.

"Why did you wait so long to tell us about this plan or proposal?"

"I just received word late yesterday about the impromptu venue. He trusts no one so to keep everyone on their toes that is how he does things."

"Are you sure that all parties and allies will attend this function?" Bynder asked.

"I guarantee you they will. When he calls, you stop whatever it is that you are doing and come. If you do not, in his mind, he sees it as rebellious and traitorous behavior."

"And Connor's role?" Selene stepped forward.

"Connor and I spoke at length about her role," I responded.

"What does that mean?" Selene asked.

"That means not one person knows everybody's role," Connor answered in my stead.

"But do you know everyone's role, Ronin?" Selene asked.

"No, not even me. I know key players but not all, especially not the minor ones, nor am I aware of how they will acquire all that is needed to succeed in this suicide mission. That way, the people in my circle can be trusted to a fault. If Monlow does not change the game plan for tomorrow, this can work. But then again, we always prepare for the worst."

I continued to answer all of their questions but I was not quite sure I reassured them. Honestly, there were no words to guarantee anyone of this takeover. How do you assure anyone of a scheme when so many are involved, and how does a villainous person ask one of honor to trust them? Truthfully, I didn't need their trust. Right now, I just desired their aid. But I needed Connor - she was the deal breaker.

"You have done so much evil and wrong to this planet alone, it's a wonder we're even speaking to you."

"I understand, Bynder, but like you said - desperate times."

"Just know this. We don't fully trust you. If you make one false move or if we feel this is a ploy to kill two birds with one stone—as in we help you take down Monlow then you take out the San—we will take you with us," Bynder warned and I expected nothing else.

"Fair enough," I agreed. "It goes both ways. If you plan on taking out Monlow and me, then have the San council members take over, it will not fare well for any of you," I cautioned.

"Not even Connor?" Tony asked from the doorway. It slammed shut when he stepped inside.

"Be careful," I warned him as he eased his way to me.

"What's wrong, Tony?" Connor asked. He stared at her as if to curse her but the answer to his sudden mood change became clear when Willow strolled in behind him. She'd told him about our living arrangements. Why else would he be so furious?

"I have a better question: Where did you stay when you lived in his palace?" He turned his hatred on me when he asked her such a personal question.

"Not here." Bynder stepped in Tony's path as he headed straight for me. "We are working on an alliance. This is not the time for personal agendas."

Tony ignored Bynder, "No answer, Connor?" One could feel the tension in the room.

I instinctively stood closer to her. She faced away, humiliated, and she'd done nothing wrong. "It's none of your business," I answered for her.

"Oh, he speaks for you now?" he looked to her right before swinging at me and missing.

"Stop!" Connor yelled, but she could have been a million years away.

I'd wanted this for a very long time and if it was a fight he wanted, then it's a fight he would get.

Tony shoved me and I slid to the center of the warehouse, but all that did was ignite my hatred for him. There, I removed my jacket and shouted, "Do you really want to do this, boy?" We may have been the same age but our lives were so different. He'd lived a sheltered life and it had spoiled him.

When I approached with tightened fists, Tony swung on me again but I dodged every single one of his blows. On his third attempt, I dropped to the floor and whacked his legs up from under him. He landed on his back but flipped up and within a second, I shot up and kicked him in the jaw. His body twisted to the left and he stumbled back. A pool of blood dripped down his face as he stared at me. He smeared it across his twisted mouth with the back of his hand.

"You think you're tough?" I gave him three quick jabs to the ribs. "You think fighting will change anything?" I yanked on his collar. "Don't you get it? If you have to fight for something, it isn't yours."

Tony pushed my arms away and fought to stake his claim but I fought to show him he could not intimidate me. Despite being born a San, I was still an Ethosian at heart. That made me cruel, calculating, and vicious—what one would call a sociopath. So every time I struck him, I tried to crush his bones. If it were up to him, I would no longer be in his world, let alone Connor's. He wanted me gone, completely wiped from reality—so 'loathsome' didn't begin to cover what I thought of Tony.

My body twisted, flowing with the momentum of my hits but he could not keep up. I'd had to fight all my life, unlike him. I might have been royalty but he was the one who lived a life of privilege. So, of the two of us, he was the only one wounded. His attacks barely affected me. I was so tired of him thinking he was superior to me, always judging me as if I were filth. He didn't know me but now he was getting a crash course into who I was.

Whatever came in our way, we used—wood for stakes or sharp objects to slash each other. Nothing stopped us. Not even when we bashed into walls, crashed through glass or dented metal pipes. We were ruthless, he and I, and it felt stupendous.

"Are you ready to stop?" I asked Tony, who stood drunk off exhaustion after I'd taken my rage out on his now bloody body and ripped clothing.

With his last attempt to charge me, I twisted him around and pressed his back to my front, then gripped his neck with my forearm and began to choke him. He struggled for freedom but I wanted him to stop moving and there was only one way I could make that happen.

I enjoyed his choking noises and that I was the one he would eventually succumb to. Time seemed to have become motionless; I came to out of a deep trance when my body was slammed to the floor by both Bynder and Erena. Shak kept Tony away.

"Unhand me immediately!" I roared. I wanted Tony and nothing was going to stop me.

"No, enough!" Erena ordered. "The longer you keep this up means the longer I have to stay here and you know I hate this place." she pressed my shoulder to the floor and held my own dagger to my throat. That was the only thing that brought sensibility back to me. She knew my temper well. "You can't kill everyone in your way," she seethed.

"Let me up," I ordered, more in control. She backed off.

"San don't hurt each other," Bynder stepped between Tony and me.

"He's not San," Tony pointed at me.

"Keep testing me," I said. Erena and Bynder held me back.

"All right!" Bynder yelled. "Like it or not, we are now allies. Ronin, we will talk soon."

"Fine," I gritted my teeth. I still wanted him but let it go for now. I faced Bynder, "If you are not back here in three hours, after our meeting, then I will know the council's answer. But know this, Connor and Willow will be going back with me. Mark my words." I glanced over at Connor and saw the look of disappointment etched across her face. I knew she was upset but she would still do the right thing. I said nothing more as I took my leave. Grabbing my sheath, I headed out the door.

Chapter 10

Connor

I stood there, speechless from being both embarrassed and furious at them fighting. Then, Ronin just left. He simply left. Barely able to face anyone, I swallowed back my shame and faced Selene. "Are we ... are we ready to go?"

"Yes, I think that's a smart idea," I headed towards the door but Cheyenne rushed up to me.

"Are you okay?" For a split second, I watched her lips, amazed that she asked about me. I half-smiled and nodded, still shaken, and she walked off while I headed out into the fresh air.

Willow stood by one of the SUVs as if she'd done nothing to cause this mess. I walked up to her, "What was that? Did you really have to say anything? We were cool back on Ether and now you pull this crap?"

"It just slipped out when Tony asked." She bit her bottom lip and looked at Tony and Ron for support.

"You know what, Willow, I cannot wait until this is over so we never have to deal with each other again." Her face crumbled into a cry and Ron swooped in to hug her like he always did. *Five minutes ago she wouldn't let him touch her but now look at her...* I could have told Ron she hadn't even asked about him the whole time on Ether but I was no Willow.

"Connor..."

I held up a hand, stopping Tony mid-sentence. It took a long second for me to muster enough resolve to even face him. "Don't," I shook my head. "Just don't before I bash your face in."

"Leave it alone, Tony," Cheyenne said. "You've done enough and so have you, Willow." Willow shot up at her best friend and left her mouth open with nothing to say.

The Keepers walked over after finishing up talking amongst themselves. "The council wants us to meet them at headquarters," Tanzia said. "For now, you can see your parents for a brief moment, then we return with answers."

I was fine with getting out of there and seeing my family. I wished it were possible to see my besties, Angel and Hope, but what would I tell them about my disappearance? Then I'd have to turn around and come up with another reason for having to leave again. Not a reasonable thing to do.

It was Cheyenne who drove me to my parents. She actually offered, which I found odd since we'd always seemed to butt heads in the past. At first, we drove in silence but halfway to our destination, she broke the ice. "How is he?" she asked, not looking at me.

At first, I wasn't sure who she meant, but then it clicked.

"He is all right," I said, not wanting to tell her the truth about Ronin, her twin; the one who'd tried to murder her.

She placed a hand over mine and stared into my eyes, "The truth, Connor."

"He is a ball of confusion, Cheyenne," she continued to navigate through the streets as I spoke. "He is angry, bitter, damaged, but most of all, hurt. He tries to hide that part of himself but I see it," I blushed at knowing him the way I do.

She glanced at me for a long second, then faced the road again. "I don't even know Ronin but he's the part of my life I've always missed. It never dawned on me that I had a twin," she took a moment before she continued. "I should hate him…" Emotions caught in her throat. "I should despise him, want him gone, but I can't."

"I know." Even though Cheyenne had both parents like me, hers were never around. Being wealthy does not mean having it all. Her father worked all the time and her mom traveled around the world, leaving her at home.

"I'm seventeen and I still have a nanny. Sadly, she's my best friend." She wiped her face dry. "He's my only family."

"And in his warped mind, he thought that by ending you he was saving you from a life of having to deal with Monlow. He must have sensed your connection or knew there was something special about you, and that is why he chose you."

"Thank you," she responded.

"For what?"

"I know he was protecting you all this time, Connor, even though he was conflicted about it and on Ether, too—but I know you protected him as well. I thank you for keeping him safe." She grabbed a napkin out of her bag and dabbed her tears. "I feel so stupid thanking you. He probably doesn't…"

"No, he does. He feels it too, Cheyenne. I think he keeps his distance because you are literally all the family he has left. And if we don't survive then…"

"I get it," she nodded. "Why get close to a person if they won't even be there tomorrow?"

I grabbed her hand and squeezed it. We rode that way for a while until we stopped off at a wooded area I'd never seen before. We were parked by a stone building that looked more like a bunker above ground than a home.

Cheyenne voice-activated Selene through her phone and her face appeared on the screen in the car's dashboard. "Connor, your parents have no clue you are alive so they've had no forewarning about your visit today. We didn't know if you'd ever return so we thought it would be best for them to accept they might never do so. They don't know about the San. Your father still doesn't have all the answers even though he is part of Mr. Conway's, Ron's grandfather's, secret society. It's imperative that you give nothing away in regards to us or this impending war. You have less than an hour. Make the most of it." I heard what she left unsaid: say your goodbyes just in case.

"What did they think happened to me?" I asked.

"I told them that you confided in me about witnessing a murder and what you saw affected you mentally, hence your behavior in the past. I told them I was a federal agent and you're our key witness to a huge crime ring and you are under our protection. They felt they should have been involved but I explained that the criminal associates knew who you were and you needed to flee immediately. There was no time. Needless to say, mine and your family's friendship has been severed."

"So, you took the fall for me?"

"Yes, but stick to that story and use your discretion. And, Connor, stay strong," Selene advised, then wished me all the best and hung up.

"Good luck," Cheyenne added.

Slowly, I got out of the vehicle and walked towards a huge stone door. I pressed the button to the right, then implemented the code that Selene gave me. I took a gold key from my pocket, inserted it into the slot and turned it three times to the right then back two times. The door slid open to the right and let me in. Down a long green lit corridor, I walked to get to the main door. I placed my hand in the middle of the green glass and it asked me for my name. I had to repeat my name twice—my voice shook so badly. The closer I got to my parents, the harder it was to function. On the second attempt, the door allowed me entry and right there, in the center of the foyer, sat my mom—in a wheelchair, but she was alive.

"Mama!" Immediately, water blurred my vision. I fell to my knees, unable to walk, much less talk.

She wheeled herself over to me. "Dear, God!" She grabbed my face in her warm hands that smelled of vanilla. "Connor," she whispered, blinking back tears. "Is it really you?" I couldn't answer. No words would form; only tears answered her. "Blaire!" she screamed for my father. "Blaire!"

My head fell to her knees, it felt so heavy. I clutched both her legs in the metal chair that she was now confined to.

"What is…?" He ran in and stopped. Falling to the floor next to me, he grabbed me and pulled me to him. I nestled my head against his chest. My mom managed to slide to the floor and we all sat there, crying senselessly.

My sister, Ebony, and younger brother, Kane, eventually joined us. All of us stayed that way for I don't know how long. My parents kept wanting to look at me like I wasn't real.

Eventually, we made it to the couch with me sitting in between my parents and Kane on my lap, wrapping his little arms around my neck. Ebony sat on the chair across from us. They asked me a million questions. "What happened? Why didn't you come to us about this murder?" my mom begged for answers and I could see the agony on her face.

I had no answers to give, "I don't know. I guess I was just confused and scared. I kept messing up and I didn't want to keep disappointing you."

"Oh, baby, you could never disappoint us. We would love you no matter what. Just talk to us," Mom said, gripping both mine and Dad's hand.

The dam broke again. "I'm so sorry," I cried. My mom kissed me on my forehead.

"Just talk to us. Now that you are back, we can…"

I shook my head, "Someone is actually waiting outside for me. They wanted us to have some time alone." I picked at my shirt—my new attire of leather pants, fitted top, and short leather jacket with combat boots.

My mom grabbed me close to her bosom and rested her lips on my head. "Connor, please," she pleaded and I clasped her hands that held my face. "We just got you back. I don't understand, what is going on? Who are these people that are after you?"

"There are things I just can't tell you." How could I tell them the truth? She'd been attacked because of me. Monlow's men used her as bait to draw me out. I wanted to break but like Selene had asked me to, I held strong.

"Please, sweetheart, tell me something," my mom begged.

"Just know that I am fine," I lied, biting my bottom lip and trying to stop it from quivering. "It's just best that you don't know too much," I looked up at her.

"Too much?" she asked. "We don't know anything other than the fact Selene and this strange man came to my hospital room. He never spoke not once, only stayed at the door. You never told Angela or Hope anything, so why tell Selene but not any of us?"

"Lizzie please..." my dad stopped her.

"What, Blaire? She is my baby!" My mom hugged me tighter.

"One day I was being followed home so I went to her house across the street instead. She knew something was wrong and it just slipped out. She said that she could protect me and since they knew who I was, I had to go into hiding immediately." That was partly true; my enemies knew where I lived and I had to flee.

"How long is this going to go on?" she asked.

"Not too much longer, I promise," I said, feeling terrible that I could not tell them the truth.

"Then you will be back for good?" Kane asked, sitting up.

"Of course." I swallowed back my misery.

"Tell her the good news, hon." My dad attempted to break the tension and the line of questioning with good news.

"Yesterday, at therapy, I finally showed progress. The doctors thought I would be paralyzed from the waist down but miraculously, I was chosen to be a part of a rare study and it's working."

My dad and I quickly glanced at each other. We knew that his secret society, a.k.a. the San, was helping her. We had access to advance technology and certain medications most medical facilities on Earth were not privy to. That last part he didn't know but he was smart enough to figure his secret group was a lot more advanced than they informed him.

"Show her your progress, hon," he said.

"The doctors said eventually I will walk again. They say I will make a full recovery." My mom grabbed a pair of crutches, stood up with Ebony's help, and slowly shuffled her feet forward.

"That's great, Mom!" I encouraged her.

She walked to the kitchen and back but by the time she sat back down, my time was up. "I have to go," I hugged her. "I'm so proud of you."

"I know there is more to this story but I cannot stop you, as much as I want to." She kissed my head again and my dad eventually pried her arms away.

"Are you sure you have to go?" Ebony asked.

I stood to my feet. "Yes," I nodded and gave everyone a hug.

"Stay with your mom, guys. I'll walk Connor out." My dad was right behind me.

In the hallway, I rushed for the door but my dad took my hand and pulled me back. I didn't want to; I needed air but instead, I fell against him and let out a river of sorrow. "I have a feeling you know you were adopted and this has something to do with that, but I won't tell your mother. It would make her worry even more," he kissed the top of my head. "I'm so sorry, sweetheart," he tried to stay strong but his voice cracked and his chest shook from deep emotions. "I'm sorry I couldn't protect you and our family better. I am so sorry, baby." He almost crushed me with his death grip.

Oh, god he thought this was his fault. He had no clue that by adopting me, he helped tremendously. Hearing my father, who in my mind was the strongest man in the world, cry ripped me to shreds. "No, Dad," I looked up. The pain on his face was heart-wrenching. "You did protect me, don't you see? The secret society you adopted me from just didn't tell you everything and for that I am sorry."

"I love you, Connor, and I know you may never come back to us." I stayed in his arms and wept. "Just know that I will take care of them, especially your mom."

I wrapped my arms tightly around him, my fingers clinging to his back. "I know you will," I looked up at him. "You're the greatest dad in the world."

He wiped the tears away from my face, "I love you, sweetheart."

"I love you too, Dad."

Peeling myself from his arms, I left. I couldn't look back, it was too hard.

"Just go," I cried when I made it back to the car.

"Okay...okay," Cheyenne agreed and drove off. She rubbed my back and kept repeating, "It will be all right."

But would it ever?

Chapter 11

Willow

I stared out the window watching nature fly by, still furious that Connor had confronted me in front of everyone. "I just don't understand how she could get so upset with me?"

"Just let it go, Willow," Ron whined like I didn't have a right to vent. He nonstop rubbed my arm like I were some wounded pet.

"I was just answering a question, Ron," I snapped at him for trying to shut me up. He always did that when we were dating but that ended as soon as he left me to die. I looked away from him, annoyed that he sat next to me in the back seat instead of upfront next to Tony who was driving me to my parents' house. "Right, Tony?" But he only faced the road and didn't respond. *What did he have to be upset about?*

Ron kept touching me but what he didn't understand was that I wasn't the same girl from months ago. I'd changed so much that I didn't even know myself anymore. I didn't want the same things, nor did I want him. I figured if I pulled back he would get the hint, so I slid over in the seat.

"What's wrong, Willow? Talk to me," Ron pleaded.

"Nothing, Ron." I wanted him to leave me alone. I felt so out of place. It was too quiet and calm here. Every nerve in my body tingled, the situation filling me with agitation.

Once again, I peered out the window as we headed to that place I'd once called home. My stomach tossed in resentment towards them all. They expected an apology from me but didn't think I deserved one. Not an ounce of pity came my way. No one had asked how I was or what had happened over there. Nothing!

When we pulled in front of my parents' mansion I didn't budge but sat there examining the place. It seemed much smaller now compared to Ronin's palace, my new home and sanctuary. The house sat back behind a gated fence protected from the rest of the world. Too bad it didn't work against the San.

"Willow, Tanzia is talking to you," Ron said, interrupting my thoughts. I scooted up so I could see her on the dashboard's screen. She was already at headquarters; not that I'd ever had the privilege of going there but that was where they were headed.

"Sorry what?" I gripped the seat, trying not to focus on where I was. A place I didn't want to be.

"We're not going to tell the council members about your presence yet…" *Of course not—why should they be allowed to follow protocol?* "Your parents don't know you are alive…"

"So, what sense does it make seeing them if I may not even survive." I felt my scars and felt ashamed. "Once a model, now a freak." My family would shun me. Shallow it may seem, but true.

"Willow!" I could feel Ron's eye on me.

"You're not a scared little freak, are you, Ron?" I barked at him.

Ron and Tony shifted in their seats—judging me, the both of them, but they didn't know what insanity I'd suffered. "I just don't think my mom seeing me is sensible. And then, telling her I have to leave again will only make things worse," I explained further. "What did you tell them anyway?"

"Since they were never exposed to our world, we told them nothing. Your mom believes you pursued a career in modeling but your dad thinks the worst."

"I tried working the modeling angle but your dad doesn't believe me," Ron interrupted. "Being a part of my grandfather's secret society he thinks that you were kidnapped or taken by the people he'd tried to save you from as a baby. He hired a private investigator but after three months of nothing, he gave up, especially after not being able to contact either my grandfather or my dad."

"I…" The front door opened. My dad, briefcase in hand, hopped into his McLaren P1, his favorite getaway car to clear his head. My dad—the man who'd never told me or my mom the truth. Maybe if he'd warned me, if he told me something, my life would have turned out so differently. But he didn't; he only held onto his lie.

My mom stood at the door watching him leave like she'd done so many times. Dressed in her white robe, she stood with mangled hair, wearing no makeup. That was forbidden, she'd always told me. She looked sickly and pale. Once young and beautiful, she had aged ten years in a matter of months. I wondered how long it had been since she'd stepped outside.

I grabbed the door handle but froze. I shut my eyes, contemplating if I should go. I missed them so much but flashes of Ether surfaced in my head. No. I was a freak of nature. It was too hard—and only to rip their hearts again, never to return. *It's wrong.*

"Your parents don't care, Willow. They love you anyway," Ron said as if he knew what I thought or how I felt. I cut him a look, warning him to leave me alone, but then heard the gate open and watched my dad ease out of the driveway and head toward the winding road. My mom stood there for a moment, searching around, then shut the door. I relaxed and let go of the door handle.

"Drive," I ordered resting my head back on the seat.

"No," Ron said. "You can't do this. At least let your mother know you are all right."

"She won't believe it. Look at me. She'll think the worst."

"The worst is death, Willow," Tony finally spoke.

"Oh, now you have something to say? Just go!" I shouted at them, furious that they kept staring at me. Ron tried to hug me but I moved all the way over. "You could have sat upfront," I spat.

"Why are you so angry?" Ron asked.

"Because you left me behind!" I screamed. "You of all people, Ron." My tone was wicked but I felt so angry.

"Hey, stop beating up on Ron. He tried everything to get to you. We even devised a plan but—"

"Well, he obviously didn't try hard enough, did he?"

Yes, I was angry. I was hurt. But most of all, I no longer felt like the San they wanted me to be. In the short months I had lived on Ether, the place had already messed with me both mentally and physically. I couldn't go back. I was too far gone.

Ron observed my mood. "Sorry, Willow. I really tried." He got out of the car and walked around to the front seat. I felt bad for him but he wouldn't get it. I'd seen too much, done too many terrible things. I'd never wanted any of this but they pushed me, so there I was. I'd suffered the worst. He had to know I was no longer the same girl who'd left Earth. He needed to move on like I had.

* * *

Outside the warehouse, Tony and I stood down by the water discussing something I really didn't care about. Though bruised, he had on fresh clothes since we had time to swing by his place so he could change. "You should give Ron a break. He really did his best." Tony was trying too hard to avoid my scars.

"He's hovering too much." I kept my arms folded, staring out from the dock's edge. The cool breeze felt nice and the air smelled refreshing, unlike certain parts of Ether.

"Yeah, but he's always done that and you love the attention, at least you used to," he annoyingly reminded me.

"Not anymore."

"He doesn't know that. He thinks you are the same person who left here less than a year ago. Jesus, Willow, most people don't change that much in what—seven, eight months?"

"Well, those people never visited Ether."

"Connor seems the same."

"Don't compare me to her." I held up a hand. "Besides, she hasn't suffered like me. She hasn't done the things I've done." I relaxed my tight grip. "Or maybe she's done more. They did sleep in the same room together and I can only assume in the same bed - *for months.*"

"All right, Willow. I don't need the details." He held up both hands in truce. "And just so you know, we've all suffered, not just you."

"How do you know she's the same?" I turned back to him. "I am so sick and tired of everyone thinking she's so precious and overlooking the fact that she's related to Monlow, you know the very monster who wants our powers and life."

He rubbed his hands over his face. "I'm not blind, Willow. I have my doubts about Connor but that's because of Ronin. For some reason she's blind when it comes to him. He may be San and Bynder may trust him enough to believe that crap he's spitting, but I don't."

"What are you saying, Tony?"

"I'm saying that I've spoken with some of Ron's grandfather's associates and they don't trust him either. They believe Ronin will be just as bad or worse than Monlow if he rules Ether."

"So what is your point?"

"My point is that some San members also agree that he cannot be trusted. We cannot take a chance. If we decide to back him and succeed, there will be measures taken."

"Like what?"

"Nothing I can talk about." He refused to tell me more.

I hurried over to him. "Are you so idiotic that you can't see he is the best option we have? You need to back off or you're going to mess things up and everything's going to backfire. Just leave it alone. He's proven himself to me, Tony."

"Yea, well, he's never proven himself to me so…"

"Connor and I are alive. He brought us back like he promised…"

"Of course he did because he wants us to help him. To make sure he gets control over Ether. He's not going to piss us off then ask for help."

"He saved my life, Tony."

"How?"

"When Monlow was going to strip me of my powers and send me to some horrible place, Ronin prevented it."

"If he saved you, then how'd you get those scars?" He rubbed his cheek.

My heart raced from this preposterous conversation. "That was Monlow's doing. I got it from a creature while I was in prison but Ronin freed me." I stepped away. "You don't get it. He forced me through a stint of challenges and made me tougher for it." I could see the disgust in his face. "Tony, I used to be afraid of everything all the time but I'm not anymore. He made me stronger than I ever would've been living here on Earth."

"But why should you have to be this way when Earth is your home?"

I turned my back to him. "I can't come back here to live," I said to the ripples in the water.

He stepped in front of me. "What do you mean you can't come back here? This is your home, Willow."

"No, it's not. Just being here makes me uncomfortable."

"I think it's called post-traumatic stress syndrome, Willow. Even war vets get therapy. You can, too."

"Just let it go, Tony. Can you please just explain it to Ron?"

"No, Willow. If you're so strong, then woman up and tell him yourself," he rudely said, then walked off the pier, back to the car.

Chapter 12

Connor

The council agreed on meeting with Ronin but since he was not allowed to know the headquarters' whereabouts, he used a hologram device from a secret location. Finally, they settled to align themselves with Ronin for two reasons: One—Monlow was our common enemy and we would most likely not win without the insight and alliances Ronin would provide, which would benefit us in the sense of making Earth stronger; Two—Ronin was in fact San. That fact they either knew or suspected but them being the council, of course, giving us answers was out of the question.

Odd how enemies could become allies for a common cause. It was a strange situation but if it prevented Earth from being taken over, then so be it.

Cheyenne and I were the last to arrive back at the warehouse. My and Willow's presence alone encouraged more tension, so I made it my business to ignore this strain with Tony while Ronin spoke to our Keepers, namely two council members, Ms. Ridgemont and Mr. Diaz.

All of us yougows were there: Ron, Willow, Cheyenne, Tony, and even Scott who, like always, showed up late.

"Connor, I am so happy to see you." He grabbed me up and twirled me around.

"I'm surprised to see you here," I said to Scott, who was up and about and no longer pretending to be hurt. When I left, he was living at the San headquarters' infirmary ward after an attack in Kiev, Ukraine, and since life was *very* good for him there, he milked his stay as long as possible.

"Now you know I wouldn't miss an opportunity to raise a little Hell," he joked, but was serious. "I want to go out in a blaze of glory." He held up his fingers, mimicking a gun.

"Still crazy as ever." I patted his shoulder "Glad you're here."

"Since you've been gone that over there…"—he pointed and winked at Cheyenne, since she was in hearing distance— "has grown soft on me."

This I had to hear. "You and Cheyenne?" The woman had always hated him but I thought it was because she'd secretly liked him.

"Yup." He literally barked at her like a dog when she kept listening. She squalled and annoyingly walked away after making a detestable noise. "She no longer throws up at the sight of me." He leaned in close. "I'm wearing her down." In all fairness, Scott was a cutie with dirty blonde hair and grey eyes but his personality was rough and rugged, the kind Cheyenne needed. She was a tough vault to crack but somehow, Scott was not fazed by her hard exterior. She probably liked that about him even though she still hadn't admitted to it.

I smirked. "Yea, I see the warmth," I said with a laugh. "Hey, if we survive this, remind me to tell you about Metadonia."

"Oh, yea, what's that?" I piqued his interest.

"Your freakin' Nirvana." I giggled. "You'd love it, Scott, I swear."

"Dang, girl, you got a guy interested for sure." He shifted and adjusted his belt.

"Trust me, you won't be disappointed."

"If I have to take Monlow on myself, then so be it. It's on now."

I could always rely on Scott to make me laugh.

"Let's go!" Bynder yelled over to the rest of us lingering back. I rushed ahead but suddenly had a bad feeling. Stopping cold, I watched everyone walk out the warehouse. It took me a minute to catch my breath, then I joined them, too.

Something's not right.

I hurried ahead to catch up with Ronin and his two companions. "What's wrong?" he asked with gathered brows.

"I don't know." I shook my head but when he pushed on, I instinctively grabbed his arm.

He abruptly stopped. "What?"

"I don't know," I repeated, trying to catch my breath. "Just be careful." I wasn't sure if I was overreacting. It was most likely nothing. I just wanted this mission to go smoothly.

"Always," he said then headed forward.

I let it go but could not help keeping extra cautious. Ronin walked ahead of us with Erena and Nordac in front as we approached the wooded area. Standing in between the trees, we yougows and the Keepers formed a circle. Tanzia said a mantra like she always did before a great challenge and I searched the expressions of everyone there—nothing but stoic and rigid faces showed, mirroring mine. Everyone wore dark combat gear black boots except for those of us who'd come from Ether wearing leather.

When Tanzia was done, Ronin shook the golden key twice and lightning struck from it as he moved the thing in the air where an ever-growing vortex appeared. Ether beckoned us.

Both Erena and Nordac stepped through first, then Ronin and me, then Byron and Selene, and so on until we'd all made it through and the portal closed. It was eerily quiet in the woods. We were a good distance from the palace, like we were earlier in the day, when we traveled to Earth.

After remaining motionless and hushed for a while, making sure it was safe to venture onward, we eased ahead, following the three Ethosians. The sky was dark purplish-reddish, their nighttime. Our eyes all glowed their vivid colors as we traveled without lights.

A chill ran up my spine like a lightning bolt. It was but a peculiar sound that caught my attention. I immediately halted and shook my head at Ronin. He turned his head awkwardly and slowly held up a finger.

All hell broke loose. Bright lights showed in our faces. It was hard to make out what was happening or who our attackers were until I heard words that brought fear to my world.

"By order of the Ethosian military, you are trespassing on foreign soil. Turn down your weapons and surrender!"

The words were spoken but in truth, they gave us no time to surrender. A loud scream erupted when Ronin was shot in the head and I realized that cry came from me. He fell back into the weeds and I could no longer see his body in the midst of the bright lights.

Chaos erupted all at once between gunfire and smoke, then an explosion occurred. I landed on my back, half blind and clasping my ears. They were ringing from the loud commotion. I wiped the scattered dirt from my face and sent a telepathic message to Tanzia, hoping she could hear me, but she did not respond. I rolled over to stand and head back the way I'd come but sharp, hot pain scorched my back. I fell forward, paralyzed.

Hands clawed me, then gripped under each of my arms. As they lifted me up, my head fell forward and I could only hope we could still escape. But when a brightness showed in my face and an unfamiliar voice said, "It's her. Bring her," I knew we walked right into a trap.

I was thrown over broad shoulders like a rag doll, unable to resist. My body betrayed me—no longer my ally. I no longer had any. Then I remembered Ronin had been shot in the head. I wanted to cry out, move, yell, do something—but it was useless.

What about the others? Are they even alive?

My body was thrown in the back of a vehicle and my head slammed against the metal floor. I quivered from the feel of cold steel. As we ascended, my stomach did the opposite. There was nothing I could do but lie there taking this undesirable trip to my ancestor, Monlow. They did not have to say it but I knew exactly where we were going. I was finally about to meet my long-lost kin, the one who wanted all my blood to save his hideous life.

Oh, god, maybe this was a dream, a nightmare I would wake up from soon. But if it wasn't, I hoped my body could move by the time we landed at The Dom.

Each twist and turn in the air did nothing to help my stomach feel at ease. It was a wonder I didn't choke on impending vomit. I tried my best to move at least a finger but I couldn't even blink. Nothing worked for me and thinking proved a challenge. My body wanted to pass out but I needed to stay alert. I listened to the mumbling of the men around me but they spoke low, or it might have been my fading mind.

When we finally descended, my fingers and eyelids were the first to move. The door lifted up on its side and I was yanked out by my both my arms and legs like trash. But as a San, I was just that. Ironically, so was their leader—only they had no clue.

I was placed on the gravel face up and a tall man leaned over me. He wore a black fitted uniform trimmed in gold and a long drape that attached to his upper jacket, trailing behind him. He held a long black rod with silver rings around the top resting upon his shoulder. Surveying me for a split second, he touched me with the tip of the rod. A jolt of lightning surged through me like hellfire and my body instinctively arched in a stiffened position. I screamed out from the electrocution.

When it subsided, I kicked the man back and leaped up, but twelve men in matching suits and hoods surrounded me at once. I should have been flattered that they felt the need to have so many men to bring me in, but being there was no joke.

"Stop!" The man I'd knocked held up his hand and eased into the inner circle. "This one is to be specially delivered to Monlow. Unharmed!" He spoke to each hooded man, then returned his attention back to me. I sensed no abilities from him. He might have just been human but according to the medal on his jacket, he was high ranking.

"Try that again, Connor, and you will be dead just like your accomplice, Ronin." He pointed the rod at me and I relaxed. From his belt, he removed a contraption. Hold out your wrists." I didn't budge, only stared at him like he was insane. Two hooded beings grabbed my arms and held them up for me. How gracious of them. He wrapped my wrists with some sort of liquid that solidified, binding them together and preventing me from free movement. "Let's go." He spun around and his drape followed behind him. I followed suit in between two rows of both supernaturals and hominids. In their belts, they carried metal rods. The men marched up in tune as if on a red carpet escorting me inside the Dom. It was breathtaking.

Two large double doors opened to the castle but it felt more like doors to a crypt. As the doors slammed shut behind me, so did my fate.

This was the grandest place I had ever been to. Sadly, it would be a short visit. Moss lined the inner stone walls that intertwined with the mountain itself, reminding me of the Renaissance era times that traveled into the future and joined forces with new age technology. Cameras lined the wood-paneled hallway walls, about twelve spaces apart, and turned in my direction whenever I passed them. A droid hovered directly over me down the long hall to my impending date, the one I had tried so desperately to avoid.

Little white and black dots on the wood shifted every once in a while. I had no clue what they were but I had a feeling if I tried to escape they would ascend upon me, most hastily, and cause great harm. In between the cameras and curious dots, swords decorated the wood. The architecture reminded me of Ron's grandfather's mansion. Although grand, it was not at all impressive. The colors were bleak and dreary, with the exception of an offset of red, and the temperature inside was beyond cold. It was glacial.

We stopped in front of an elevator and only six sentinels stepped in with me, while the man who'd shocked me stood in front of me. Two rods were pointed at my head.

As we rose, inching closer to my dreadful kin, I wanted so desperately to be afraid, to scream, to fight, but a part of me wanted to meet Monlow. I was both intrigued and ready to meet the man or beast who called himself Ronin's father, the one who'd caused my kind and his, years of suffering. The one who'd tortured my biological mother. I just wanted this to be over.

After the elevator stopped, the doors parted and we were greeted by another long hallway. Like before, we marched in silent tune.

Eventually, what I yearned for came to pass. The closer we drew, the more anxiety rose inside me. Not fear, but a sensational fire grew within my gut. It took my breath away and I had to stop. The power he held both dazed and consumed me. I had never felt anything like it before. Every nerve in my body reacted to him and I had yet to lay eyes on him.

"March!" the human spoke. He shoved me onward and instinctively, my hands went around his throat. It took all of the six men to pull me away. As they pinned me to the floor, I stared up at him with such contempt, but it wasn't him that I was irritated with. He rearranged his drape and leaned over me once again, his flat expression reflecting mine. "You're lucky that I cannot truly harm you, girl."

"And you're lucky they're here," I growled, losing control.

"Lift her," he said, pointing his weapon in the direction he wanted me to venture. I did just that after they released me. At first, my steps were in tune with my escorts' but then I hastened to double the pace until I eventually passed them.

My journey ended in front of two large white doors. I could sense him. My heart pounded wildly and I could not help but rest my head against the cool door. His breathing was audible. I gripped my stomach the same time a lone tear found its way down my cheek. It was surreal, this moment in time, one that had me stand so close to a blood kin, one so close to death. It would soon be over, this life I was forced to lead. The life that had not been my own for so long would soon be over, no matter the outcome.

I jerked back when the doors cracked, allowing me entry into the dim chamber. The foulness the doors concealed overwhelmed me. Unfortunately, I knew what death smelled like and Monlow was no doubt dying. It seemed as if time slowed when my feet moved before my brain could register its next thought. I had not waited on my escorts but instead, turned the corner and kept going.

Monlow sat in a gold chair reeking of putrid decay. He stood up at the sight of me and his long black robe touched the floor. Seconds seemed like minutes the narrower our distance became. It never once registered for me to hesitate; I just kept going.

My surroundings were a blur he was the only thing that mattered. Monlow was spellbinding. His orbs shined a glossy black, his height twice that of mine and his presence immense. Not godly, but commanding. My eyes took in every inch of him—what I could see of him—and the sight was disturbing. As much as I hated him, in my heart lingered a slither of treacherous sympathy. He'd taken in so many abilities, he lived a life of confinement. After all he'd accomplished in his lifetime that within his body, he'd jailed himself, like he had done to so many others. How ironic.

Not five feet away from my kin, reality hit. My stomach churned, realizing that I was completely on my own. There was no way out. No plan.

Monlow lifted long boney fingers and removed his hood. His veins ran plump with tar and his skin was translucent. The flesh on his nose was gone and all that remained was split bone.

"Yes." He sniffed the air around me. "You are in fact Connor. I could feel the greatness in you before you even arrived." He spoke through pencil thin lips, his voice deep, animalistic, with a hint of a growl underlying each word.

"And I you," I said snidely, not using a respectful tone. Heat rose up my back and ignited the resentment I felt for him once again. It was irrational. He could end me at any second and yet, the fact of being backed into a corner only added fuel to my own survival instincts.

"Leave us!" he bellowed to my escort behind me. And as he spoke, something about him stirred a wildness inside me. It even chilled me because a tiny part of me was in awe of him. "I sense something in you...awe yes - admiration, my child. We are more alike than I'd hoped. Although, I do not smell fear from you," he said to me.

"No, I do not fear you." I moved to the other side of him. His glossed-over globes followed my every move like a cat in a hunt. "You should not have harmed my kin or Ronin." My stomach twisted at the mention of them but I rebuffed any detrimental emotion.

"Ronin!" He screamed. Monlow tossed his chair across the room then glided down the steps, moving like no human that I'd ever known. "Clever boy, hiding you here on Ether. I never suspected. He knew me well, that son of mine. How long had he been protecting you?"

"You would have to ask him ... oh wait, you can't because you killed him."

A loud growl escaped his throat. He rushed up to me with such speed, my skin crawled, then halted an inch away from my face. But the strangest thing occurred; instead of hurting me, he simply touched my head with that of a finger. "You cared for him." I jerked away and he scowled down at me as I was not privy to the secret joke. Then, with just a flick of his hand, he broke me from my liquid shackles.

I slowly backed away, rubbing my wrists. He kept his distance. "From what he tells me, you never cared for him."

"I cared for Ronin!" the room rumbled with his voice.

I lurched back. *Did he actually care for Ronin?*

He turned his back to me and addressed me with a softer tone. "You're under the impression that this is a family reunion. Your tongue is far too liberal," he warned. "That human inside me no longer exists for I am far greater than a mere human."

I heard his warning but I did not heed. "You don't seem to be far greater. You're dying. And for someone so powerful, you need this mere human to save you. But what happens in another two or five centuries when I'm long gone?"

Spinning around, he bent over and his body stretched to where his face was not too far from mine. "You seem to think that all I want is blood from you. What your body produces will allow me to live for a very long time. Longer than any known being."

"What?" A chill found its way up my spine.

"Yes, think about it. You think I've hunted you down just to live another few centuries when I can live a millennia?"

I was sickened to my stomach. "Clones?" I shook my head at the thought of it. "I would never let you."

"I don't need your permission, my child."

"Stop calling me that!" I yelled.

"But that is precisely what you are." He stood back up. "Your mother gave me a child - you..."

"What?" I backed away, confused.

"Yes, Connor, you are indeed my daughter, *not* my distant relative. It seems as if you follow in your mother's footsteps. She cared for an Ethosian as well but back then I was more…" He waved a hand over his body. "Human, so to speak. Although truthfully, she had no clue what a monster I truly was until the day she told me we formed life." He glided to the far corner of the room. "But with the help of another, she was able to escape my palace while pregnant and hid you from me. My own child."

"I don't believe you," I whispered to myself. My thoughts became clouded. "You can't be." My stomach caught in my throat, I was so repulsed. I'd often wondered about my father but not this. Never him.

"Oh, but it is, *daughter*." He paced around me so closely, I could feel his searing breath on my body, which wanted to pass out from what I'd heard. "After that, I placed a bounty on every San who ventured here in the hopes of finding her or you. It wasn't until years later that I discovered she'd returned to Earth where she delivered you. When I sent scouts to find her and bring her back to me, she did the noble thing and took her own life."

"You lie." There were no words to comprehend this twisted perversity. "You're sick." I walked away from him to clear my mind. "No, it will never happen." I shook my head at him.

"Yes, the lab can do amazing things. We've perfected it. Your planet is so far behind us in technology that the possibilities never dawned on you. Your clones will be my very own medicine for years to come. They will be born and reared in a lab. I may even keep you around to watch the ones, made of you, grow," he said with a twisted smile, but then it slowly faded and with it so did the room's warmth. "No, I won't. I will punish you for your mother's actions. She took you away and she robbed me of the opportunity to end her life myself." His expression might have been flat but he got off on hurting people, on doing his utmost to break them. I could only imagine this was the same careless behavior he'd had when he tortured Ronin.

"Mark my words, Monlow. This will never happen." I glared at him overwhelmed with such loathing. *I don't know how or when but I will stop him.* This I vowed to myself.

"Like I said, you don't have a choice in the matter. I like your bravery. You remind me of me so long ago, but no more. I grow tired of you." His lips curled upward as his eyes scanned the length of me. "Sentinels!" he roared, and the same six men entered. "Take her."

As the men approached, I did my best to fight them off one by one. I'd never fought so hard for my life. But Monlow was there to make sure I didn't escape. He loomed over us like a dark shadow and with a thought, my body soared across the chamber. I bounced off a glass case, took down swords with me, and landed on something jagged. The last thing I remembered was the darkness that enveloped me.

* * *

I jolted awake to unfamiliar sounds and a strange language. My thoughts were foggy, my head heavy. My lids fluttered open as the light shone brightly and it took a minute for my sight to adjust. I tried to move but my body would not obey and, even though I was in an upright position, my arms and legs would not budge. They, as well as my chest, were strapped down by black bands to a table.

"She's awake," said a being with orange slits for pupils. Its oblong shaped face was covered in a clear mask and wore a full white body suit. Another seemingly human male dressed similarly responded to the supernatural but in the foreign language.

The human came toward me with a pointy contraction in hand and placed it on a tray next to me with other metal objects. I could not even begin to imagine what they were all needed for. My pulse quickened as I noticed the tubes of blood that sat on the tray.

My blood.

They had already begun the process. I struggled to free myself when they had a large device, big enough for my body to fit through, situated in front of me.

"Let me go!" I tried to shout but it came out more like a high-pitched mumble.

"Silence!" orange eyes ordered me and its voice reminded me of what a tiger would sound like if it could talk. It gave me chills. The creature tightened my bands and that's when I realized my clothes had been changed. My shirt had been replaced with some thin white material and the same for my bottom half that stopped mid-thigh. How troubling that my midsection was left bare. I let my head fall back on the table, knowing they'd left my skin exposed for a reason, but with no idea why. My brain would not work.

What did they give me?

I squirmed but the straps were too tight. I was stuck. "Hurry, give her more medication to calm her before we start the procedures. They said her metabolism was high." The human male walked over to me and removed his mask. For a monster, he had a pleasing face. "I would have you put to sleep but Monlow wants you awake to feel each and very prick. You should feel lucky that you're aiding in an extraordinary experiment. It's revolutionary. No one will remember you, of course, but aiding in Monlow's recovery is most imperative."

"Go screw yourself, you bastard." I hocked mucus on his face. Nonchalantly, he wiped my DNA away with a gloved hand and put it in a clear jar. *They're keeping everything!* He smiled down at me. "You may proceed," he ordered, then replaced his mask.

Orange eyes pressed a cold canister to my shoulder and it released a hiss. It both stung and gave me a cold sensation. Its numbing affect was immediate and, without hesitation, a droid hovered over me. The table slowly lowered back until it was horizontal to the floor. This was it. I was out of time.

I was trapped in a serious situation with no plan of escape. I had to free myself, but how? *Think, Connor.* My brain was so foggy from the drug they'd given me and my thoughts were jumbled. I licked my dry mouth and my body trembled terribly. I wasn't sure if it was because of the cool temperature, the drug's side-effect, or fear.

The droid's sudden humming refocused my thinking. A red light from the robot shone on my abdomen and began to slowly slice me from left to right. I could feel every heated, serrated cut. My body tensed up from being cut open while alive.

Focus, Connor!

I was furious that Monlow was actually winning, that he was going to live for centuries to come and I was the reason why. My own *father* was killing me. But I could not think; my brain was too muddled. All I could picture was Earth being taken over and that everyone I ever loved would either die or be enslaved. My family…

"Her eyes. Cover them!"

I focused on the droid above me, aimed it sideways, and it sliced a third masked worker who'd remained quiet the whole time. When that person dropped, the other two scattered.

Anything within my visual path I sent flying across the room, all the while fighting the impending fog in my head. Moving the huge contraption in front of me, I pinned the human against the wall. Orange eyes tried to cover my face but tripped over fallen equipment and bumped into my table, crashing us to the floor. One of my straps cracked. I twisted my arm free just when the creature got up. With my free hand, I caught the arm of the creature and snapped it. It made such a horrendous yowl, I reached over, grabbed the tranquilizer and shot it in the neck.

"Shut up!" It finally did and fell on top of me.

I shoved it over and laid there, out of breath. It was only a few seconds before an alarm sounded and I wondered if, somehow, the sentinels had been notified, but then the palace shook. Covering my head from the falling ceiling, I waited it out until it calmed.

As soon as it stopped raining debris, I maneuvered all my limbs free and managed to get up. With bare soles, I stepped over broken equipment and the shattered blood vials. Picking up some gauze from the floor, I used it to apply pressure to my open stomach. It was bleeding pretty badly but I didn't have time to find a laser gun and seal it. I held onto the counter for stability and searched for my clothes. They were in the back, thrown in a metal trash bin. That sight alone held a finality to this whole situation, making me feel so insignificant. Grabbing my clothes, I dressed myself while grunting over my open wound. This was the first time I appreciated the clothes' material. It would not absorb the blood, only apply needed pressure. After applying my boots, I rushed out to see why the alarm sounded, but something within me made me stop.

I turned back to examine the lab. Walking back over to the counter, I noted different types of liquids in clear tubes. Some of the liquid appeared thick, some looked cloudy, and some particles moved inside the fluid that sat still in their slot.

I thought of my blood and the need to get rid of it. If I did not survive this lunacy, there was no way Monlow would have anything of mine left to use. Spotting tubes with my name on them, I poured their contents down the basin. As a matter of fact, I felt the need to destroy each and every tube in that lab. Whatever he was using to prolong his life, I wanted to make sure he had no more of it.

Once I started, I could not stop. I destroyed canisters, bottles of medications, cylinders I removed from the injectors, smashed centrifuges, and specimens of any kind. I broke microscopes, all the lab's equipment, computer hard drives, computer chips, and even glass computer screens. By using my hands, it felt more therapeutic.

Through my insanity, my wound bled uncontrollably, but I was too consumed with obliteration. I screamed aloud as my emotions grabbed hold and I took it out on this horrifying place, thinking of all who had senselessly paid the price for Monlow's greed—my Keepers, my family, my friends, and now, Ronin. I was truly alone. I hated him for what he'd done to us. I hated him for who he was to me. He was no father of mine. My real father was back on Earth.

Once the room was in disarray, I stepped back and looked at the cuts on my hands, realizing how easily I could get hurt. There was no way I could defeat this monster on my own. This fight and all the planning had been for naught. I shoved anything left on the counter onto the floor. Standing there in the wake of my ruin, I started to think of my next move, but another explosion pulled me out of my trance and back into reality.

When there was nothing else to destroy, I decided it was time. I gripped the handle to the exit but once again, I halted. To my far left stood a frosted glass vault. I could not see what was behind it but thought it odd that it would be sitting alone, away from everything, as if important. A cold chill ran up my spine as I walked over to it.

Punching the glass with my bare fists, I noted a single large black case. Reaching in, I pulled it out and sat it on a nearby counter. I easily snapped it open; oddly, it wasn't even locked. I stared at the case for a moment, dreading to see the contents. I reached for it but stopped and stepped back, hesitating. The hairs on my body stood on end but I needed to see. Stepping forward, I reached over and yanked off the top.

My stomach hit rock bottom when nothing other than Monlow's blood stared back at me. Without confirmation, I knew it to be his. Three pipes sat alone, encased in velvet. I grabbed a tube, easily smashing one to the floor and taking pleasure in somehow destroying a part of him. Then, the next crashed as well but as I picked up the third tube, the voice of the professor rang in my head: "your blood is the key". I gripped the last tube tight and fell against the counter, at which point it dawned on me what the professor had meant. If my blood was the key to saving his life, then that meant our blood is as one. Reality hit me hard across my chest.

Did the professor know that Monlow is my father all along?

My hands shook, thinking of what I was about to do. In all honesty, there was no other way. Now having met Monlow, I had but one choice. He might be weaker now than in his youth but he was, in true form, a monster. I had to become more than what I was to defeat him, even if that meant my life would never be the same. I looked at the tube again and saw Dr. Pausat had signed it. It was he who left the tubes for me.

But like the professor had asked: What was I willing to sacrifice in order to save our kind and my planet?

"This was it, professor," I whispered.

With shaky hands, I reached over to the injector and sat his tube of blood inside. Holding it in one hand, I did the one thing I could and would never come back from. Doing the unconceivable, I injected Monlow's blood into my very veins with much remorse but out of sheer necessity.

I slid down the counter once all of my kinship slithered inside me. At first, my heart tried to leap out of my chest, then it slowed to a mellow beat and my body felt cold. My hand fell over and the injector, my culprit, rolled out of my palm onto the floor. Tears streamed down my face as euphoria set in. My mind felt like it was soaring high about my body and, although my sweaty body trembled, I could not help but enjoy the ride. Now I understood why Monlow wanted to hold on to his power. He could not get enough. It was addicting.

More debris fell on top of my head as a flood of pictures that were not my own washed over me, like memories. I both liked and hated the flashes that imposed my mind. It sickened me deep down inside, yet I liked the anguish caused by me; only, it was not me but Monlow—and it was revolting.

As the world around me spun out of control and I fell over onto the ground. My back arched in anguish as my body took to this foreign matter. My bones ached, my teeth grinded, my eyes gave me the perception that I could see through anything. It was both agonizing and thrilling. I hated it but I wanted more.

Once my flight descended, I lay panting after the surge of power subsided. I opened and closed my hands several times, not really feeling like they were mine. I gripped the chair to stand and broke it with a slight tug. I looked at my palms, not understanding how I'd done that. My head turned towards the shooting and screaming that was far away from me and yet I could hear every last utterance.

I stood on my own and looked at my reflection in the glass. I appeared the same but felt so different. In actuality, I felt nothing—not doubt, not anguish or pain. My stomach wound had already healed. I had accelerated healing, but never this fast.

Facing the room, I lifted each and every object in the lab with barely a thought, some raised or lowered; others I spun all while levitated. With just a thought, one by one, I dropped each object back down. It was incredible. No bloody nose nor any residual effect from using so much power.

A crooked smile crept across my face upon thinking of the possibilities, but then withdrew any wickedness that tried to plague me. I had to remind myself that what I did was to stop Monlow only.

Having wasted enough time in this room, I rushed out the door with no thought to my welfare. Passing several labs of testing equipment, I lifted everything up and smashed it to the floor with one swoop, never having to stop once to do it.

Up the stairs I went, two at a time, dodging falling bricks as the Dom was starting to crumble around me. The brick staircase spiraled like I was exiting an old dungeon. On the landing, several sentinels blocked the first-floor entrance. I walked halfway down the corridor and stopped, angled sideways.

"Hey!"

Immediately they aimed, and without hesitation, shot their weapons. Stopping the electrical current coming towards me, I redirected the charge back in their direction, shocking them instead. I was at the door before their bodies hit the ground.

Up more stairs, I ascended but froze on the second-floor landing. Through my escape, I hadn't stopped to think what all the commotion was. There were huge holes throughout the castle and pirates were climbing up the mountain and through it, taking down sentinels one by one. Bombs took out several at one go. On each level, the same thing occurred: fighting, bombing, and sentinel attacks.

On about the fifth level, after I'd taken down several protectants, I came across the caped sentinel who'd kidnapped and brought me there. My blood boiled when he glared back at me, but as I approached him, he did the oddest thing. He bowed and I was taken aback. When he regained footing, he said with the utmost seriousness, "I'd hoped you'd subsist. I wish you countless blessings, Connor."

I fell against the partition and the words Ronin had spoken came to mind, "Connor, you will simply walk through the front door, invited." *Oh, God, Ronin.* My heart leaped, thinking of his death. But like he'd said, we would not know everyone involved. The more I thought about it, this sentinel was the one who'd made sure the hominids and supernaturals did not touch me and released me from my paralysis hold.

I addressed the human with a nod, then hurried through an opening made by an explosion, sending person or being flying out of my way until I reached the top. On my final stretch, outside on the mountaintop, Aiden and his men were fighting Military Protectants. They fought valiantly with either fists or swords, but I could not tell who was winning. The whole place was a madhouse.

Then, a loud piercing sound erupted my thoughts—Monlow. I could sense him close but smelled him even closer. I rushed onward, dodging, blocking, and fighting everyone in my path. Everything seemed surreal as though I was there but not, as one would describe an out of body experience.

Sentinel after sentinel I passed in order to get to the one man they protected relentlessly. I trudged forward without forethought of what could be my end. The building shook again as it took another hit and I dodged fallen statues or barriers that came crashing down. There was so much screaming and shouting, I wondered if anyone could understand what others were saying. Terrified workers ran past me as I ascended higher, closer to the being that ruthlessly controlled Ether.

I thought of his blood coursing through my veins, blood that was already there but now, it had become the tainted blood of all those he'd taken against their will.

Then, as if a whisper from an unforeseen presence passed through me, I diverted my course and ran toward an opening that overlooked several levels below. I could not believe my eyes. As if the dead had arisen, I saw both Ronin and Tony back to back, fighting off protectants. And for the first time since I'd injected myself, I felt something: humanity. I touched the stone, the one that upheld this palace, as if I could touch him, even though there was no logic to it. But, I could somehow breathe again. And not too far off stood Bynder, Selene, and Cheyenne. But the castle had split in two and they were on the other side.

In the midst of the bedlam, Ronin removed himself from a fight and looked directly up at me. A sudden rush of relief washed over the both of us. I should have known that he was still alive but I had turned off all my emotions and felt nothing. Now, though, I could feel him, and he was the added strength I held on to, the drive that pushed me forward. His face showed anguish, knowing what I had done, realizing that I now harbored darkness within me. He'd never asked me to do it—only gave me the choice to inject myself—but I chose this route in order to save the ones I loved.

Protect them. I told him, and he placed a hand across his heart.

I turned away briskly and, as I did, Tony yelled after me. I could not look back. On my own accord, I entered Monlow's chamber that was no longer pristine or held order.

So much commotion stirred inside his throne room, away from the rapid fire. I rushed past a session room and saw the professor's lifeless body. I entered the room and knelt next to the man who sacrificed for us all. His throat had been slashed. Closing his lids, I thanked him in silence for all he had done for us and uttered a verse for his soul to enter a better world in the afterlife.

The sound of a hideous growl yanked me out of sentiment. Monlow hissed ugly threats at anyone who opposed him.

As I headed toward the hideous monster, my body soared back from where it had just come. Chanting filled my ears but it was not coming from me. Regaining my footing, a stunning woman wearing a long black robe matching her long dark mane ascended upon me.

The sorceress. Her skin was porcelain white and she was as evil as she was pretty. Her stare was hypnotic as her hues changed color with the slightest turn of her head.

"So young, so pretty," her raspy voice said as she approached. "You should be on our side." She sauntered up to me, then around me. "We can do the unimaginable and be unstoppable, you and I." She stroked her finger across my back then gently coiled her fingers in my hair.

"It's hard to side with the one who wants you dead, or did you not know?" My gaze followed her steps.

"Oh, Connor." She ever so gently stroked my cheek, like a mother to a child, then, without comprehension, she disappeared. I spun around but she was nowhere in sight. "Monlow was never going to kill you, only take what he needed. Don't you see you are his greatest accomplishment? His heir. His blood. He needed to see if you could survive. What fight you have. It was none but a challenge. Now side with him, with us, and reign alongside him as his rightful successor." Suddenly, she appeared in front of me. "With you at his side, there will be nothing you both could not do or take." She clasped her hands together in joy.

As much as what she said revolted me, it atrociously stirred something pleasing within. "No." I shook my head, trying to rid myself of the disgusting nausea that wanted to say "Yes."

"You feel it, do you not?" she said, sounding sickly sweet, but she wasn't. "You are his daughter after all, and now…" Her long black tongue licked my cheek and as I jerked back, she held onto me. "Now more than ever."

Without my permission, I wavered in her direction. She placed a cold finger on my hand but it felt so inviting. I admired her movements; she was the most beautiful entity I'd ever seen. I wanted to coil myself in her arms to feel safe.

"Yes." I swayed toward her splendor. I wanted to be like her. I wanted to be her.

"No." I quaked, needing to remove such deceitful sentiment. It was false. "I need air."

"Give in, Connor," she demanded with a charming smile. "You desire it so."

"I can't." I stepped back but she held tight to me. I shut my lids refusing to let her mesmerize me and allowed my other senses to take over. I suppressed my humanity and tapped into the darkness that now swirled within me. I could smell her vileness and it soured my stomach. When I opened my lids, the enchantress no longer held her sway. "I said no." I shoved her away.

"Yes!" she shouted and raised her hands, but I blocked her flow of energy and we remained mentally locked. I saw her true form of decayed flesh. She was an elder sorcerous, a most powerful one. This I knew from the tainted memories that invaded my mind.

It was a mental struggle but I refused to give in to the ugliness Monlow had birthed. "NO!" My scream echoed, and with a gush of wind, her body flew out onto the mountaintop with the pirates who ascended upon her like a mighty force. Her wails were hideous but they soon stopped, and I could no longer hear her beating heart.

Her murky impression upon me ceased and I refocused my thoughts. Heading towards the back, I walked into the private chamber that housed Monlow. He fought off the Military Protectants and sentinels that betrayed him. Both uniformed men and men dressed as rogues fought each other. I didn't know who to trust but I knew one for sure who was not an ally, Monlow.

The room was a war zone of bodies, fallen wreckage, and flickering lights. Monlow took down several men at a time. He needed no sword or weapon. He was the strongest weapon known to Ether and, if he wanted to get rid of you, he would.

A strange coldness enveloped me at both the sight and stench of him. There was no hesitance on my part with regard to the instinctual need to rid the universe of the damnation named Monlow. Whatever reservation one might have had, I held none—not even the need to survive.

With haste, I raised my arm and with it came a bolt of lightning, an ability he'd stolen from another that I now beheld. The protectants fled across the room as Monlow's abdomen seared from the gash I had just given him. He raised his head in search of the culprit and found me standing there. For a split second, he almost seemed betrayed, and if he had the power to kill with a gaze, I would have lain dead in an instant.

"Connor!" His voice boomed across the room that stood hushed except for the distant uproar outside.

The men retreated further when they saw me enter and, with each step of mine, Monlow's wound healed. "You are most certainly different," he snarled. "What have you done?" He glided awkwardly towards me. "What you've done only proves who you are indeed."

"I did what I had to," I spoke emotionlessly to the man who claimed to be my father.

I aimed every sword in the room at him, but he twisted them around towards the men instead and pinned me to the back of the chamber. Breaking his hold on me, I blocked the steely weapons aimed at the men's heads and diverted them to the floor, right before they discharged.

"You are but one. Do you really think that you alone can take me down?" he asked.

"I may not, but I will die trying." I sent his body soaring through a two-glass barrier to an adjacent room and he landed face down. Our surroundings erupted into a war zone again as Monlow's sentinels fought one another, but to me, it was only the two of us.

Monlow had yet to move, but I knew it was only a matter of time. He was toying with me, making me think he was weaker than what he truly was. As I eased upon him, an arm moved then a leg until he stood, towering over me. I directed shattered glass toward him and more than twenty large shards penetrated his body, but one by one, he pulled them out, all the while, his cold black orbs daring me.

Heat rose inside me. My insides felt like they were searing and I could smell my own flesh burning. I fell back on his stairs, trying to find a mental escape from the feeling—but there was none. The agony was unmeasurable but if I gave into it, the battle would be over before it started, so instead, I allowed it to do its damage.

Standing up, I refocused on Monlow's mind, trying to break his concentration. I flew back in the air and my shoulder popped out of its socket. I slammed it back in place. Regaining my footing, I tried to ignore his havoc on me and focused on his mind. As if an unseen fist hit me in the face, I twisted to the left and blood spewed down my nose.

I spat out the gore and sent an energy charge toward him, twirling him in the air. His thoughts were hard to break through but I tried to make him yield. He was so strong though, so very strong. It was difficult to penetrate his cognizance.

"Do you think I will break so easily? He growled, landing in one swift motion. "Do you really want to penetrate my thoughts?"

"I've already seen what drives you but your morbid memories have shown me your weaknesses." They had not. I was unable to decipher all the distorted recollections.

Monlow sniffed the air near me. His back arched then he released a howl. His cracked lips distorted into what would be perceived as a grin. "Yes… yes, that's it. That is why you are different but you put too much faith in what little blood of mine courses through you."

"I may, but now I know why you hate being San. The council tied your hands and forbade you from taking others' powers." I kept a lock on his mind, hoping that he would either slip up or break. "You felt you deserved more recognition for your gifts; you felt you deserved a more powerful role because of all you could do—but they saw it more as a perversion."

He stomped his foot in protest and, with it, the floor beneath us cracked. The lights failed as more bombs were discharged. Still, neither of us moved. His body rounded and he growled, releasing a pungent wind from his mouth. As my feet slid back, half the men in the room fell through the damaged bottom out into lower levels. I formed wind under the men, by use of the room's air, and they landed softly on the level below us.

In a flash, he stood in front of me, lifted me upside down, and attempted to rip my legs apart. I palmed his slimy skin and burned his flesh with a pulsating scorching heat. With a wail, he dropped me. I rolled out of his reach. In a fit, he knocked over twelve Vusazen statues which plowed into both friend and foe.

He crawled onto the side wall, then the ceiling, like a creature that no longer belonged to the human species. He moved methodically towards me in an attempt to frighten me but, in all honesty, I was in awe. What chilled me was the fact that I felt wonder at his abilities. I should have feared him but that part of me which felt connected to him prevented such reasoning.

He dropped in front of me, larger than life. He backed me up and I did not block him or even attempt to. It was as if I needed to know what I could withstand from him. It made no sense even to me. Was I toying with death? I rose in the air and levitated in front of him at his request.

"I sense no terror from you, Connor, or maybe you've always desired the malice that's energizing your heart and bonding within your flesh now. It is clear to me, your heart is not fully in this fight." He tossed me across the room and I landed upside down against a mantle.

More men entered the chamber to take on Monlow but I wanted him for myself. I witnessed him take on several of them. He was not stopped or phased by any kind of weapon, even from the continuous electrical blast of droids. Ronin could be seen right between the retaliators and I had no idea what it was going to take to stop him. But why was I hesitant? Why wasn't I fighting harder?

I got up to one knee and was immediately stopped by the largest hound I'd ever laid eyes on. Blue-black in color, it bore its double K9's. The mongrel kept me at bay while Monlow finished both man and species that tried to take him down. The thing must have weighed well over two hundred pounds. Leaping on top of me, it tore at my bruised arm. I screamed out as its teeth dug into my bone. Forcing my hands in its mouth, I yanked onto its bottom jaw and it finally let go of my limb while turning towards my face. I held it back by its massive throat and managed to kick it off of me. I scrambled up as I did it, but in an instant, it was shot to dust. I looked over to my right and saw a tattered Ronin running towards me.

For the second time today, relief engulfed me. I wanted to ask him how he was still alive when he fell to his knees and slid over to me, ripping a piece of his shirt in the process and began to wrap up my bleeding arm. This time, the pain was unbearable but I realized that it was sentiment causing such a sting. I quickly retracted any emotions of concern and did not even dare ask about the others. There was no time for such pleasantries.

"Don't give into it, Connor. Fight the influence he now has over you." I stared at him for a long while. How did he know? Of course he knew. I'm failing them all, the ones I love. It twisted my stomach. I needed to not let this false idolization of Monlow consume me. These were not my desires but his.

I shot up and blocked Ronin when two swords came for him. I took the lives of the two men. I felt nothing as I did so.

"You may appear to be the most powerful one here, but in reality, you are the weakest." It was me who ascended upon Monlow this time. "It's not that you want power. You need it. No matter how much you steal it will never be enough, and for that, I pity you."

Monlow hissed at me and I shot both fire and energy toward him and hit him mid-center. Between the two, he went spiraling through the glass panel down into his torture chamber. I jumped in after him, using the surrounding energy to slow my descent.

He landed on a large sharp object that penetrated the middle of his chest. He lay still for a long moment and for a split second, I'd thought that was it, but then his abdomen tightened, he lifted up his arms, and raised his body off the spike.

Once on his feet, he ripped his robe down, revealing his form to me. His chest healed before my eyes as he grew in size and became gigantic. His girth must have been over ten feet wide as he stood twenty feet tall. His body was greyish white and like his face, mostly translucent. I could see the vivacious vessels underneath his whole body. He was completely hairless—no longer a man, and although he had two legs, his feet were curved stubs. And if that was not enough, he bore a long, jagged tail that swayed continuously.

Hideous.

As I was revolted by his appearance, his tail cracked bones in my face and I went up in the air, my leg landing on a mounted pitchfork. It was excruciating but I gripped it tightly and began to wiggle my leg off it. Before I was free, he grabbed the spear and tossed me up and down several times, never once giving me time to react.

"You could have reigned at my side!" he rumbled.

My back and leg took the brunt of his banging but I persisted, trying to think of a way out. It was troubling. On the last hit, he slowed down and the blow wasn't that hard. Monlow was getting tired because he had to physically lift me. On the last trip, I aimed my fury at his limb and snapped it in half. I fell to the floor, ignoring the breaking sound my leg made and sent a piercing spasm to his brain. He stumbled back. It worked. He was definitely weaker. I levitated the spike, driving it straight to where his heart should have been.

He faltered but for only a second. He stared right at me when he pulled the spike clear through to the other side. He stomped hard, shaking the castle, and released a most loud and hideous noise while doing so.

What the Hell was going to take him down?

Out of nowhere came Ronin, leaping out of the window above. In his hand, he held a wooden bow with a black arrow, laced with silver liquid. The scent was familiar, moondar serpent's poison. Ronin had it aimed, ready to fly. That must have been the weapon Erena and Nordac were searching for on the other planet.

As monstrous as Monlow was, a look of sadness sat upon his face. "How could you?" he bayed at Ronin. And I could feel his hurt. As damaged as he was, he truly loved Ronin.

"Through all your lies and deceit, I know you are not my father," Ronin shouted at the black-eyed creature who loomed over us.

"I am your father." He beat his chest.

"Even in impending defeat, you still hold to dishonesties." Ronin pulled back on the strings of the long, wooden contraption but the arrow did not fly in the air, instead it miraculously appeared in Monlow's chest. He peered down, amazed.

Monlow raised his head to gaze at his beloved son. At first, tears fell, then fury engulfed him when he slapped Ronin across the chamber room. As much as I wanted to help him, Monlow needed to be stopped.

If the black arrow did not work, then what would? Is this all for nothing?

Several rebels hurried down the stairs and unloaded every weapon known to fail on him, and he still didn't fall. He took every hit but nothing stopped him.

As Monlow kept us at bay, the black arrow shook in his chest as if trying to do something. Monlow appeared to be sweating. *Odd.* A cold sensation tingled through me.

Then, the most peculiar thing happened: his face showed panic. Suddenly, a warm gust of wind encircled the room then zig-zagged around us, until it plowed into my body. I locked in place, taking in what Monlow unwillingly released. The power that entered me felt glorious. My body went up in the air as the wind kept flowing around me, through me. Monlow fell to his knees in his weakened state and fought to keep his strength as I fought to stop the energy he'd lost control of. It was too much.

As if my actions were not my own, I articulated the riddle I had once been told on Earth, the day my brother was taken: "*There were twelve, then ten, then who at the end? What goes up then goes down but never all around? Blood begets blood, which one shall be the victor?*" "Yes, Monlow, you have taken from us, your own kind, and I gladly came to your world—but the outcome is not as you expected. True. Your blood courses through me, but I shall be the victor in the end."

I raised each and every torturous object in the air and aimed it at him. One by one, weapons of all kind plagued his body. As the current that flowed in me subsided, I lowered myself down and walked over to the weakness called Monlow, and pushed the black arrow all the way in.

I wasn't even aware when Ronin woke but he stood next to me, as well as twelve others, watching Monlow take in his last breaths. He was slowly withering away. The noises that escaped him were the sound a dying animal would make and it was almost hard to listen to. We needed to see. We needed to bear witness to his demise. His face sunk in, his skin melted away, and he slowly fell on his back. He stared up at us with hallowed cheeks, attempting to say something, but no words escaped his lips.

Gasped sounds were faintly heard and he no longer focused on anything. His eyes dulled and he released a long exhale. His body finally turned to dust. He'd lived longer than any San should have.

When he no longer existed, a mood of elation exploded in the barbaric place, but astonishingly, a cold chill crossed my heart. A loud horn sounded outside, signifying his passing. I wanted to be happy, I wanted to cheer, but I could not. He no longer lived but a part of him still existed inside of me. I would be forever connected to him.

I looked about the room to the happy faces but my mind was swirling. Not from feeling lightheaded or weak—for all my wounds had healed. My body felt unfamiliar. Everything seemed to move slower—either that, or I was moving extremely fast. I wasn't sure. Was my animated gait a result of the foreign power within me?

Someone hugged me but, at first, I hadn't a clue who. Ronin shook me. "Connor." I looked up at him and lastly felt fear. I needed this strength to fight Monlow but now, what would I do with it? How would I get rid of it? "It will be all right, Connor. I know what you've sacrificed for us." He whispered in my ear. I fell against his shoulder and released sadness; he let me, but as soon as I heard the others coming, I pulled back the dam.

Selene was the first one of the Keepers and yougows to rush over to me. "Connor, you don't even look like you have been in a fight at all." She examined me like she always did. "But you don't look well."

"I don't feel well," I explained. Several others spoke to me but it was hard to concentrate on what was being said.

"Well, firstly, let's get out of this ghastly room," Selene said looking around at all the horrible contraptions Monlow had used to torment people with. Bynder was the last to leave as he stared down at the ashes of Monlow.

All of us hurried out of the room like Selene suggested and returned to the large throne that had once belonged to an evil ruler. The room was destroyed but the victory was ours. Only two Keepers, Bynder and Selene, were in the room with Tony, Ron, and Willow of us yougows. Everyone else was scattered around the castle.

People still rushed into the room to see the ruler they loathed, only to be disappointed for there was nothing left of him but ash. Monlow's followers were brought back to the chamber and as they beheld Ronin, each man and woman bowed to him. Not only did the ones in the room give him his respect, but all throughout the castle and even those on the grounds. It was breathtaking to see. A scene so moving, it overwhelmed me. We all stood back and gave Ronin his rightful moment. He might have been San but he'd been reared an Ethosian and deserved this title after all the enforced injustice he'd endured to survive.

He looked out upon his people. "This victory belongs to all of us. I did not fight alone here today. Were it not for all of you and my kin, the San," he said, gesturing to us. "Then none of us would be standing here today. Rise up and accept your win!" They did as instructed and cheered for their new ruler.

While Ronin took care of the ones loyal to his father, Bynder pulled me aside. "How are you, truly?" he asked, after observing my state. "You're different." I nodded. "You did what you had to do, Connor, or none of us would be here today if you had not sacrificed."

"I know." Feeling unstable, I leaned against a post. "I feel sick. How is it possible to be so strong and feel like this?"

"Why, what's wrong?" Tony asked as he approached.

"Honestly I had no clue what I was going to do after I first met Monlow. He was a monster, Bynder. Then, in the lab, I had no other choice, or did I?" I asked him for reassurance.

"What did you do?" Tony asked again, then others came over to us.

"Injected herself with Monlow's blood." Ronin joined us after clearing the chamber.

"You did what, Connor!" Tony screeched, then turned on Ronin. "And you both knew what she was going to do?" Tony asked Bynder and Ronin.

"He didn't know for sure, Tony, and no one asked but there was no other way. I needed to be faster, stronger and … it needed to be done." I searched everyone's face.

"Then there is your answer, Connor. You don't need my reassurance," Bynder said.

"Bynder, you went along with his?" Tony asked sounding furious.

"It was her decision. This is war, Tony," Bynder explained. "What did you think we trained so hard for? Did you think we were going to go back to our lives the way we left them? It's a wonder that we are all still standing. Everyone has sacrificed, including Connor."

"But does she always have to pay the biggest price?" Tony asked.

"I'm all right. I mean, I will be." I hoped. "Besides, it was my decision, not anyone else's. Even though it was never discussed, it was an option." My whole body felt like it was on fire. Every noise was amplified and the smells were multiplied. Things looked different—more detailed. I could see the smallest detail on every object.

"And why exactly did they both need to know, I mean, if this isn't a bad thing?"

"In case they needed to take me down, Tony." I explained.

"Exactly," Bynder answered.

"So, this is a bad thing." he replied, shifting his feet in frustration. "Like I said, Connor has to sacrifice."

"Let it go, Tony. I don't need to be sheltered. It had to be me as he was my kin…" I hesitated. "He was my father, so I had no choice."

"We've often wondered," Bynder said. "And you believe…"

"Yes." I answered, before he could finish. "As soon as I met him, I felt it." No one else said a word. What was there to say about the vile man who hurt so many others? My own father, the one I had to end?

"So, how do you feel, stronger?" Willow appeared out of nowhere. The hairs on my body rose on end.

"That, and a lot of other things." I didn't feel I needed to explain that I felt unlike myself. That it felt unnatural. And that I wanted to find a corner in a dark room to refrain from all the new heightened senses, especially the bright lights.

"Well, we won and it's all over," Willow said to me, but something clicked. Her tone was off, her heart raced but, mostly, she could not keep eye contact with me.

"Not quite," I replied, studying her behavior. As I stared at her, Willow's body took flight and landed against a barricade. "What did you do?" I questioned not believing her lighthearted performance.

"What!" Willow squealed as her body remained bound against stone.

"Connor!" Selene shouted.

But I only focused on Willow and not the disapproving remarks behind me, and there were a few. "Tonight, I had to do something I can never take back, Willow." I stressed every word with such contempt. "Maybe it was meant to be or maybe not, but regardless, it was forced." I fumed, no longer trying to control my temper.

"What are you talking about, Connor?" Ron asked.

"She is the reason why I was kidnapped today, Ron. She, the one who never asked about you, her friends or her family, and the same person who now considers Ether her home."

"What? Not possible!" Ron defended her like he always did. "Let her go!"

"No!" I snarled. "I can see things a lot clearer now. Just tell me—how long have you been working with them?" I asked her. "Was it from the very beginning, when Ronin released you from jail, or was it when you crossed the wall to see the professor? Funny how when Ronin confronted you about wanting more power, you were suddenly able to fight to change the conversation. Fear always gave you away."

"You're insane! Bynder, it must be Monlow's blood making her act crazy." Willow whined like the helpless girl she'd always pretended to be.

"Connor, let her go. That is for the San council to determine," Selene said.

"Tell us!" I shouted, watching Bynder gripping his gun tightly—not because of my behavior, but for Willow's questionable actions. "I can smell the wet stench of treachery sliding down your back."

"How else would they know when and where to come for us?" Ronin questioned her as well. "It had to have been on Earth. I never used the portal by my palace at any other time before today. There is no other explanation except it had to be a person who left Ether with me. That was Connor, Erena, Nordac, and you. And Erena can smell swine a great distance away."

"Willow, no," Selene whispered, shaking her head. "Was once not enough for you to learn?"

"Yes," Ronin said. "Khan confessed to me that it was you who'd approached him, knowing he had switched sides as you felt it worked in your interest, of course. And it was you who came up with the idea of the blood, not him. But it was he who switched the vials in the end. You never once needed convincing." He held his jaw tight. "You honestly think that a tiger changes its stripes?"

"Ronin, you couldn't trust him. Khan was a traitor. I was innocent in all of this." She kept playing the victim role.

"Of course I do. What does a dying man have to lie about?" He walked closer to her. "Actually, this plan was contingent upon your betrayal. I only needed to get you so far, then the rest was up to you. I told you from day one that I never trusted you. I just gave you a false sense of security and you fell for it. You're the main reason why I kept Connor so close to me, not as much as my father. If she was alone, then it could have ruined things."

"I don't want to believe it, but they're right." Ron stood next to Ronin, his expression blank, no longer the protective man who cared for Willow. "Every time you're scared, your powers react. They always have."

"Ron."

"Enough," he begged. "Enough. Willow, let go of the lies."

"Fine!" Her jaw clenched. "Yes, over the wall I was approached by a Military Protectant but they had no clue who I was until I made a deal with them on Earth, right before we took a portal back to Ether. I'm not dumb; I knew my fate even before we left. You think I'm going to let you turn me in to the council after what fresh hell I went through here? I don't think so. Then you…" Her big browns rolled over Ronin in disgust. "Fighting over her." She faced me. "Now she's damaged goods. I am so damn happy that she is sick." Bynder grabbed hold of her.

"And there it is, the wicked truth," Ronin said. "Your deceit is the reason why Connor got into The Dom. Thank you," he said sarcastically. "The professor and I figured you were approached behind the wall and you contemplated the move but you needed to weigh your options. All it took was the threat from the San turning you over to the Council and you changed sides that quickly. I figured when you switched. Needing to give pertinent information to make a deal, you told your contact, on Earth, the date we were to attack. So, once we took a portal back, we each had holograms ready, but you were none the wiser. Someone like you never takes credit for their wrongdoing, no matter who it harms. Not blood, but self-preservation runs through your black veins."

"I hate both you and Connor!" She stopped, trying to wiggle out of Bynder's arms. "I trusted you, Ronin."

"But I never trusted you." Ronin curled his top lip. "I told you that early on." He turned from her. "Take her away." Ronin ordered two sentinels by the door. "You can take her when you portal back to Earth," Ronin advised Bynder.

"About time you all see the light," Scott said, strolling in as if he owned the world, with Cheyenne at his side. "I told you that I never trusted her after the crap she pulled."

I was amazed that Cheyenne said nothing; actually, she didn't even look phased. "As much as I didn't want to believe you could betray us a second time, I had to think of who had the means and opportunity, and immediately I thought of you." Cheyenne stood next to me.

"I would have told you about the plan, Connor, but I had to make sure and, like I've said before, you work best under pressure," Ronin said to me. He was right; furthermore, if he had told me, then I would have stressed about it all the time.

When the sentinels attempted to add wrist shackles, Willow jerked away and turned her wrath on Ronin and me. "You two deserve each other. I am just glad that I don't have to watch you two together anymore. You both repulse me. I hope he turns out to be just like Monlow. Oh, wait, maybe it's Ronin who needs to worry now that you are so much like your father." She laughed, ever the sadistic one, then removed her smile. "Tony," she called to him, but never shifted her gaze from me. "Don't waste your time on this one…" Willow waved her finger at me. "They have some sick, perverted connection. You don't stand a chance. I hope Ronin kills you, Connor just like Monlow killed your mother, his love."

"Take her away," Ronin repeated, fighting to hold me back.

"No!" Willow's body lit up like a lightning bolt and her outer body set on fire. Anyone next to her leaped out of the way but she shot me with a bolt of electricity, dead center. I went flying back but lowered to my feet.

"I knew you were holding back in the sessions," I glared at her fire-ridden self that headed towards me.

"I hate you, Connor. You ruined my life and you still get everything in the end." The heat she emitted was severe. "You're the reason why my world turned upside down. You're the reason why I'm such a freak. I wish that Monlow had killed you!"

"We've all sacrificed, Willow." I sidetracked a fireball. "Of course, you would see it as power but now, I'm cursed with something I can never get rid of, you selfish Bitch."

"I hope it eats away at you and kills you from the inside out. I hope I'm there the day you die." Willow's words cracked.

"Not if you're dead first." I tossed her into a glass case.

Bynder lunged at her but she knocked him back. Ron ran around her, trying to divert her attention and, for a moment, Ronin and Bynder grabbed her even though the touch seared their hands. Everyone tried to block her in but Willow broke free and lit them on fire. Then she turned to the room and lit it up—the curtains, furniture, anything made of wood. Lifting her up, I slammed her down and swore I heard her neck snap, but she got up.

Ronin shot an arrow at her but, through electricity, she diverted it back towards him. He tried to dodge it but the arrow nicked his thigh. I punched her in the gut and she flew through a wall into the other room. She lay limp all but for a second and those of us still standing rushed over to her. She sent two bolts of lightning to the ceiling, blocking our path.

Lifting the debris off us, I ran after her. She kept shooting electricity over my head and, even though I knocked her down several times, she'd roll over and get back up. She was no longer able to maintain the fire and although bloody and singed, she kept going. By the time we reached the edge of the mountain, she was barely breathing and her skin had become charcoal.

"Don't do it, Willow!" I shouted.

"Now you can have it all," were her last words and she fell backwards off the cliff. I ran to the edge to see her staring at me with such a content look on her face as she plummeted down.

I was about to leap off the mountain after her, but Bynder held me back by my waist. "No." The water is infested with predators. We both watched her splash down into the water. "She'll never survive and neither will you."

I stood at the edge for a long time but she never came up, and I was not satisfied. I was furious that she got away.

We walked back to the chamber and told everyone what had happened.

"She was sick," Bynder said, hands on his hips. "This might have been a victory but, in fact, we still lost overall."

"How was she that strong?" I asked.

"She ingested 'madness'—something equivalent to a psychedelic drug in your world. She must have acquired it when she was in Nede. But it only lasts for a short while and its very addictive," Ronin explained while Selene patched his leg. "Sorry, Ron."

Ron left the room to be alone and I felt for him. The love of his life jumped off a cliff to her supposed death, but I had a feeling she was still alive. A very strong feeling. Willow was more conniving than we thought and if any one of us would survive predators, it's her.

Chapter 13

Connor - Aftermath

Later that night, we all gathered at Ronin's palace. He had a feast prepared in celebration of our victory. He kept it intimate. It lasted well into the night and even though I was tired, it was the first night I didn't have to look over my shoulders.

During the dinner, Ronin pulled me aside needing to talk. We walked out under the stars and sat down by the veranda. His face held sorrow and it started to scare me. "What is it, Ronin?" He hesitated. "Just say it."

"I want you to live here on Ether. You've sacrificed everything by taking in Monlow's blood and, unfortunately, that was a great price to your sanity. You now hold part of the madness that plagued his mind and body."

My mind started to spiral out of control. Did he really just ask me to stay here on Ether? "Ronin, I…"

"Wait, Connor before you answer." He took hold of both my hands and I tried to suppress my ever-rising nerves. "I was reared under such wickedness. You will need my guidance in controlling what now ails you and, in return, I will need your mortality as the ruler of Ether."

I was blown away by what he asked me. It was all so much, so fast, but in truth, it's been months. "I can't believe it's over, I thought this fight would never end so, Ronin I never stopped to think about that afterwards."

"We are San, the fighting never ends for us. I know that you are strong but you have no clue what's to come next. The enemies that will surface and the battles that we will undergo."

I pulled my hands away from him and leaned against a nearby column. A wave of guilt swept over me and landed in my stomach. "I wanted to say yes to the sorcerous. It took all that I had not to. How can you trust me when I'm no longer sure that I can trust myself?"

"That is why it is imperative you stay here on Ether. I want to be here for you, to help you and to pull you back from those moments of obscurity." He came to stand in front of me and interlocked his fingers with mine. "There is a reason we met. We share a unique link, one I was never pleased with. Actually, I detested it at first, but now, I feel we have a bigger purpose. All that we've witnessed and all that we've withstood lead us to the path we must journey together. We balance one another. We will keep each other sane or at least human. That I now know."

I stared up at him in wonder, not knowing what to say. My pounding heart drowned out my thoughts. 'Yes' would be my answer but I needed to think this through with my mind and not my heart. "I don't know what to say." My mind spiraled away as he stood so close to me.

"Say yes." By the small of my back, he pulled me closer and, when his lips touched mine, I no longer contained a thought. His tight embrace let me know that he would never let me go - I never wanted him to. No matter what he'd done in the past, being in his arms felt right. To Hell with what's right or what's wrong, I wanted Ronin. I could no longer fight it. And as his lips found my neck, I desired nothing more than sinful pleasures.

* * *

A week had passed since the overthrow of Monlow and, during that time, we discussed the future of Ether and San's part in the new world. We deliberated over who would take on roles and what those duties would be—a tedious but necessary task. There would be foreigners that would try and take control of Ether's for it had enemies. During a takeover, a government was at its weakest so this was the best time for adversaries to strike, that included ones who still believed in Monlow's rule. With Ronin being a young sovereign, he expected to be challenged —but Ether's Military did not hesitate to bow to him. He did not have many allies besides us Earthlings now.

Over the past week, I've done a lot of thinking about what I wanted and what I needed. I had to accept the dynamics of this new person that I've become and figure out my path, besides being a protector. I've had moments of incoherent thoughts, or indecipherable memories which has brought about feelings of maliciousness. It could be debilitating. In this time, I've come to realize that Ether managed to somehow slither into my soul. How could it not? After all the terrible things I've done and all the horrendous things I've seen, I've come to need its chaotic environment. Ronin asked me to rule at his side, but he has a dark past and I have a dark future, so we needed support and guidance if I were to travel between worlds. That's why I chose Selene as my trustee and Bynder would be Ronin's. Tanikka would be the go between for us four. I wouldn't have it any other way.

Cheyenne, Ronin's twin, proudly accepted a role to stay on at Ether and be a part of his board and life. That suited her well. Cut-throat as I knew her to be, he would never worry with her at his side. She would now be around family and that was something she'd always desired. Even though they were new to each other, twins had a bond like none other.

Ronin asked Shak and Tanzia, to be public relations of the San, as liaisons and they accepted. Tochia was asked to join the San council board on Earth. She had made connections with them during her stint at headquarters while she healed after the Tanner incident.

As for Scott, Ether was his new home as well. With him having an estranged relationship with his father, it was expected. Metadonia was his new life. I'm still holding out for him and Cheyenne, even though she remains stubborn.

Both Ron and Tony opted to stay on Earth full-time; they felt Ether held far too many unhappy memories. Tony was not pleased with the turn of events between me and him, but he soon realized that I was not the same person as when we first met. We were civil at least. We had a long way to go but this was a start.

When the time came for us to return to Earth, Ronin pulled me aside. We stood outside his palace grounds but he needed to make sure we spoke alone. At least we tried. As he did months ago, Ronin grabbed my arm and slapped a burgundy metal rod on my forearm. It sealed into a bracelet like its predecessor that had saved my life. "What is this?" I twirled it around my wrist.

"This one sends a beacon to mine." He held up his arm where he wore a matching one. "That way, I will always be able to find you, no matter where you go or how far away you are. It may not pinpoint your exact whereabouts, but at least I would know what planet you are on. And yes, this means we are officially steady." He kissed me in front of everyone and I no longer held onto guilt for how I felt.

"Connor Equibel, come back soon or I will come after you. This I promise." I could not help but blush. Showing affection in front of others was a new concept to me.

When the portal opened, I looked back at the new ruler of Ether. He stood proud, with his hands clasped behind his back, dressed in black and gold imperial garments with sentinels at his side. He was finally safe. He was indeed my Destiny, no matter how hard I tried to deny him. I was overwhelmed with joy. It was hard to leave him.

"I will see you soon, Ronin," I promised, and walked through the portal back to my other home—Earth.

I needed to rebuild many relationships, between my family and friends. Although they didn't know everything, they did know that I was different. My family still had no clue about the San but my father, my real one, somehow understood me better. If the time ever came when they'd truly find out, we would deal with it then.

For now, my bestie Angela still did not know about Ronin, whom she knew as Vincent, her adopted brother, so he kept his distance. We figured it would be best that way. There would be far too many unanswered questions.

My mind traveled to dark places that frightened me. Flashes of another's life overwhelmed me and sometimes proved difficult to climb out of that nightmarish hold. At times, my emotions were erratic. I knew right from wrong, and although I never wanted to harm anyone, when Monlow's memoires came, so did his emotions, the ones that liked malice. He had been an evil individual. I'd lost the person I once was, but I was working on finding the new me, a better me. On a daily basis, I fought the obscurity within, and without question, my friends, Angela and Hope, were there to support me when I fell. They helped me find a lighthearted Connor.

But Ronin was always there to help me through the murkiest of times. Being on Earth could be suffocating and sometimes living in the black just made more sense. He suggested fighting malevolence on other planets and this helped me remain somewhat mentally stable by taking my twisted side out on the corrupt. It was therapeutic for the both of us because he was always at my side. Even though he ruled Ether, he and I both needed the fight. That was in my blood and in his nature—something we just couldn't deny.

So, I now reside on two planets and somehow, balanced the time between both realities and worlds. Honestly, I would not have had it any other way. I've kept Ronin humane when he had doubts about how to run his order. He's needed help to find his humanity and I've needed help to keep it. Like he said, we balance each other. Even if we did not we could never let the other go. That's part of the San Destiny- irrational love bordering on insanity.

My deepest regret was Willow. She was presumed dead but I believe she is still out there and I plan on finding her. This, I promise.

Dictionary

Keepers: Guardians of the young. They teach the San history and help the yougows hone their skills as they grow up to be protectors of planet Earth. (Selene, Bynder, Shak, Khan, Tanzia Tochia).

Yougow: (you-gow): Younglings, young San teens in training to become protectors of Earth. (Connor, Tony, Cheyenne, Byron, Ron, Willow & Scott)

Dianads (Dee-a-naud): Defender of Earth.

The San: Humans with abilities. They predate humans today and have lived quietly on Earth for centuries fitting in with beings without abilities that have come to evolve. They can live up to 200 years old and don't start aging until round 100 yrs.

San-I (Saun-I): The San language.

Butals (boo-tauls): They are San fighters who have enhanced combat skills and amazing agility.

Pausan: A pain deliverer and form taker. Pain can be delivered in any form, from stimulus to physical. They can also shift into any living form.

Forest folk: Old beings that live in the shadows of Ether until hungry then they search for gullible minds. They feed off of memories.

Caring House: San front for an adoption agency on Earth. Where all the yougows were taken after birth then placed in human's without abilities homes for protection sake.

Feelers: San hunters but not fighters. They hunt by use of impressions they receive from visions. They have extremely heightened senses and have the ability to warp reality.

Woler (whoa-lers): Creature from Earth. Hired muscle, half human half giant. They grow to about eight feet tall, their skin turns a pasty purplish color, have ripped muscles and move extremely fast. They are known for their tracking but their only loyalty is money.

Dictionary

Keepers: Guardians of the young. They teach the San history and help the yougows hone their skills as they grow up to be protectors of planet Earth. (Selene, Bynder, Shak, Khan, Tanzia Tochia).

Yougow: (you-gow): Younglings, young San teens in training to become protectors of Earth. (Connor, Tony, Cheyenne, Byron, Ron, Willow & Scott)

Dianads (Dee-a-naud): Defender of Earth.

The San: Humans with abilities. They predate humans today and have lived quietly on Earth for centuries fitting in with beings without abilities that have come to evolve. They can live up to 200 years old and don't start aging until round 100 yrs.

San-I (Saun-I): The San language.

Butals (boo-tauls): They are San fighters who have enhanced combat skills and amazing agility.

Pausan: A pain deliverer and form taker. Pain can be delivered in any form, from stimulus to physical. They can also shift into any living form.

Forest folk: Old beings that live in the shadows of Ether until hungry then they search for gullible minds. They feed off of memories.

Caring House: San front for an adoption agency on Earth. Where all the yougows were taken after birth then placed in human's without abilities homes for protection sake.

Feelers: San hunters but not fighters. They hunt by use of impressions they receive from visions. They have extremely heightened senses and have the ability to warp reality.

Woler (whoa-lers): Creature from Earth. Hired muscle, half human half giant. They grow to about eight feet tall, their skin turns a pasty purplish color, have ripped muscles and move extremely fast. They are known for their tracking but their only loyalty is money.

Credo: (Cra-dou): Invisibility. Means to mask oneself, fade or disappear. The San all have this ability.

Bostuge (boss-toog): Blue creatures who protect Ronin on Ether. They're built like humans but are blue, extremely tall. Their features are exaggerated with long fingers, wide mouths, big brown eyes that blink slowly.

Vuszen (voo-zayn): Ether military Crest. Similar to what a wolf and eagle looks like on Earth. Considered be one of the most ill-tempered animals and it's vicious like the military of Ether.

Hominids: Ethosians that look just like humans.

Sodder: Ethosian hominids with altered body parts —or Bostuge, the blue creatures. The animal breeds were a whole other life force. Beings here were bigger, faster, smarter and usually stronger than ones on Earth.

Gadarts (gaud-autss): Massive Ether creatures with green reptilian skin, big brown-yellowish eyes, wide mouth and a noisy tail. Afraid of light.

Volger, (voul-gaur): An Earthling creature. It's a possessor. They are beings with the ability to jump into one's body and it take over.

Ether: Foe of Earth and ruled by Monlow. The beings that live there are called Ethosians.

Strouka (stroo-ka): A gentleman's club on Ether.

Tget toss (t-gat, touss): Time traveler, a problem preventer.

Munar (moon-aur): A seer, one who can predict future events.

Nunan (nu-naun) aka abnormal(s): The unnorm, nonhumans from Earth.

Boun: A levitating light.

Etsna: Means terrible or horribly bad.

Shugna: Curse term in Elonium.

Glutton: Either black or charcoal grey, but always large with a wide girth. Stands seven feet tall. Its nose is long, its lips are red and wide, and always smell like a barn.

The Key to Ether: Its round shape is made of gold with eighteen gold claws, that of the Vuzen, surrounding it. There is a small round ball on the inside and when it goes up and down it ignites, causing electricity to shoot from the middle, which is what you need to open the door.

Flappezt: A green scaled creature with a long neck and four arms. Very similar to a dinosaur. It was not the most vicious being but it was far from the kindest. Can grow to twelve feet tall.

Decouas & Wettle: Two closely related species who stand equal in height with four arms and eight feet. They weigh close to three hundred pounds since their bodies are made of stone. The Decouas, a far more vicious species, stole territory which ended their close unionization.

Moondars: Huge creatures with red glowing eyes that match their dry skin. It stands over ten feet tall and is built like a truck. On their head lives a long black beautiful, ponytail of deception. Its hair splits into three serpents that spits a fatal toxin. It's one of the meanest creatures on Ether and nearby planets. They were not known for their small talk and can kill you in an instant.

Military Protectant: Under Monlow's rule that protect Ether and are higher ranking than Enforcers.

Sentinels: Guards who protect both Monlow and Ronin in and out of their palaces.

Enforcer: Ether police.